Bury in Haste

Bury in Haste

Jean Rowden

ROBERT HALE · LONDON

© Jean Rowden 2007
First published in Great Britain 2007

ISBN 978-0-7090-8394-8

Robert Hale Limited
Clerkenwell House
Clerkenwell Green
London EC1R 0HT

2 4 6 8 10 9 7 5 3 1

Typeset in 10/12pt Sabon
Printed and bound in Great Britain by
Biddles Limited, King's Lynn, Norfolk

Chapter One

Constable 'Thorny' Deepbriar sat straight backed, unaware of the hardness of the chair beneath him. Although he was witnessing the most appalling crime, his face displayed no hint of emotion; a lesser man might have closed his eyes, or covered his ears, but that was beneath his dignity. An officer of the law had to maintain certain standards of behaviour, whatever the situation.

This situation was as bad as they came. Just ten feet from him murder was being committed, and he was helpless to prevent it. The constable was no coward, but intervention was simply not an option. He could only endure.

Not everyone gathered there as witnesses to the crime had the constable's fortitude. Some of those around him were fidgeting, while others had that far away look in their eyes which suggested they had managed to absent themselves mentally from their surroundings. The man next to Deepbriar was pulverising a pasteboard ticket between his hands, the pressure of his fingers gradually obliterating the legend 'Tonight's Performance – 1/6d'.

Only the individual who was responsible for the slaughter was at ease, indeed she was clearly enjoying herself. Mrs Emerson took a deep breath and reached for top C, giving it all she'd got, and only missing by a smidgen. Deepbriar winced as the glass in the windows of Minecliff's village hall rattled ominously, wondering where Puccini was buried, and whether the ground would be heaving as the poor man turned beneath it.

Trying to distract himself, Deepbriar stared at the solitary picture on the wall, a photograph of the young Queen Elizabeth, taken at her coronation a few years ago. She didn't have to listen to the likes of Mrs Emerson, he reflected morosely, she could go to Covent Garden and listen to the best singers in the world. That thought brought no comfort.

He tried to concentrate on something else, reminding himself of the book he'd picked up from the library that morning. He'd been looking forward to reading the latest Dick Bland mystery for weeks. Unless there was some crisis that required him to don his uniform and return to duty, he would have the whole of tomorrow afternoon to lose himself in the adventures of his favourite private eye.

Something about Dick Bland had an irresistible appeal to Deepbriar's phlegmatic soul; his fictional life was one of constant excitement, his mental prowess being much in demand for the untangling of the most horrific murders, while a week rarely went by when he wasn't required to face some deadly threat to his life.

Another full-blooded shriek made Deepbriar shudder; it was no good, the anticipation of future pleasure wasn't sufficient to distract him from his present pain. More characters appeared on stage, among them the reason he was enduring this torment. Mary Deepbriar wasn't her husband's match in height, nor in girth, but she was well rounded, with the natural colouring of an English rose, now a little past its first bloom. No amount of make-up or generosity of spirit could make her believable as a Japanese woman. As for Mrs Emerson, with her fleshy face framed by the fringe of greying hair which refused to be hidden under the black wig, a less likely *Madame Butterfly* was hard to imagine. At least Mary could sing in tune, Deepbriar thought gloomily.

As *Madame Butterfly* approached another high note, the tension was broken by the sound of a door opening at the back of the hall, then came the soft rhythmic creak of footsteps as the intruder tried to walk quietly down the aisle between the chairs.

A slight figure came into view, 'Psst.' Harry, the son of the couple who kept the local pub, was gesturing wildly from the end of the row. Phyllis and Don Bartle half rose to their feet, but Harry shook his head at his parents and waved them back down. They subsided, looking disappointed.

'Mr Deepbriar,' he hissed.

From the stage *Madame Butterfly* glared down at Deepbriar as he picked up his trilby from under his seat and eased his six foot and thirteen stone out from among the tightly packed chairs. The naked antagonism in her stare made him suddenly clumsy and he almost fell into the empty seat at the end of the row, next to young Emily Spraggs. He recovered enough to smile an apology to Emily but she didn't notice. She had looked up in anticipation when the door opened, doubtless hoping to see her husband. Disappointed, she was now visibly distracted, her fingers picking nervously at a button on her coat. Deepbriar shook his head indulgently; she and Joe had only been married a week, so they were still at the love struck stage.

'What's up, Harry?' Deepbriar breathed out with relief as the two men stepped outside into the cold night air. 'Not that it's a hardship to leave, but I'm off duty.'

'Sorry, Mr Deepbriar, but it's old Bronc. He came to our back door a few minutes ago, in a right state. Says he was knocked down on the road, and the car didn't stop. It sounded fishy to me, he's sure it had no lights on. I said I'd come and fetch you.' Harry's eyes shone. 'He reckoned they were up to no good.'

Harry spoke with the enthusiasm of the amateur sleuth. To date his single success had been achieved at the tender age of ten, when he proved that the rag and bone man's pony had caused the damage to the village pump while its owner was in the pub. Now twenty-two, he lived in hopes of solving other more serious mysteries, refusing to be disheartened by the almost total lack of crime in Minecliff.

'This had better be good, Harry.' Deepbriar gave a none too reluctant glance back at the village hall; an excuse wasn't to be sniffed at, but it needed to be a good one. 'Mrs Deepbriar isn't going to be happy if I'm not back in there for her next chorus.'

The heir apparent of the Speckled Goose looked wistful. 'Show going well is it? I heard a bit as I came in, it sounded lovely.'

The constable sighed. There were advantages in being tone deaf, Harry didn't know how lucky he was. 'It wouldn't be half bad, if only that wretched Emerson woman hadn't taken the lead. There's a limit to how much a music lover can take.'

'You should worry,' Harry said sorrowfully. 'They won't even let me audition for the society. That's Mrs Emerson for you.'

Deepbriar maintained a diplomatic silence. Minecliff was a small village, and there were never enough people to fill the ranks of the chorus; Mrs Emerson probably would have welcomed old Bronc, the tramp, if only he'd been able to sing. Harry's lack of musical talent was legendary; a sound that was a cross between a scalded cat and a hippopotamus in love could often be heard coming from the pub's cellar. Unfortunately he was quite unaware that his voice was less melodious than a foghorn. There was even a rumour that this was why he'd spent the entire two years of his

National Service guarding a fuel dump at an isolated spot in the Scottish highlands.

'Quiet tonight I expect, Harry?' Deepbriar tactfully changed the subject. 'Nice for your mum and dad to have the night off. Though I suppose they'll be home in time for the drunk and disorderlies.'

Harry laughed, acknowledging the little joke. His parents ran a decent pub, and he couldn't remember when they'd last needed Deepbriar's assistance to keep order. 'It's the quietest night of the year. Even old Bert Bunyard isn't in yet.'

'He's laid up. The Colonel's gamekeepers won't be sorry, they'll have a quiet time of it for a few weeks. Bert fell down the market hall steps in Belston on Monday. He's got his leg in plaster.'

'I hadn't heard about that,' Harry said.

Deepbriar grinned. 'Really is a quiet night, when you don't even get to hear the local gossip.'

Harry laughed. 'Old Bronc's a bit ripe,' he said, as they reached the back entrance of the public house. 'I knew mum and dad wouldn't want him in the bar, so I put him in the back porch and gave him a cup of tea. Maybe I'd best fetch him a spot of brandy to put in it. He's had a bit of a shock. What about you, Mr Deepbriar? Can I get you anything?'

'Best not,' the constable replied reluctantly. He might just get away with missing the rest of the performance, but there'd be hell to pay if he returned home with the smell of the Bartle's best bitter on his breath.

The old tramp sat huddled on the wooden bench in the back porch of the Speckled Goose, a mug cradled between his gnarled hands. It was impossible to guess his age, and he made no claims, but there was a rumour that he'd fought in the Boer war. He was a small man, and thin, but he didn't look it under the many layers of clothes that swathed him, evidenced by the multitude of grubby layers around his scrawny neck, making him look not unlike a tortoise.

When Deepbriar had seen him some seven months before, Bronc had sported a disreputable trilby hat, but now he wore a green deerstalker. The constable's spirit's lifted; as a detective, Sherlock Holmes was a little eccentric for his taste, but nevertheless the appearance of the famous man's trademark seemed like a good omen. Maybe Harry had finally discovered a mystery.

'Here we are, Bronc,' Harry said cheerfully. 'I've brought the law, like you wanted. You can tell Constable Deepbriar all about it.'

Bronc drained the mug and held it out. 'Bit o' somethin' to warm the cockles would help, Mr Bartle, Sir,' he said.

'I'll see what I can do.' Flattered by the title most customers reserved for his father, the landlord's son took the mug and nodded, turning to Deepbriar on his way out.

'Thought he'd better not have anything stronger than tea till you'd seen him,' he whispered. 'Shan't be a minute.'

Deepbriar seated himself on the other side of the porch and took out his notebook, trying not to breathe deeply; Harry was right, the old tramp smelt none too sweet. 'Well now,' he said. 'What's all this about?'

'Car nearly ran me down, it did,' Bronc said. His voice was low and gravelly from years of sleeping rough. 'Look at the tear in me coat. Gurt black machine it was, goin' like a runaway train an' not a single light showin'.' He shivered suddenly. 'Not nice, meetin' it so sudden. When a man gets to my age he don't want to be thinkin' about dyin'.'

'No need for that sort of talk, you still look pretty lively to me, Bronc,' Deepbriar said. 'When was this?'

'A while back. Gave me the fright of me life. I had to jump into the ditch.'

'Were you hurt? Did it hit you?'

'Naw,' Bronc grinned. 'Never touched me. I'm quick on me feet for an old 'un. Came close, though. Caught me coat.'

'In the village was it, or on the main road?'

'On the road. I landed in the muck.' The old man looked up at the constable, his eyes pale and bright. Then his expression changed subtly as his gaze wandered to some far distance. 'Landed in the muck,' he repeated. 'Came right at me it did. Just along by old Ma Fisher's stall.'

'Ma Fisher?' Deepbriar frowned. 'Must be before my time, Bronc. I don't recall any Fishers in Minecliff.'

'Who said anythin' about Minecliff?' The old man growled. 'I'm talkin' about Falbrough market. Hers was the first pitch round the corner from the church.'

Deepbriar's heart sank. 'But you're in Minecliff now. You were telling me about a car that nearly hit you when you were on your way here.'

'Naw, was I? I dunno 'bout that. Had to jump for me life I did.

In the midden up to me knees I was, an' them folks all laughin'. Disgrace it is, all that muck in the street.'

'I think you're getting muddled up with another time. Come on, Bronc. Think about it. You were on your way to Minecliff. Go on from there.'

'Minecliff.' Bronc rubbed his forehead with grubby knuckles and looked rather vaguely around him. 'I'd be heading for Job Taylor's then, would I? Pulls a good pint, does Job, not mean like some I could name, neither.'

'Let's get back to this car,' Deepbriar prompted. He couldn't remember the exact year when Job Taylor, one time landlord of the Speckled Goose, had died at the ripe old age of ninety two, but it was before the war.

'Gurt roarin' noise it made,' Bronc said. 'Scared me half out of me wits. Saw it all of a sudden like, skiddin' sideways round the corner.' He brightened suddenly. 'Must've been on a Tuesday. Ma Fisher don't go to market on Fridays.'

Deepbriar sighed. This was getting worse. There had been no Tuesday market in Falbrough since 1930. He put away his notebook.

'Tell you what, Bronc, I reckon that car's been and gone these twenty years and more. I don't think there's much chance we'll see it again.'

The tramp's brow furrowed, then his face lit up in a childlike smile. 'Not with no lights on, eh? But it tore me coat, constable,' he added, plucking at a strip of material that hung off the hem of the threadbare Burberry he wore as a top layer. Deepbriar inspected the damage. There was nothing to suggest how it had been done; most likely old Bronc had caught it on a barbed wire fence.

'Maybe we can find you a new one.'

Harry arrived then with a measure of brandy. 'Sorry I was gone so long,' he said breathlessly, 'somebody came in for a beer and the barrel was empty, then the bulb had gone on the stairs to the cellar. Have I missed anything?'

'No. He's a bit confused. Says the car knocked him into the midden, on the corner by the church in Falbrough, with everybody laughing at him. And it was a Tuesday, because Ma Fisher was at the market.'

The young man looked baffled, then deeply abashed. 'He had it clear enough when he told me. I'm really sorry, Mr Deepbriar.'

He drew his brows together, concentrating. 'Let's see. He said he'd called at Quinn's farm and had a bit of bread and cheese, then he was almost to the village when this car came at him round the sharp bend. Reckoned it didn't have any lights on. Though come to think of it, he went on a bit about dying, I don't know what that was all about, and he did say it was Silas Quinn he saw.'

'That would be Ferdy's grandfather.' Deepbriar stood up. 'There's not a lot I could have done anyway, not unless he noticed the make of the car or the number. Biggest car in these parts is the Colonel's Humber, and that's grey, not black. Not to mention he never gets it out of second gear. No harm done anyway, except to Bronc's coat. I said I'd try and find him something else. I thought maybe the rector might be collecting for the next jumble sale.'

'I can do better than that.' Harry vanished again.

Bronc tipped the glass high to savour the last drops of brandy, then he set it down beside him with a sigh. 'That was a bit of all right,' he said. 'A man's insides get a mite cold, this time o' year.'

The inner door opened and Harry returned, carrying a thick tweed overcoat.

'Gent left this in the bar two years ago. You remember? Mum took it into Falbrough to the lost property, but nobody ever claimed it. It's too big for me, and Dad didn't want it. What do you think, Bronc, reckon this'd be a good fit?'

'Thank you Mr Bartle, Sir. You're a real gent.'

'Looks very fine,' Deepbriar said, as the tramp put the overcoat on over the torn Burberry. 'You got a place fixed for tonight?'

Nodding, the old man winked. 'I do that. Thank you kindly, Sirs. Any chance of another drop to keep me warm before I go?'

Harry grimaced. 'Don't tell anyone, or Dad'll have it out of my pay. You sure you don't want a drink, Mr Deepbriar?' He lowered his voice. 'I've got a little package for you, if you've time to come into the bar. That one I told you about last week. You won't miss much of the show, it'll be the interval by now, you could have a quick pint and be back in time for the second half.'

Some time later Deepbriar stepped out into the night, putting his hat on. He drew in a breath of fresh clean air and looked up at the stars, enjoying the sense of solitude. The little item Harry had given him made a slight bulge under his coat, and he patted it happily. It was a shame to have to return to the village hall, but he felt fortified now, ready for anything.

Always the policeman, even when he wasn't on duty, he

glanced down the hill towards the wooded shadows at the end of Violet Lane. The glow from Minecliff's three street lamps didn't reach that far, but he had the impression that a shape was moving against the trees.

The constable stopped, staring into the night and wishing he had a torch with him. If that shadow had been a man he wasn't tall, but bulky. A bit like Bronc, but the tramp was still sitting in the porch of the Speckled Goose, making the most of the drink Deepbriar had bought him. If the man wasn't incapacitated, Deepbriar might have thought it was Bert Bunyard. Far away a dog barked, but all else was silence.

He weighed up the likelihood of finding a suspicious character loitering in Violet Lane. Apart from the footpath that set off across the fields, there were only three little cottages down there, and not one of them with anything worth stealing. It had been nothing but a shadow. He was getting as bad as Bronc, imagining things. Squaring his shoulders he headed back to face the demise of *Madame Butterfly*.

It was a cold thirty-two-degrees Fahrenheit outside, but the atmosphere at the Deepbriar's breakfast table was a great deal chillier. Mary had barely spoken a word to the constable the night before, and her back faced him when he'd followed her to bed.

He was trying to find something to say as he drank his second cup of tea, but he couldn't think what; Mary was normally such a peaceable soul, not given to displays of temperament. It was a relief when the telephone rang.

'This is Ferdy Quinn,' the voice at the other end rattled off briskly. 'I've got a complaint to make. Bert Bunyard's been on my land again. I'm giving you warning, constable, if you don't stop him playing his tricks I'll go down to that run-down old heap of ruins and wasteland he calls a farm and settle him myself.'

'Perhaps you'd best calm down, Mr Quinn,' Deepbriar said stolidly, picking up a pencil, 'and tell me what's happened.'

'I've no time to talk now. It's not just me, Will Minter's involved as well. We've got to get our beasts sorted out. If you want to do something useful you can come and help, or better still, go and lock up Bert Bunyard!' The phone was slammed down.

Deepbriar sighed. Obviously Quinn hadn't heard that his arch-enemy was out of action, hobbling on a pair of crutches. Bunyard couldn't possibly have walked or ridden the two miles to Quinn's farm. He had an ancient lorry, but it was rarely in working order, and when Bunyard did manage to coax it into life it made such a terrible noise that the whole village could hear it.

'Got to go out,' he said, swapping his pullover for his tunic. Mary nodded, saying nothing. Deepbriar put on his cycle clips. As he reached the door the telephone rang again. 'If that's Ferdy Quinn ...' he began, but his wife was on her way upstairs, obviously having developed a sudden deafness.

With another sigh he picked up the phone. 'Minecliff Police,' he said.

The voice at the other end was quick and breathy, the accent distinctively upper-class. 'Oh, constable, I'm so glad I found you at home. I do hope I'm not disturbing you?'

'What can I do for you, Miss Lightfall?'

'Well, I was wondering if you were free this morning. At eleven. Morning service at St Peter and St Paul, you know. Only Cyril Crimmon sent a message round to say he can't come, some sort of family business I gather. Since you don't play regularly at Minecliff now, I thought perhaps you'd be able to help us out. I don't know what we'll do about evensong either, if Mr Crimmon isn't back by then. Of course there's the Wilkins boy, but he's only eleven, and with his legs not really being long enough to ...'

'I'll see what I can do,' Deepbriar said, cutting across the flow. 'But I have to go out and deal with a police matter first. You'd better have young Nicky Wilkins on hand, Miss Lightfall, in case I can't get to you by eleven.'

As he pedalled through the village Deepbriar's thoughts wandered. The request for his services at St Peter and St Paul reminded him of another reason for his dislike of Mrs Emerson. Within six weeks of moving into the village she'd supplanted him as Minecliff s church organist, and now he had to make do with the crumbs dropped from her table. He mostly got funerals, because she didn't care for those, saying the atmosphere interfered with her artistic aura.

Appeals from other parishes, like Possington, were welcome. St Peter and St Paul's had one of the best organs he'd ever played on. Somehow a group of parishioners had managed to raise the huge sum of seven thousand pounds to have it repaired. The instrument was far grander than the one at Minecliff, with fifteen stops and three manuals, and a swell to great coupler. Since its refurbishment the tone was truly magnificent, with none of the unwanted noise from the tracker action. The stoppers on Minecliff's organ rattled so much they almost drowned out the quiet passages.

If he wasn't too long at Quinn's farm maybe he'd reach Possington in time to play some music of his own choosing as the congregation arrived; Father Michael had eclectic tastes, and allowed his organists full rein. The thought cheered him, and he leant more heavily into the pedals.

Deepbriar almost fell off his bike when Emily Spraggs ran out of her door and into the road right in front of him. Last night her pale little face had shown signs of worry. This morning she looked positively haggard, and there were tear stains on her cheeks.

Chapter Two

'Mr Deepbriar.' Emily Spraggs gulped. She was twisting the front of her bright pink pinafore tight between her hands. 'Please. I don't know what to do. Nobody's seen him. And you know Joe, he wouldn't go off without telling me ...'

'Your Joe? What's he been up to then?' Deepbriar dismounted and propped his bicycle against the wall, taking the girl's elbow to lead her back into Honeysuckle Cottage. The newlyweds' home didn't live up to its name, being the last in a terrace of six council houses, but Emily and Joe had already given it a charm all of its own. Pots of colourful begonias filling the windows between bright yellow curtains had something to do with it, but the romantics in the village declared that the two young people's love for each other shone from the very walls.

'He didn't come home last night. He said he'd be working late, and he was going to come straight to the village hall. For the show, you know. He took his best coat with him specially, to put on over his work clothes. Only he never came.'

Deepbriar cleared his throat noisily. 'You – er – you didn't have an argument? Yesterday morning perhaps?'

'Of course not.' Another tear trickled down her cheek. 'We've never argued, not about anything.' She flushed. 'We're still on our honeymoon. Joe promised to spend as much time as he could at home this week, because we can't afford to go on a holiday, what with having the house to do and everything.'

'Well, I'm sure nothing serious has happened to him. I expect that old lorry broke down and he never got back to Wriggle's yard. Tell you what I'll do. It's not far out of my way, I'll go and check.'

'Thank you. I should have walked up there last night, but I didn't like to, not on my own in the dark. And it was late by then ...' Fresh tears flowed.

Deepbriar was already out of the door and astride his bike. 'You stay indoors, in the warm, and don't you worry,' he called reassuringly, as he pedalled away.

He glanced at his watch. Five minutes to ten. So much for being at Possington with time to spare; he'd have to ride fast to fit everything in and still reach the church in time for the service.

Deepbriar looked for the tower of St Peter and St Paul's, just appearing above the trees; he dwelt briefly on the pleasure of playing the best church organ in the county and tried to push on a little faster. He had to see Ferdy Quinn first, and he had the disappearance of young Joe Spraggs to investigate; the thought gave him an enjoyable quiver of excitement, quickly quashed. English villages didn't produce mysteries worthy of Dick Bland and his ilk, he mustn't let his imagination run away with him. Still, even a little bit of a puzzle made a change. If only he wasn't so short of time.

That led him to wonder if Joe had been reluctant to waste a Saturday night on the Minecliff Operatic Society's latest offering; there was only so much a man could be expected to endure. Then again, he was newly married, and he'd made a promise to his pretty young wife.

Remembering his own misdemeanour of the previous night, Deepbriar was suddenly immersed in gloom. If Mary didn't relent he could be in trouble; she might 'forget' to put the Sunday joint on to roast. She'd done it once, when Minecliff won the area cricket championship. He hadn't intended to stay out quite so late celebrating, and he hadn't realised he'd pushed her wifely patience just a little too far when he finally rolled in at four in the morning. A slight feeling of resentment lingered, even after eight years; for a man with a healthy appetite he'd always thought the punishment had far exceeded the crime.

The constable turned on to the muddy track that led to Wriggle's Yard, which was a rather run down patch of land containing piles of bricks, wood, slates and other building materials. Deepbriar jolted slowly round the last corner then braked sharply. The wooden gates in the paling fence stood wide open. Propped against the left hand gate was a bicycle, which every soul in Minecliff would have recognised as belonging to young Joe. It sported a bright blue saddlebag, which had famously been a wedding present to the happy couple from Joe's boss. Not a generous man, Alfred Wriggle, Deepbriar reflected, grinning as he recalled the wisecracks in the pub when Joe told them about the gift.

Wriggle's ancient lorry was parked in its usual place, facing the outside world, ready to make its next delivery, one headlamp glass cracked right across, tyres nearly bald, the canvas cover creased and sagging. Unsurprisingly, Wriggle never replaced anything until it fell apart.

Dismounting, the constable left his machine leaning against the hedge. He advanced slowly, walking on the firmer ground at the side of the lane to avoid the puddles and preserve the shine on his boots. 'Joe? You there, lad?'

There was no response. Deepbriar marched past the abandoned bicycle to inspect the lorry. Both the cab and the back were empty. A tea cup, white china with a pattern of pink and yellow flowers, stood precariously on the old Atkinson's bonnet. It had several chips out of the rim and there was a smear of dirty fingerprints around the sides. By craning his neck he could see it contained a scummy residue, possibly tea.

Despite his earlier resolution to avoid speculation, something stirred in Deepbriar, belying his outwardly prosaic nature. A country bobby spent a lifetime dealing with little things; the most serious crime he'd ever encountered was a spot of black marketeering during the War, and even then the real detection work had been done by men from Falbrough. There was a part of him, hidden deep and rarely allowed to see the light of day, that yearned for something more. He peered closely at the cup with something like fondness in his eyes, noting the outline of a perfect greasy thumb print; it was just the kind of evidence you'd expect in a Dick Bland story.

The tiny hut which served as an office was locked, and the window was too filthy to see through, but Deepbriar soon located the key, hidden under a stone round the back. Inside the hut was a rickety table half covered with papers, a wooden chair, a small filing cabinet, and a cupboard which wasn't large enough to conceal a child, let alone Joe Spraggs. Deepbriar opened it anyway, careful to touch only the outer edge of the door, but the cupboard only contained a dirty saucepan and an empty bottle, and a heap of mouse droppings. On the window ledge was a cup similar to the one that had been left on the lorry, but cleaner.

It took several minutes to make a methodical search of the site. Wriggle never threw anything away, and there were weed-covered heaps of half-bricks and broken sinks, scattered between enormous piles of wood, some of it rotting silently into dust. There were also the remains of several old vehicles, most of them so rusted as to be unrecognisable. Eventually the constable was satisfied that Joe Spraggs wasn't hidden anywhere in Wriggle's yard, nor was there any evidence of anything untoward having happened. Without really admitting as much to himself, he had been keeping an eye open for such things as freshly dug earth, pools of blood and spent bullet casings.

But there was Joe's bike. Deepbriar investigated the saddlebag; it contained a few bread crumbs, scraps of cheese, the dead-spider stems from two tomatoes, and an ancient linen napkin worn thin by years of use, which had evidently been used to wrap some kind of pie. It seemed young Emily had sent her husband off to work well provided.

Despite the lack of evidence, Deepbriar was happily intrigued. He couldn't yet be sure that a crime had been committed here, but at the very least he'd walked into the scene of a mystery. He inspected the lane outside the gate, and it was there that he struck gold. True to form, the tyres on Wriggle's lorry were so worn that the tread had almost gone, yet tracks in the mud showed that a vehicle with much newer tyres had been in the yard. As well as the elderly Atkinson, Wriggle owned an Austin 7, but the tracks were too wide to have been left by that.

After making some notes in his notebook, Deepbriar added a drawing of the pattern left in the mud by the wheels and measured them, then he followed the tracks, and was intrigued to find they led round behind one of the large stacks of timber.

Perhaps the car or van had been hidden out of sight when young Spraggs drove in. Had he interrupted a robbery? But then why would he have stopped to make himself a cup of tea? Maybe the fingerprints on the cup didn't belong to Joe Spraggs at all.

Reluctantly Deepbriar left the cup untouched. If a crime had been committed here then he could only hope that nobody else would arrive on the scene until he'd reported it. He noted the time in his book. Ten twenty-four. Sergeant Hubbard would want such details when Deepbriar phoned his report to headquarters.

Even the chance of missing his Sunday roast paled into insignificance beside the prospect of having discovered a major crime. This would make a change from Bert Bunyard's poaching escapades and children scrumping or playing truant from school.

Deepbriar wheeled his bike back along the lane, checking the hedges. By the time he arrived at the surfaced road he was sure Joe hadn't pushed through into the fields or been overcome by some illness and fallen into a ditch. The hedges belonged to the Manor and the Colonel kept them well maintained; they were thick and impenetrable, while the ditch held nothing but mud and an occasional puddle of water. It was a mystery right enough. Had Joe returned from his day's work, and drunk a cup of tea? Perhaps. But why had he then gone off and left his bike behind, not to mention Emily?

For the moment there was nothing more to be done, but Deepbriar felt a swelling excitement as he set off towards Quinn's Farm. He reached a sharp bend where the road turned through more than ninety degrees, following the edge of one of Quinn's fields, and he slowed down a little, recalling the previous evening's encounter with Bronc. The tramp had been coming from Quinn's farm, just after dark. And this was where he'd claimed that a 'gurt black machine' with no lights showing, had knocked him into the ditch. Could it have been on its way to or from Wriggle's yard?

The tyre marks were there too, imprinted in the mud on the bend. Deepbriar propped his bicycle against the hedge out of the way, and bent over them, taking out his notebook again to be sure they were the same. Bronc hadn't been imagining things. But then, the old man wasn't stupid, merely suffering from the loss of memory that often comes with old age. With a little gentle prodding he might well produce more information about this car. A shame it was black; any other colour would have made it almost instantly recognisable.

Deepbriar resumed his journey, cheerfully contemplating the next stage of his investigation. Then he remembered another man who went missing from the village, and his mood changed in an instant; Joe Spraggs's disappearance was beginning to look altogether too much like the case of Ed Walkingham.

A man of independent means, Walkingham had lived in Mill House, a large and isolated dwelling on the edge of Minecliff. Three years ago he had disappeared from his home in the middle of the night; the front door had been found standing wide open, and a valuable collection of silver was gone from a cabinet in the living room. Mrs Walkingham had reported the crime, tearfully insistent that her husband must have discovered burglars and been spirited away by them. Then, as in this case, there had been evidence of a vehicle coming and going.

Deepbriar had summoned Sergeant Hubbard, fearing the worst; kidnapping perhaps, or even murder. Coming to the scene, the sergeant had duly called in the CID. What followed became the biggest manhunt Falbrough had ever known, with reports of sightings of the missing man coming in from as many as fifty miles away.

When Ed had finally been located, alive and well in a bed and breakfast establishment overlooking the beach at Brighton, it turned out he'd run away with a barmaid from the Falbrough Arms. He'd sold the silver to a local antique dealer and was living off the proceeds. His ladylove, a bright girl who had learnt to drive during the War, had brought a car, purchased in secrecy the week before, to fetch him in the middle of the night.

Members of the neighbouring constabularies, pulled in to help with the manhunt, never missed a chance to remind the Falbrough officers of the incident. Ever since then, 'missing persons' were dirty words as far as Sergeant Hubbard was concerned; he wasn't going to be happy when Joe Spraggs's disappearance was reported. Deepbriar allowed himself to descend into his customary gloom. By expecting the worst he found life rarely disappointed him.

Deepbriar opened the gate at Quinn's farm and pushed his bicycle into the yard at exactly ten forty, only slightly out of breath.

Ferdy Quinn came dashing from the barn, a short stocky man with a florid complexion. Carrot coloured hair stuck out from under his cap and sprouted generously in front of his ears. He was followed by two of his men, old Bob, looking every one of his seventy years, and Alan the cowman, Bob's grandson. Both men were watching their boss, like a pair of well-trained sheep dogs alert for the slightest signal from their master.

The farmer greeted Deepbriar with a flood of words, none of which was a welcome. 'About time! I was thinking of fetching my shotgun. And don't you go telling me this was just some harmless prank. I've had enough of that old rogue trying to make a fool out of me.' He took off his cap and ran a hand over his bright red curls. 'Bunyard's gone too far this time.'

'Steady on, Mr Quinn,' Deepbriar took out his book and opened it, casting a fond glance at the notes and diagrams he'd made at Wriggle's yard before turning to a fresh page. 'I'll need to know what this is all about. I'm not a mind reader.'

'It's my heifers. When Alan here came out this morning he found the field gate wide open. I'm telling you, constable, if you don't deal with Bunyard ...'

'Keep to the facts, if you please,' Deepbriar said, giving his pencil a lick and writing swiftly. He glanced at the cowman. 'What time was this?'

'About seven,' Quinn said quickly, giving the younger man no time to reply.

Deepbriar sighed and turned back to the farmer. 'And everything was as it should have been last night?'

'Yes, I walked round with the dogs at ten, same as always, so he must have come later than that.'

'Then this morning your heifers were gone.'

'Yes. Alan went up to the corner and there was the top gate open too, on to the lane. He was getting right worried by then, and he shouted for Bob to fetch me. I tell you I was in a state, thinking my beasts had been stolen. It was in the paper a month back, how a farmer over at Woolbarton lost a dozen prize Herefords that way. But once we got up top we noticed Will Minter's gate was open too, and there they were.' His face creased in indignation. 'Twenty two pure-bred Jersey heifers let loose with Minter's Aberdeen Angus bull! I'll skin that man!' Quinn shook his fist in the direction of Minecliff, so furious he was barely able to form the words.

'If you're talking about Bert Bunyard,' Deepbriar said levelly, looking up as he finished making his notes, 'you've got it wrong this time. He's got a leg in plaster. He can barely hobble out of his own front door.'

'What?' Quinn's face, already flushed, turned the colour of beetroot. 'That's impossible!'

'I saw him myself yesterday. Whoever it was let your cows out, couldn't have been Bert Bunyard.'

The farmer looked about ready to spontaneously combust. His two men backed off a little to get out of range, as if an explosion was a real possibility. 'Then he must have persuaded somebody else to do it, or ... or he paid somebody,' he finished desperately.

The idea that Minecliff's meanest man would pay anybody for anything was so laughable that the constable didn't even bother to consider it. 'Can you think of a single soul who'd do Bert Bunyard a favour?'

'What about that son of his?'

'Humphrey hasn't been off the farm in five years,' Deepbriar said, snapping his notebook shut. 'Somebody's played a nasty trick on you, Mr Quinn, but it wasn't Bunyard, not this time. No other damage was done? The gates were opened, not broken?'

Quinn shook his head. 'No. But look, it must have been Bunyard,' he added, almost pleading. 'There's nobody else would do a thing like this.'

'Two miles across the fields with his leg in plaster? It's impossible, even a young man couldn't do it.'

'He could've ridden that old nag of his,' Quinn suggested.

'Doubt if he'd even make it on to her back. Easy enough to tell. The ground's wet, a horse would leave hoof prints. Either he'd have come up the lane, or through that gate.' Deepbriar pointed and they went together to check. There were signs of large-booted feet, but nothing to indicate that a horse had passed that way recently.

'I'm sorry, Mr Quinn,' Deepbriar said, heading back towards his bicycle, 'I have to say, even if we find the culprit, there's not a lot to be done. Criminal damage would be hard to prove, seeing it's Minter's bull that may or may not have done the harm.' He half turned. 'Was old Bronc here yesterday?'

'Yes, he called in for a chat and a spot of tea.' Quinn was dismissive. 'He was on his way before dark, this is nothing to do with him.'

'I didn't think it was. Tell me, did any of you happen to see a big black car on the road any time during the afternoon? Or maybe a while after Bronc left?'

The old man and his grandson shook their heads in unison, still apparently struck dumb.

'Not that I recall,' Quinn said. 'What are you getting at? Nobody's going to go trying to steal animals in a car, they'd be in a lorry. Anyway, nobody stole them did they, just let them in with Minter's bull. There's no knowing what might come of this. My heifers ...'

'I don't need instructing in the ways of the birds and bees, thank you, Mr Quinn,' Deepbriar said, raising his hand to interrupt him. 'But I'm blowed if I know what we could charge anybody with, even if we prove who let your heifers out. I'll call on Mr Minter tomorrow, see if he's got anything to add to what you've told me.'

He focused his gaze sternly on the excitable little man. 'I'll need your word you won't go making any more wild accusations in the meantime. Bert Bunyard's done his fair share of daft things and he steps over the line now and then, I won't deny, but this time you're barking up the wrong tree.'

A little hot and bothered from cycling nearly three miles in ten minutes, Deepbriar sat down at the organ in Possington's ancient church. With a wink he tossed a threepenny bit to young Nicky Wilkins, and the boy returned happily to his place in the choir.

With a nod to Miss Lightfall, her plain face expressing her relief at his arrival, Deepbriar launched into the first hymn. As usual the joy of releasing music from beneath his hands and feet lifted him above the cares of the day, and the earlier part of the morning was banished from his mind. A rare smile spread across the constable's flushed face as the sound swelled to fill the ancient building.

During the sermon Deepbriar's mind wandered, but not to Joe Spraggs or Ferdy Quinn. The vicar had chosen to preach on Psalm 145 verse 15: 'The eyes of all wait upon Thee, and Thou givest them their meat in due season.' He couldn't help but think of Mary and her unnatural spell of bad temper, and wonder if there was a roast dinner awaiting him. His mouth watered.

As the sermon came to an end the side door creaked open. Every member of the congregation could be heard holding its breath, listening to the stealthy footsteps as the newcomer tried to walk silently across the flagstones. A meagre man, with non-descript features, came into view. He had thin mousy hair and a feeble stringy moustache, and his eyes were the colour of winter puddles. With his right hand heavily bandaged, and his every movement an apology, Cyril Crimmon crept to the side of the organ, keeping his gaze unwaveringly on the vicar, as if his attention might compensate for causing such a distraction.

Deepbriar had left his helmet on the rail that ran round behind his seat. Doubtless expecting to see Nicky Wilkins, the newcomer finally took his eyes off Father Michael and looked up, to find himself confronted by this symbol of law and order. He gave a violent start, his feet coming off the floor briefly, and jarring back down with an audible thud. A barely suppressed ripple of laughter rang from the choir stalls, with a fainter echo coming from the pews.

Father Michael announced the last hymn, and with a friendly nod to Mr Crimmon, who looked as if he was about to faint clean away, Deepbriar applied himself to his task. Luckily the vicar had chosen 'We plough the fields and scatter', and as every voice was lifted to make the most of the cheerful tune, the interruption was forgotten. By the time Deepbriar looked up again from the instrument, the man who usually played it had gone.

Making the most of the trumpet stop, Deepbriar played the congregation out of the church. Glancing at the retreating parishioners he noticed Mrs Wriggle among them; of course, she must be visiting her daughter, who lived in Possington. Seeing the wife of Joe's employer made him forget Cyril Crimmon's odd behaviour. Suppose something serious had happened to young Spraggs? Deepbriar was very much aware that he hadn't yet made a report, but if this was a genuine missing person case the sooner action was taken the better; regardless of Sergeant Hubbard's inevitable displeasure. Distracted, he missed a note, creating an unpleasant discord.

A few minutes later Deepbriar climbed from the organ's high seat, having given his all in the final voluntary once the parishioners were mostly out of earshot and wouldn't complain about the volume. He found Father Michael awaiting him.

'Thank you so much for stepping in,' the vicar beamed. 'I'm sure Mr Crimmon was most grateful. I gather he had some family business to attend to. His brother has been a bit of a trial to the family. Barnabas that is, of course, not Aubrey. Aubrey performs an admirable service for the community, a most discreet sort of a man.'

He looked around as if expecting to see his erstwhile organist, but the church was empty apart from the two of them. 'Poor Cyril. I'm afraid he suffers from nerves. Our organ has become a passion with him, especially since the renovation. That's hardly surprising, considering how much of the money he himself raised for the repairs.'

'It looked as if he'd had a bit of an accident,' Deepbriar said. 'He had a bandage round his fingers.'

'I'll call on him on my way home,' Father Michael assured him. 'If it's serious we may be requiring your assistance again.'

'I'm happy to come whenever I'm free,' Deepbriar replied.

'Wonderful.' He shook the constable's hand enthusiastically. 'Please pay my respects to the inestimable Mrs Deepbriar. You'd better be on your way, or I shall be unpopular. I wouldn't like to think of your Sunday dinner getting cold on the table.'

With false confidence Deepbriar told him there was no chance of that, but he wasted no time getting back on the road. Hunger was beginning to gnaw at him; a big frame like his needed frequent nourishment, and he'd missed his elevenses.

Almost against his better judgement, the constable slowed as he approached the track to Wriggle's yard. He checked his watch. It was two minutes past one. As he hesitated the image of little Emily Spraggs rose up to prick his conscience.

Throwing caution to the winds Deepbriar pedalled fast through the rutted mud. He would just take one more look. The memory of Ed Walkingham's disappearance haunted him; he must try to see the evidence with Sergeant Hubbard's eyes, and prove to his own satisfaction that the case needed further investigation, before he made the irrevocable telephone call.

Again he leant his bicycle alongside the one belonging to Joe Spraggs and walked into the yard. At first glance nothing had changed; the tea cup was still in place, the old lorry sagged on its worn tyres.

Deepbriar blinked and stared. The door of the lorry wasn't quite closed. He ran to look into the cab. There, curled up on the seat, with eyes shut and face as pale as death, lay the figure of a man. It was the missing Joe.

Chapter Three

'Joe?' Deepbriar's fingers, questing at the young man's wrist, found a pulse. He sighed with relief; he'd known Joe Spraggs since he was a child and just a week ago he'd watched him take his wedding vows. It was good to find him still alive. Even if some small and less admirable corner of his mind regretted that he hadn't discovered a murder, the unworthy thought was swiftly quashed, as was the reflection that there were other people whom Minecliff wouldn't mourn: Bert Bunyard came to mind.

Deepbriar held the palm of his hand in front of Joe Spraggs's half-open mouth and felt the warmth of breath. 'Come on, Joe,' he said, giving the shoulder nearest to him a good shake. 'Wake up, there's a good lad. Your Emily's been worrying about you.'

Spraggs didn't stir. It wasn't easy to check him over for injuries while he lay curled up in the cab, but Deepbriar did his best. He could find no visible wounds, so he stepped down off the running board and hauled the limp form out of the lorry. Without waking, Joe gave a brief snort and laid his head comfortably against Deepbriar's broad chest. One thing was sure; however he'd returned, it hadn't been under his own steam.

The young man was wearing a thick tweed overcoat, and the constable recalled what Emily had said; how, expecting to go straight to the village hall after work, Joe had taken his best coat with him the previous morning. The garment now looked decidedly the worse for wear; there were patches of grey dust on both front and back, and a jagged tear at one shoulder.

It was a puzzle. Joe wasn't the type to get himself into trouble; as a youngster he'd been inclined to spend his spare time helping his father with his allotment, rarely joining the other boys when they got into mischief. And as far as Deepbriar knew he'd never developed a taste for drink, he hadn't even made a night of it before the wedding the way most lads did. The constable suppressed a grin; if this was the first time Joe had taken a skinful, he was going to have one heck of a hangover. Deepbriar set his burden down on an old door that lay abandoned and rotting by the fence, to keep him out of the mud. As he straightened he realised he'd noticed no hint of alcohol on Spraggs's breath. He leant down again, checking that he wasn't mistaken.

Deepbriar felt himself touched by an undeniable thrill. If Joe wasn't drunk then what was wrong with him? There *was* a mystery here. Somebody had brought the unconscious young man back here this morning, but where from, and why? He must certainly speak to old Bronc again; perhaps there really had been a car travelling without lights, carrying Joe and a gang of kidnappers. Scanning the entrance to the yard Deepbriar noted that there were new tracks in the mud, overlaying the ones he'd copied so meticulously, and seemingly identical. The villains had timed it well, with everyone in church. As for why they'd abducted somebody like young Joe, at the moment he couldn't think of a remotely likely reason.

Spraggs's waxy white forehead was cool; he wasn't suffering from a fever, though he muttered incoherently at Deepbriar's touch. The constable sniffed again; a scent of some kind clung to Spraggs's clothes, a musty stale smell. Where had he been? And why wouldn't he wake up? It wasn't the time for speculation though, the detective work would have to wait. Cycling back to the village to call an ambulance would mean leaving Joe alone; unlikely though it seemed, suppose he disappeared again? Besides, it would take a long time, far better to take him straight to the doctor in the village.

Deepbriar had never learnt to drive a motor vehicle. Fortunately the lorry was facing the exit and the crank handle was in place. All he had to do was get it started and steer. It couldn't be that difficult.

He put the unconscious Spraggs into the back of the lorry. Placing him on an old army blanket that had been stuffed down the side of the cab to keep out the draughts, he tucked the cushion from the seat under the man's head.

His eye fell on the flowered cup, still standing on the bonnet of the old Atkinson. It looked such a promising piece of evidence he felt it must be preserved; he couldn't believe Spraggs's condition would turn out to have some perfectly mundane explanation.

Lifting the cup very gingerly with one gloved hand he placed it by the door of the shed.

Deepbriar grasped the crank handle. As a child he had seen a man's arm broken when a reluctant engine kicked back, and the incident had made a deep impression upon him. Warily he jerked the handle round. Nothing happened.

By the sixth attempt Deepbriar was red in the face and running out of breath. He removed his gloves, spat on his hands and took a firmer grip. This time he flung all of his considerable weight into the task. He met resistance and exerted more force. The handle spun then stopped abruptly. Caught off guard Deepbriar slipped in the mud and sat down hard.

The Atkinson, having given a rather amused cough, juddered a little. The engine spluttered and the machine rocked rhythmically, blue smoke belching from the exhaust. Deepbriar hastily lifted his bicycle alongside the recumbent Spraggs, climbed into the cab and sat down, instantly discovering why Joe had used the cushion, as a metal protrusion dug into an area already tender as a result of his fall.

Ignoring the discomfort, the constable studied the controls; it looked simple enough. He released the hand brake and put a tentative foot on the right hand pedal. The engine coughed again, derisively. Recalling that the vehicle had to be in gear in order to move, Deepbriar waggled the gear lever. The Atkinson screeched in torment, and the constable snatched his hand back as if it had been scalded.

Deepbriar thought, staring at the various buttons and levers. Finally he looked beneath his feet. Of course. There was another pedal. He had to engage the clutch. Pressing down with his left foot, he tried the gear lever again, and it settled into a new position. He let out a pent-up breath, and eased his left foot up, while gradually increasing the weight on the right.

The elderly lorry leapt forward with a snort, like a startled horse. Deepbriar, clinging hard to the wheel and wincing at the pressure on his rear end, thrust both feet to the floorboards. The engine roared but the vehicle rolled to a halt. He then lifted his foot from the accelerator. Grumbling throatily, the engine subsided.

His second attempt sent the lorry hurtling through the open gates, the cab shuddering around him, before he once more thrust his size ten boots to the floor.

He decided to experiment with another gear, stirring the ancient lever until it settled again. This proved to be less than successful, since his next leap was made backwards, the Atkinson's mudguard barely missing the gate post.

The constable took a deep breath, squared his shoulders and tried again. Slowly the Atkinson wheezed forward, its bare tyres skidding a little in the mud as it ground along the rutted lane.

Knuckles white, forehead creased in concentration, Deepbriar eased the lorry out on to the road and headed it towards Minecliff. It took him twice as long to reach the village as it would have done on his bicycle, but finally the Atkinson arrived outside Dr Smythe's house. Deepbriar lifted both feet from the pedals, and with a violent jerk the lorry came to a halt and the engine died. At least that solved the problem of how to turn off the motor. He heaved on the hand brake and wiped a film of sweat from his face.

'Strange,' Dr Smythe mused, rubbing thoughtfully at his chin. 'He's had something he shouldn't, but I'm blowed if I know what.'

'Poison?' Deepbriar asked, his eyes widening at the thought. Dick Bland's last case had involved a triple poisoning; very nasty.

'No, no, just something that's sent him to sleep, I'd say. He's showing signs of coming round, though I doubt if you'll get much sense out of him for an hour or two.'

'All right if I leave him with you then, Doctor? I'll pop along and see his wife. And mine, come to that,' Deepbriar added, as his stomach rumbled hungrily. The thought of roast beef made his mouth water, and he'd forgotten his earlier fear that there might be none awaiting him.

The Doctor nodded. 'No rush I think. Come back about three. And tell young Emily she can call in a little later, with luck he'll be able to go home this evening.'

Emily Spraggs was tearful when she opened the door. It was a relief to be able to offer her reassurance, though by the time Deepbriar left a few minutes later she was looking baffled. That made two of them, the constable reflected, for he too was mystified.

'Mary?' Deepbriar called tentatively as he let himself in at the back door of the police house. The silence told him the worst; nobody was home. On the cold cooker stood a plate, covered with a saucepan lid. He lifted the lid and looked sadly at the congealing gravy that failed to disguise the overcooked state of the meat. The shrivelled potatoes and limp Yorkshire pudding didn't look very appetising either.

He found the note on the hall table, brief and to the point, with no affectionate greeting or signature; Mary had gone to visit her sister at the other end of the village.

Having eaten his meal, Deepbriar returned to the doctor's house as agreed. Joe Spraggs's face was no longer so pale; he looked now as if he was merely asleep.

'His eyes are moving more,' Dr Smythe commented. 'He'll be with us shortly.'

Sure enough, a few minutes later, Joe stirred, half turning over.

'Back in the land of the living then?' Deepbriar quipped. At his words the young man came abruptly bolt upright, his eyes wide with terror.

'What's going on?' Spraggs demanded wildly. For a long moment he stared at Deepbriar then at the doctor with an expression of horror on his face, showing no sign of recognition. Slowly the glazed look left him. He gulped convulsively.

'I thought ...' he began, then broke off, looking round the room before bringing his gaze back to the constable. 'Mr Deepbriar?' he said uncertainly. 'What happened?'

'We were hoping you might be able to tell us that,' Deepbriar replied, taking out his notebook. 'You were saying you thought ...'

Spraggs swallowed again. 'Sounds daft,' the young man said hoarsely. 'I thought I was dead. Until the man came back.'

'Drink this,' the doctor urged, holding out a glass. 'It's only water,' he added as his patient hesitated.

Spraggs drank thirstily, draining the glass. 'Thank you,' he said. 'I didn't know I was so dry. How did I get here?'

'The constable found you, in your lorry I gather,' the doctor said, taking the young man's wrist to check his pulse. 'How are you feeling now? No pain? How about your head?'

'A bit muzzy, that's all.' He looked from one man to the other. 'I haven't smashed up the lorry, have I?'

'No, no.' The doctor raised his eyebrows. 'He's with us, I think. You can go ahead and ask your questions, constable.'

Deepbriar nodded. 'Let's begin at the beginning, Joe. Saturday afternoon. You were working late, is that right?'

'Yes, I normally finish about four on a Saturday. I'd already done one delivery to Falbrough, then there was a rush job, taking a load of timber to Gristlethorpe. I'd told Emily I'd be late, and I was going to meet her at the village hall. She wasn't too happy, what with this weekend being sort of a honeymoon.' His brow furrowed as he tried to work things out. 'I've missed it, haven't I? *Madame Butterfly*? Emily'll be upset. She was keen, because her auntie was in it.'

'Yes, I'm afraid you have missed it.' He refrained from further comment, keeping to the business in hand. 'What time did you get back to the yard?'

'Must have been about a quarter to seven. Emily had given me something for my supper, a nice bit of meat pie. I was going to sit in the cab and eat it. I went to fetch my coat first though, from the office. And that's when I saw it.'

'Saw what?'

'Tea. Already made. A whole pot of it, steaming hot. I thought Mr Wriggle must have just left. I poured a cup and took it back to the lorry, because I was checking the plugs. I remember I drank it after I'd eaten the pie ...' a puzzled expression drifted across his face.

'That may well be it,' the Doctor put in, 'hot tea, especially with plenty of sugar, will disguise quite a strong flavour.'

Deepbriar nodded, still watching Spraggs. 'Would that be normal, your boss leaving tea for you?'

'No, not really, but I didn't think much about it. I mean, the office wasn't locked either, but he forgets sometimes.'

'You locked it then, did you?'

'No, not much point. I'd be putting the cup back, wouldn't I. Only ...' he faltered. 'I don't remember doing it.'

'You remember drinking the tea though,' Deepbriar prompted. 'What happened next?'

'Blowed if I know.' Spraggs rubbed a hand round the back of his neck. 'Did I have an accident?'

'I'm not sure,' Deepbriar confessed, 'but I don't think so.'

'This is rum.' The young man lifted his head and stared out of the window. Bright sun slanted across the village green, lighting up the red and gold of the fallen leaves. 'What's the time?' he asked.

'A quarter past three,' the doctor told him, 'on Sunday afternoon.'

'You're kidding!' Joe leapt to his feet. 'My Emily will be worried sick!'

'No, she won't,' Deepbriar said, putting a restraining hand on his shoulder. 'I've seen her, and told her you're here. She'll be along in a while and the pair of you can go home. Just you sit yourself down. Let's get back to when you finished work. You didn't see anything when you drove into the yard? Or along the road?'

'Like what?'

'Another lorry maybe, or a car?'

Joe shook his head. 'It's always quiet, Saturday teatime. Didn't see a soul.'

'All right. What about when you first came to?' Deepbriar consulted his notes. 'You said ... "I thought I was dead. Until the man came back." What was that all about?'

Joe gave him a guarded look. 'I'm not sure. Maybe it was just a dream. My head's in a proper muddle. I don't understand half of this. Can't I go now?'

'In a minute. Fact is, Joe, you disappeared. At half past ten this morning I searched all over Wriggle's yard and you weren't there, but when I got back for another look just after one o'clock I found you lying unconscious in your cab. If there's anything else you can tell me, no matter what, it could help us find out what has been going on.'

Joe stared at him. 'I disappeared? That's crazy.'

'Maybe, but that's how it was. Perhaps there's some simple reason for what happened. You're back safe and sound, so maybe the hows and whys don't matter.' The constable watched as Joe considered what he'd said. 'If I was you I'd want to know,' he went on, 'and I'll do my best to help, if that's what you want.'

Slowly the young man nodded.

'Right,' Deepbriar said. 'The man you mentioned. Tell me what you remember.'

Spraggs was silent a moment, gathering his thoughts. 'I was lying on the ground. It was dark. And bitter cold; I mean, it's been cold for days, but this was worse somehow, right into my bones. I felt sort of funny, my arms and legs were all weak, like I'd been ill or something. After a while I managed to sit up and I groped about a bit. Couldn't see a thing. I tried shouting.' Joe shuddered. 'It was like I was buried, deep underground. My voice didn't sound right.'

'What do you mean, it didn't sound right?'

'Quiet. Sort of echoing, but muffled. I thought it was because it was so dark, like nothing could get through. I wasn't exactly wide awake, but I was scared that I'd run out of air.' The young man shook himself and tried to smile, but without much success. 'Sounds daft.'

Deepbriar shook his head. 'Not at all. Any idea how long you were in this place?'

'No. It seemed like forever. But then I saw light, just a bit of a glow. I wanted to get up and go over to it, but my legs wouldn't work properly. I suppose that's when I decided it must be a dream, though when I tried to wake myself up I couldn't. Then suddenly this man appeared. There must have been a bit of light coming in, not much though, because he wasn't much more than a shape looming over me. He seemed to come out of nowhere.'

'Did you see his face?'

'No. I tell you, he was just a shadow.'

'Was he tall? Thin or fat?'

'Not small. I'm not sure. I was scared half out of my wits.' Joe flushed, a deep shade of pink spreading across his face. 'All this could have been a nightmare, couldn't it?' He looked at Deepbriar pleadingly.

'It could, but I don't think it was, and you don't either, not if you're honest with yourself.' He gave the young man a searching look and Joe shook his head miserably.

'The ground you were lying on, what did it feel like?'

Joe considered for a while. 'Hard. And rough. Like stone.'

Deepbriar nodded thoughtfully. 'That matches the dust on your coat, it had to come from somewhere. I'm sure you weren't dreaming, Joe. Go on, this man appeared, then what?'

'He threw something over my head, and then these hands grabbed me.'

'You mean the man took hold of you?'

'I don't think it was him, not at first. There must have been more than one of them. I tried to fight and I was shouting at them to let me go. They got me rolled up in a blanket or something, and it was so tight over my face I could hardly breathe. There was a funny smell, sort of sickly. I don't remember much more after that.'

'You didn't hear anything? These men didn't talk to each other?'

'No.' Joe shook his head. 'Hang on, though. Right at the end I was in a bit of a panic, I was going fair crazy. Somebody yelled. I think I might have kicked one of them. I hope I did,' he added fervently. 'I hope I got him right where it hurts.'

Dusk was falling as Constable Deepbriar opened the door of the police house. There was still an ominous silence within. The telephone rang, and he went to answer it.

'Good afternoon, constable.' Father Michael's cheerful voice greeted him. 'I hope I'm not disturbing you.'

'Of course not,' Deepbriar replied, 'what can I do for you?'

'I had a word with Mr Crimmon, and I'm afraid it will be several weeks before he's able to play the organ again. I gather he shut his hand in a door. I've asked young Nicky to play for evensong today, but we've a couple of weddings coming up, as well as the regular services. I'd be grateful if you could fill in for us.'

'My pleasure. I'll have a word with my sergeant, and see if I can arrange my duty to leave me free when I'm needed, if you'll let me have the dates.'

'Excellent! I'll ask Miss Lightfall to contact you with the details.'

'Tell Mr Crimmon I'm sorry to hear about his hand. I thought he looked a bit upset this morning.'

'Ahh yes. He's inclined to be a little jealous of his position, I don't think he likes to see other people sitting in his place, as it were. No matter, a little hardship is good for the soul. Give my regards to Mrs Deepbriar.'

'When I see her,' the constable muttered gloomily, as he replaced the receiver. Feeling like a martyr he made himself a cup of tea in the deserted kitchen and sat down at the table, staring at the new Dick Bland which lay on the dresser where he'd put it the previous day. Alongside it was the package Harry Bartle had given him. He got up and fetched it, unwrapping the brown paper to reveal a garish paper-covered book.

A woman of the less respectable kind, wearing a red dress that showed off far more of her figure than would be considered respectable in Minecliff, glared at a dark man in a homburg hat. A cigarette dangled from her painted and pouting lips. 'Mitch O'Hara and the Thousand Dollar Dame,' the title proclaimed.

Like Deepbriar, Harry was an avid reader of detective stories, and devoured all he could get his hands on; this book was a gift to the young man from his cousin, a local girl who had married a GI during the War and now lived in Wisconsin.

Deepbriar placed this new offering alongside his library book. He usually enjoyed a good read on a Sunday afternoon, but today his mind was too full of his own mystery.

On the other side of the hall was the little room that served as Minecliff's police station. Deepbriar decided to write his report about the disappearance of Joe Spraggs while it was still fresh in his mind. Since Joe was back home and apparently unharmed, the case probably wouldn't be taken seriously by his superiors, not with the affair of Ed Walkingham still hanging over them. But there could be no doubt Joe had been the victim of assault; if the abduction had been a practical joke it was a pretty heartless one, and it had definitely gone too far.

Deepbriar stared blankly at the paper in the typewriter. Why, he wondered, would somebody want to drug Joe Spraggs and hold him captive overnight? There was no sign of any other mischief being done at Wriggle's yard.

It might have been easier to understand if only Joe wasn't such a sober and sensible young chap. He wasn't the kind to have upset anyone, and Deepbriar was sure he was an honest man. There wasn't much of a criminal element in Minecliff, and although Falbrough and Belston had their share of rogues, Spraggs didn't mix with bad company. What possible motive could anyone have for kidnapping him? No answers came to mind and Deepbriar sighed. When it came to real life mysteries he didn't have the Dick Bland touch.

Monday morning brought the first white frost to the fields around the village of Minecliff, but the cold air outside was nothing compared to the atmosphere inside the police house, which hadn't warmed up since the previous day. After he'd eaten his breakfast, the constable was relieved to receive another summons from Ferdy Quinn.

On second thoughts he wasn't quite so sure it was a welcome development; the reappearance of Joe Spraggs had completely driven the matter of the straying heifers from Deepbriar's mind, and when he heard Quinn's irate tones at the other end of the line, he steeled himself to admit that he hadn't yet reported the affair to his superiors. He needn't have worried; the farmer was no longer concerned with his cattle, he had something else to complain about.

'Get out here!' Quinn bellowed, almost incoherent with rage.

'He's gone too far this time!' As his voice rose to an hysterical squeal, Deepbriar winced and held the handset away from his ear.

'Take a deep breath, Mr Quinn,' Deepbriar advised, 'or you'll be giving yourself a heart attack. I'll be along, just as soon as I can.'

He telephoned Sergeant Hubbard and explained why he wouldn't be making his report in Falbrough until the afternoon, then he wheeled his bicycle out on to the road, calling a farewell as he went. There was no reply from the scullery, where a rhythmic splash and thud told him that Mary was tackling the week's wash.

If Ferdy Quinn had appeared furious the previous day, this morning he looked almost insane with rage, his face redder than his hair as he paced to and fro, his two dogs keeping a wary distance from his stamping feet, reminding Deepbriar irresistibly of the men who had acted in similar fashion the previous day. They were evidently making themselves scarce; sounds of metallic hammering came from one of the sheds, while the cows were milling about in the yard as they left the dairy. Will Minter stood by the cattle byre, watching his irate neighbour and looking as if he'd prefer to be somewhere else.

'About time!' Quinn snapped as Constable Deepbriar free wheeled in through the farm gate. 'Come on!' He stomped across the yard and off up the hill without another word, waving an arm to call Minter and the constable to join him, evidently too furious to explain where they were going.

Chapter Four

'Morning, Thorny,' Will Minter nodded. A slow-thinking, slow-moving man, he fell into step beside Deepbriar. 'Been a bit of a fire.'

'A fire? Here?'

'Over yonder.' he pointed. 'Was me what found it. Smelt smoke when I come out this morning and sent one of my lads to have a look.'

'It's my barn, down in the hollow,' Quinn bawled, half turning round but not stopping. 'Burnt to cinders, along with what was left of last year's hay.'

'Bit hidden down there,' Will Minter added, 'nobody would have noticed, any road, not in the middle of the night.'

'I hope you've not been trampling over the evidence,' Deepbriar said. 'If the fire was set deliberately they might have left signs.'

' "Set deliberately"?' Quinn looked ready to explode. 'You danged fool, of course it was set deliberately! It was Bunyard! Who else could it be?'

'We went through this yesterday, Mr Quinn,' Deepbriar said stolidly. 'You could get yourself into trouble if you go slandering people. I agree Bert's done a few things contrary to the law in his time, but he's only human. He can't walk two miles on a broken leg, and that's a fact. We'll go and take a look at the damage, and meanwhile I'd thank you to keep a civil tongue in your head.'

Ferdy Quinn took a deep shuddering breath. 'Yes,' he said at last. 'I'm sorry, constable. But I just know Bunyard's behind all this somehow. He must be!'

The three men walked on across the fields with Quinn muttering angrily under his breath until the steepening slope silenced him. A few wisps of smoke became visible, rising over the crest of the hill.

At last the barn came into sight, or all that was left of it. A steep-sided valley sheltered a smouldering heap of charred wood.

'Lucky I didn't have any beasts in here,' Quinn growled, kicking at a blackened doorpost.

'Last year's hay, you said.' Deepbriar began writing in his pocket-book. He glanced up to see a range of emotions flit across Quinn's flushed face, and quickly looked down again to hide his smile. The farmer was regretting his honesty; given time it might have occurred to him to claim something of more value had gone up in smoke; until now he'd been too upset to think about the insurance.

'That wasn't all,' Quinn said, picking up a stick and poking at the ruins, uncovering what might have been a large metal buckle. 'Kept my old harness in here, too.'

'If there's any evidence of foul play you're going a fair way to destroy it,' Deepbriar commented, and the farmer threw down the stick and retreated a few steps.

'Thought you didn't keep horses any more.' Minter put in.

'I don't.' Quinn was defensive. 'But that doesn't mean I can afford to lose that gear. Might have needed it again some time. Or I could have sold it.'

Patiently Deepbriar wrote down the items Quinn listed, then he walked round the site of the fire, studying the ground, sniffing at the ashes. Not that anyone would need petrol to set a hay barn ablaze. 'Could be the fire brigade might want to come and have a look,' he said, having satisfied himself that the frozen ground hadn't preserved any footprints. 'Nothing more I can do here.'

'Never mind, Ferdy,' Will Minter said cheerfully as Deepbriar finished his inspection, 'let's face it, that barn was pretty old, it would have fallen down in a gale one of these days, any road.'

Quinn scowled at him. 'Easy enough for you to say, you're not the one getting picked on. Suppose he comes back to do the same to the rest of my buildings?' He glared at Deepbriar. 'Who's to stop him?'

'I'll be talking to Bert Bunyard later today,' Deepbriar said. 'But unless the man can fly I can't see any way he could have got here.'

'What about Bunyard's son?' Quinn growled. 'You say it wasn't him, but where's your proof?'

'Humphrey's too scared of the outside world to come all the way over here,' Deepbriar assured him. 'But I'll check, like I said.'

'I've not seen that boy in years,' Will Minter said. 'Not quite all there, is he?'

'He's harmless enough. If it wasn't for Humphrey looking after their beasts I reckon him and Bert would have starved by now,' Deepbriar said. 'He might not have been overly bright at school, but he always had a way with animals, did Humphrey Bunyard. There wasn't a dog in Minecliff wouldn't tag along behind him when he was a boy. But I can't see him coming over here at night, I remember his mother telling me he was terrified of the dark. That would only be three years or so back, not long before she died.'

'People can change,' Quinn said. 'I don't know what the world's coming to, when respectable folks can't sleep in their beds without scoundrels opening their gates and setting their property on fire.'

'I'll be getting off home, Ferdy,' Will Minter said. 'Got a day's work to do. So long, Thorny.' He winked cheerfully behind his neighbour's back and headed off across country towards his own farm.

'Bye, Will.' The constable sighed, resigning himself to Quinn's grumbling all the way back; it was almost as bad as listening to Mary's reproachful silence. They were trudging across the last field when a shrill call cut across Ferdy Quinn's lament.

'Telephone!' Mrs Quinn's voice, trained over the years to reach her husband as he went about his work in the fields, carried clearly. 'For Constable Deepbriar.'

Deepbriar increased his pace, happy to leave the farmer's tirade behind.

'It's Ada Tapper,' Mrs Quinn said disapprovingly, as the constable hurried up the steps into the house, 'but she won't tell me what it's about.'

Deepbriar picked up the receiver. Ada Tapper was a local character. Charlady for half a dozen households in and around Minecliff, she was to be seen almost daily walking the lanes with her huge, elephantine legs encased in thick Lyle stockings, and her big frame wrapped in an ancient army greatcoat which had probably seen service in the First World War. She carried the tools of her trade in a decrepit basket, which she protected on rainy days with a large umbrella.

'This is Mrs Ada Tapper,' she announced, delivering the words into the telephone slowly, but at maximum volume, as if she had to make them travel the three miles without benefit of wires. 'I'm in the telephone box on the corner, by the church. I telephoned to the police house first, and they said to try at Quinn's farm.'

'This is Constable Deepbriar, Ada. There's no need to shout. I can hear you quite well. What's the trouble?'

'It's Mr Pattridge. I went to do for him at nine o'clock this morning, same as always on a Monday, but I can't get in. He's got all the doors locked. I think he's in the parlour.'

'How do you know that?'

'There's a gap in the curtains. I can see one of his legs. I've been knocking and calling, but he hasn't moved.'

'I'll come and take a look,' Deepbriar said. 'It'll take me about ten minutes to get there.'

'I don't think it'll make much difference how long you take, constable. His shotgun's on the floor beside him.' And with that she put the receiver down.

Deepbriar scowled at the telephone as he dialled the number for Doctor Smythe's surgery.

'I've got one more patient to see,' Smythe said, once Deepbriar had explained. 'I'll meet you out there.'

They arrived at Oldgate Farm simultaneously, the constable turning in just ahead of the doctor's car. Ada stood, stolid and immobile, outside the back door. 'There's nothing open,' she said, as Deepbriar tried the door handle, 'I've been all round.'

'I have to check for myself, Ada,' Deepbriar said, 'so I can write it down in my report.'

'Writin'!' Ada sniffed dismissively, with all the contempt of the unlettered. 'Never felt the need of it.'

The catch on the kitchen window yielded to the force of Deepbriar's penknife, and he climbed in, then opened the door for the others. 'Stay in the kitchen,' he told Ada.

She sniffed again. 'Won't be nothin' I ain't seen before.'

When he entered the parlour and saw what awaited them there, Deepbriar doubted that. In nearly twenty years of police work he'd never seen such a scene. Often, he thought bleakly, the heroes of detective stories discovered the bodies of suicides, or more often, since they concerned works of fiction, apparent suicides. The phrase, 'he blew his brains out' was a familiar cliché, but he'd never imagined it being so graphically exact. A double barrelled shotgun did an efficient job. The contents of Colin Pattridge's skull were scattered over half the room.

'Found 'is dog,' Ada said from the doorway. 'Dead in its bed in the pantry, an' stone cold. Bin poorly a week or two, it 'ad, reckon it was the only reason 'e went on this long, kept 'im goin' like. Blimey,' she said dispassionately, coming to stand at Deepbriar's side. 'That mess'll take some clearin' up.'

'I told you not to come in,' Deepbriar said.

'Seen worse,' she sniffed. 'I was in France during the war, the first lot, 'elpin' out in an orspital. Only a slip of a girl I was. Used to be sick sometimes at first, the fings we 'ad to deal wiv, but you got used to it in the end.'

That probably explained the greatcoat. It was hard to imagine the solidly built Ada as a slip of a girl, but Deepbriar no longer doubted the strength of her stomach.

'I'd be grateful if you'd brew a cup of tea for when the doctor's finished, Ada,' he suggested, ushering her away and closing the door behind her.

'Not much doubt about the cause of death,' Smythe said a few minutes later. 'At a guess I'd say it happened some time yesterday.'

Deepbriar had been inspecting the room. There was nothing to suggest that Pattridge hadn't taken his own life, including his own knowledge of the man. A small collection of items lay on the table in front of the corpse; three photographs in tarnished silver frames, a letter, the ink rather faded over time, and a pocket watch. A little further away lay a single folded sheet of paper, with the word TONY written in large capitals across it.

The spread of blood and brains had gone in the other direction; only a couple of tiny red specks had landed on the glass of the closest photograph. It showed Colin Pattridge, a good deal younger, smilingly flanked by two boys, each of them grinning at the camera and holding up a watch.

John and Tony. As unalike as it was possible for brothers to be. John had been the one who worked hard alongside his father on the farm, while Tony got into every kind of mischief. And John had been the one who had volunteered for the navy in 1942, as soon as he was old enough, and drowned in the Atlantic after just six months at sea, while Tony had grown to manhood a few years later and sulked his way through national service before drifting into a life of petty crime, coming home only when he was broke.

The old letter was from one of John's friends, evidently one of the few survivors when their ship was torpedoed. He wrote to apologise, saying how much John had wanted his father to have his watch, but that it had gone to the bottom along with its owner. There was nothing he could send back he said, except memories, and he had filled two pages with stories of the brief time he had known John Pattridge, the ink blurred in places as if he, or maybe the old man, had shed tears over the telling.

'Tony hasn't been back in a while,' Doctor Smythe remarked, straightening from the desk at the side of the room, where he'd been writing the death certificate.

'No,' Deepbriar mused, surreptitiously wiping dampness from his eyes and replacing the letter on the table.

'I hear he's got in with a thoroughly bad lot. It would have been no wonder if his father turned him out.'

Deepbriar nodded. He picked up the watch. This must have been the one that belonged to the younger son. And while John had treasured his, Tony evidently hadn't cared enough to keep it with him, though he hadn't pawned or sold it, and maybe that meant something.

With a feeling of growing discomfort, Deepbriar flicked open the single sheet of note paper. It bore no salutation other than the bald word printed on the outside. 'It's all yours now,' it said, 'I've sold off the last of the stock, and sent some money to the church to make sure John's memorial is kept in order. With everything you did, I never stopped loving you. I had your watch repaired a year ago, thinking I'd see you. I can't bear the thought of another Christmas like the last, waiting, hoping you'd find a few minutes to visit. It wouldn't have hurt you to go on pretending that you cared, for the sake of John's memory, if not for me. I hope one day you'll be happy.' It wasn't signed.

Aubrey Crimmon looked nothing like his older brother; for a start he was about twice Cyril's size. He too wore sombre clothes, but he gave the impression that this was only of necessity, because it was expected of an undertaker, or as it stated discreetly on the black briefcase he carried, a funeral director. The huge man had a cheerful air about him as he breezed into the house.

'Good morning, constable,' Crimmon extended a large black-gloved hand. 'A sorry affair,' he went on, 'I take it there are no immediate relatives to consult?'

'No. His surviving son hasn't been around for a year, and as far as I can make out there's no other family.'

'How sad. Perhaps you'd be good enough to give me the few

details I need, then, for the paperwork. Unless that's the job of the plain clothes policeman I saw outside?'

Detective Sergeant Jakes, summoned by telephone as standing orders dictated when a body was found, had arrived five minutes before Crimmon. He had taken one look at the mess inside the house and then gone straight outside to rid himself rather explosively of his breakfast.

'I'll see to it,' Deepbriar said sombrely. He could hardly blame the younger man, he'd been grateful that some hours had passed since he'd eaten his own meal.

It only took a minute, then Crimmon summoned his assistant who had been waiting outside, and they prepared to remove the mortal remains of Colin Pattridge from his home. Deepbriar stood by the window, half watching, though his thoughts wandered. Crimmon took hold of the sheet which Ada Tapper had brought to cover the body and began to remove it. He froze, just for an instant, his plump features tense so that for a few seconds his face looked almost gaunt. Deepbriar came abruptly out of his reverie in time to see that the man's hands were trembling.

'Are you all right, Mr Crimmon? Something wrong?'

'No, nothing at all.' The undertaker gave an unctuous half smile. 'We see all sorts, of course, I don't know why this should have shocked me. I beg your pardon, most unprofessional.'

But, Deepbriar thought, it hadn't been the sight of the shattered head that had brought the man up short. Only the dead man's hand and arm had been uncovered in that first smooth motion. When the gun had fallen from Pattridge's grasp, his nerveless hand had dropped to the arm of the chair. Deepbriar hadn't noticed anything odd about it, but now, coming closer, he saw that the third and fourth fingers of the right hand were slightly webbed, making them appear shorter than the others.

'Strange, that,' he said, pointing. 'I've known Mr Pattridge for years, but I'd never noticed it before. Was that what surprised you?'

'Well, yes.' Crimmon nodded. 'How very astute of you, constable. It's just a coincidence, I believe I remember seeing a similar hand on another of our clients. I dare say it's a common enough thing, a little abnormality like that appearing now and then. Mr Pattridge must have been related to a lot of people in this area, even if he doesn't have any close family still living.'

*

Lunch, like breakfast, was a silent affair, with Mary slapping a plate of bread and cheese and pickle down in front of her husband then returning to her laundry without a word. Deepbriar stared down at the food, not seeing it. His mind was still full of the scene at Oldgate Farm. He wondered if Tony Pattridge would turn up, like the proverbial bad penny, once he heard what had happened. Would he shed a tear for his father? Folk often didn't know what they'd got until they lost it; maybe he'd come to regret his neglect of the old man, now it was too late to do anything about it.

Deepbriar listened to the sounds from the back of the house, identifying the moment when Mary picked up the peg bag and a basket of washing to take into the garden, letting the door slam. He had to find some way to appease her, but so far all his attempts to apologise had been rebuffed.

Of course what he'd seen and done that morning was official police business, but he'd always been able to share a little of the burden of such things with his wife, knowing he could trust her not to gossip. He ate his meal without really tasting it, then made a pot of tea, taking a cup through to the scullery.

'Thank you,' Mary said stiffly. 'Put it down there.' She nodded to the shelf above the wringer.

'Listen love,' Deepbriar began awkwardly. 'I'm really sorry …'

'Not now,' she said, elbowing him aside on her way to the door. 'I'm busy.'

With a heartfelt sigh Deepbriar retreated to his office. There were still a few things to do before he cycled in to Falbrough to give his weekly report, and the best remedy he could think of for a spot of melancholy was hard work.

Deepbriar sat staring at Alfred Wriggle across the table in Emily Spraggs's kitchen. He'd summoned the builder's merchant with a telephone call, suffering no pangs of conscience when he exaggerated the Doctor's concern for Joe's state of health, insisting that Wriggle must fetch the ancient Atkinson, since Joe wouldn't be fit to drive the lorry for another day at least.

Wriggle was a spare man, with fine thin hair and skin stretched tight over his facial bones, as if his parsimony extended to the matter of his own flesh. He wore a threadbare jacket fastened with one remaining button, and a worn flat cap lay in front of him on the scrubbed boards.

'You didn't do that vehicle of mine any good yesterday,

constable,' he said, jerking his head towards the window. 'Easy to see you don't know much about motors. Reckon it'll be needing a de-coke.'

'Is that so?' Deepbriar consulted his notebook. 'Then while that's being done you might like to get the headlamp fixed. Otherwise you could be getting a summons.'

Wriggle looked innocently puzzled. 'What headlamp's that then?'

'The one that's been broken since midsummer,' Deepbriar replied. 'I notice it's not even got a bulb in it, so I'm fairly sure it won't be working. Consider this a warning, and make sure it's fixed by the end of the week, eh? But I didn't come to talk about that, I need to ask you a few questions about what happened to young Joe.'

Pursing his lips, Wriggle shook his head solemnly. 'The pranks these youngsters get up to. Wasn't like that in my day, we were too busy earning a crust to go messing about playing practical jokes.'

Deepbriar studied the man's face; if Wriggle was dissembling he could see no sign of it. 'So you think it was a practical joke?' he said at last.

'Can't think of any other explanation. It must have been a couple of his friends, giving him a hard time because he just got married. Not that I'd expect that sort of monkey business with Joe, he's a quiet lad. He turns up on time and doesn't whine if he has to work late now and then. What else could it be?'

'I don't know,' the constable said. 'Suppose it wasn't Joe they were after? As far as I could tell there was nothing stolen from the yard, but I'll need you to check. You didn't have anything special there this week? Anything particularly valuable?'

Wriggle shook his head. 'Had some marble slabs in for the Colonel, but Joe delivered them to the Manor last Tuesday. Though there's a lot of stock out there, I wouldn't want you to go thinking any different. It'd be a fair haul if somebody raided my yard, that's for sure.'

Having seen the state of most of that 'stock' Deepbriar contented himself with a noncommittal nod. 'No sign of them removing anything. Only Joe. Somehow I don't think this was any sort of robbery.' The idea that thieves were responsible for Joe's disappearance didn't hold water. They could have waited for him to leave and had the place to themselves. Drugging a man's tea and leaving it there, hot and inviting, was a strange thing to do. It spoke of careful planning.

Deepbriar got an assurance from Wriggle that he'd look over his stock and let him know if anything was missing, then the old man left, driving the elderly lorry back to the yard, having rather grudgingly agreed to give Joe the entire day off without docking his pay. Once his boss had gone Joe came downstairs, his young wife flitting solicitously along behind him.

'Hello there, Joe. Feeling better?' Deepbriar asked.

'I'm fine,' Spraggs replied shortly.

He didn't look fine, the constable thought. There were dark marks under his eyes, and his face had no more colour than when Deepbriar had found him the day before.

'I heard Mr Wriggle drive away,' Joe went on, taking the seat his boss had vacated. 'The old man's none too good with that lorry. It needs nursing.'

'He seems to think I damaged it. Says it needs a de-coke.'

Joe grinned. 'That's as maybe, but it's no fault of yours. The old bus is on its last legs. It's only the way I take care of it keeps it going.' He covered a wide yawn with his hand. 'Excuse me. Didn't sleep too well. Daft really, seeing I still felt so tired. Doctor says I should be wide awake by tomorrow morning.'

'I don't suppose you've remembered anything else?' Deepbriar asked.

'No. I've been wracking my brains but I can't think of a thing. If I do then I'll let you know.'

'If he does, then I'll come and tell you,' Emily put in, laying a proprietorial hand on her husband's shoulder. The young couple exchanged fond glances.

'You do that. I'd best be off then. Take good care of him, Mrs Spraggs,' he said, smiling as the girl blushed on hearing her title; it seemed no time at all since she'd been little Emily, youngest of the Hopgood clan, offering him an apple on her way to primary school.

'Mr Deepbriar.' She spoke in an undertone, stopping him as he stepped out of the front door. 'Is he safe now? Whatever this was about, you don't think anything else bad is going to happen to him?'

'I wish I knew,' Deepbriar said ruefully. 'I certainly hope not, and I'll do my best to make sure it doesn't. Try not to worry. And if he remembers anything else, no matter how small a thing, you be sure and let me know.'

Chapter Five

Deepbriar telephoned Falbrough yet again, to advise them that he was further delayed, thanks to the discovery of Colin Pattridge's suicide. When he did finally get to the station he'd be in trouble, since there was no hope of catching up with the paperwork; it looked as if he'd be spending the next few evenings in his office. With Mary still barely speaking to him maybe that wouldn't be such a bad thing.

From the road, Hurdles Farm looked like a junk yard, and the view didn't improve inside the gate. Parked forlornly by the ramshackle barn was an ancient lorry, standing on four flat tyres, and with grass growing up through the rotting wooden floor. An old sofa with the springs sticking out leant against the tumbledown porch, and a scrawny chicken ran clucking from beneath it as Deepbriar approached.

There were sounds of movement on the other side of the door when Deepbriar rapped on it with his knuckles, but they faded rapidly into silence.

'Anybody home?' he called, knocking again, persisting until he could hear a slow thud, thud, thud growing gradually louder as somebody approached the door from inside. The hinges squealed a loud protest when it swung open.

'Well?' Bert Bunyard's moon-shaped face appeared, glowering. He clung to the side of the door, his other hand leaning heavily on a crutch, the plaster cast on his leg thrust before him like a trophy.

'Don't recall invitin' you to come visitin',' the farmer said ungraciously. 'Hope you got good reason for gettin' a sick man out of his bed of pain.'

'Just a routine call, Bert. Maybe I'd better come in. If you're sick you'll not want to stand in the cold while we talk.'

The farm kitchen was as messy as the yard, but warmer, thanks to a battered black stove in the chimney breast. Bunyard dropped awkwardly into the only armchair, leaving Deepbriar to fetch a rickety wooden stool from against the wall. He sat himself down and met Bunyard's gaze.

Minecliff's most notorious rogue was in his forties but he looked ten years older, the fleshy face criss-crossed with purple veins, his hair a greasy grey thatch. The farmer dressed the same whether he was indoors or out, with a red neckerchief knotted at his throat, and a filthy old stock coat bulging over his stomach and tied round his waist with string. There was one change though; the right leg of his trousers had been cut from the bottom up to knee level to accommodate a plaster cast, already grubby, and splotched in places with dark stains.

'How's the leg?' the constable asked.

'How d'you think?' Bunyard favoured him with another glare.

'Bad break was it?'

'When you get to my age any break is bad,' Bunyard growled. 'If it weren't for these 'ere crutches I 'ad in me cow shed I couldn't even get down to the shop. Starve I would, if I waited for me neighbours to come an' 'elp. What you want? Don't tell me you came 'ere to ask after me 'ealth.'

'I came to see if you know anything about what's been happening over at Quinn's.' Deepbriar said sternly.

Bunyard's eyes widened, his face showing nothing but innocent surprise. 'Somethin' goin' on over there? I don't know nothin' about it. Man don't get to see much when he can't 'ardly 'obble out 'is door.'

'You've not heard about gates being opened in the middle of the night, or a building set alight?'

The man grinned, showing uneven teeth stained brown. 'Can't say I 'ave, but tell me more. That ole misery gettin' his comeuppance is 'e?'

'I'm sure you can make it to the Speckled Goose if you want the gossip,' Deepbriar replied. 'I won't deprive you of the pleasure of hearing it with all the trimmings.' He took out his notebook, though he doubted if he'd wheedle anything useful out of Bunyard, the man was so mean he wouldn't give his neighbours the time of day unless he thought there was a profit in it.

Flipping the pages open Deepbriar noticed the sketch he'd made of the tyre marks at Wriggle's yard. To him that seemed a far more important case, though Ferdy Quinn wouldn't agree.

'Have you seen a big black car driving through the village any time in the last few days?' he asked. The question took Bunyard by surprise, and for the briefest moment Deepbriar saw something in the man's face, before it was once again wiped clean.

'Can't say I 'ave. Only been to the shop twice since I got this,' he said, gesturing at the plaster.

'Right.' Deepbriar looked down as if consulting his notes, sure he'd struck some chord. It was frustrating, but he'd get nowhere trying to force the issue, Bunyard could be a stubborn old goat. 'How about Bronc, have you seen him recently?'

'No. He don't come 'ere. Don't have nothin' to spare for tramps, enough trouble keepin' body an' soul together for me an' my boy.'

'Talking of Humphrey, I don't suppose he's been out and about? Visiting someone perhaps?'

Bunyard snorted. 'Last time my boy left the farm was the day they threw 'im out of school. Hasn't seen no reason since then, likes it better at 'ome. Anyways, he wouldn't know a black car from a grey one like that old wreck of the Colonel's.'

Deepbriar nodded. Doris Bunyard had somehow persuaded the school board to allow Humphrey to attend classes until he was fourteen, although he wasn't capable of learning much. Luckily he'd been a biddable child, not given to disrupting the lessons, happy to sit quietly at the back of the room.

Humphrey would be nineteen by now. Since his mother's death he'd withdrawn further into himself, forgetting much of the language he'd learnt. Deepbriar had always felt sorry for the boy, teased and bullied by his peers, and exploited by his father. Small wonder he preferred the company of the farm animals and refused to venture into the wider world. It was more likely Bert had found a way to fly across two miles of fields to Quinn's farm than that Humphrey had been persuaded to go there.

'Still, I'd like a quick word with him.'

'He's in the yard. Got a cow down wi' the sprindles. Be lucky if it don't turn into chabby foot.' The farmer gave Deepbriar a challenging look. The constable kept his own expression carefully neutral. He had an idea that Bunyard invented these outlandish names for his animal's complaints; he regularly brought out new ones, most notably in the pub when there were strangers in the public bar. Often some gullible city dweller would be impressed by his country yokel act and buy him a drink, thinking he'd encountered a true rural character of that elusive old England he'd come to find. Deepbriar had yet to meet anyone, either veterinarian or farmer, who had heard of any of Bunyard's diseases.

Deepbriar rose to his feet. 'I'll go and find him then.'

'Close the door be'ind you,' Bunyard grunted. 'An' don't you go upsettin' the lad. 'E's got a lot o' work to get through, what wi' me bein' laid up.'

'I'm sure he's run off his feet on that account,' the constable said sardonically, aware that Bert did very little, even when he was up and about. 'Don't worry, me and Humphrey get along all right, I'll not trouble him.' He left by the back door, stepping squeamishly over what looked like the inedible parts of a chicken lying in the mud, and squeezing past a rotting wooden cart with a scruffy cockerel glaring beadily at him from the top of one wheel. A dog barked frantically as Deepbriar crossed the yard, straining to reach the intruder as it thrust against the chain tethering it to its kennel.

Humphrey Bunyard was in the cow shed, on his knees beside a cow that lay flat out on its side. The young man was stroking the beast's head, crooning soft meaningless sounds and rocking back and forth with his eyes closed. Even in repose Humphrey had the look of a bewildered child. As the constable approached the animal seemed to sense his presence, for it lifted its head then hauled itself heavily to its feet. Humphrey got up too, the apprehension on his face turning swiftly to a smile as he saw who his visitor was.

Deepbriar pulled a bar of Dairy Milk from his pocket, bought for the occasion before he left the village; it was lucky the rationing was over at last, he didn't think Mary would have understood the need to give young Bunyard her weekly supply of sweets, not the way things were between them just now.

'Hello, Humph,' Deepbriar said. 'I've brought you something.'

Falbrough police station was dozing in the mid-afternoon lull when Deepbriar arrived. He made the most of his chance, taking over a typewriter and writing his report on the abduction of Joe Spraggs, deeming that more important than the acts of criminal damage at Quinn's farm. Pulling the last sheet of paper from the machine with a flourish, he turned to find Sergeant Hubbard behind him.

'Bit busy out your way then, Thorny,' Hubbard said ponderously, leading the way into the cubby hole that served as his office. 'I gather that old scoundrel Bunyard has been up to his mischief out at Quinn's farm again. I've had Quinn on the phone twice this morning, seems to think you aren't taking him seriously enough. In the end I told him if he didn't get off the line I'd have to charge him with wasting police time.' He sank into his chair, puffing as if he'd just run a mile, and waved at Deepbriar to take the seat opposite. 'Reckon you should persuade those two to bury the hatchet.'

Deepbriar didn't waste his breath explaining the impossibility of that enterprise. 'It's not Bunyard,' he said, 'not this time. Can't say I've much idea who it is though, not yet, and I haven't had time to write a report on it. To be honest I was more concerned with what happened to young Joe Spraggs.'

He handed over the sheets of paper and waited for the sergeant to study the typescript, watching the man's face and seeing the frown appear beneath his dark brows as he read about the events at Wriggles yard.

'I'm surprised you bothered me with this, Thorny,' Hubbard said at last. 'It was a practical joke.'

'I don't think so,' Deepbriar said. 'Joe's not the type to get involved with the local scallywags. Besides, you saw what Dr Smythe said. They probably used chloroform the second time, but something more serious the first, in a cup of tea, if you please. Where would his friends get hold of stuff that would knock a man out like that?'

Hubbard harrumphed. 'I don't know and I don't care,' he said, tearing the sheets quickly into shreds. He leant across the desk, dropping his voice. 'You know the sort of things they'd be saying if we start another missing persons investigation!' he hissed. 'You might have forgotten the Walkingham case, but I haven't.'

'But this isn't like that,' Deepbriar protested. 'There's got to be a reason....'

'The boy's safe back home, and with no harm done. It was a prank that went a bit too far, nothing more. Drop it, constable. That's an order.'

The Speckled Goose hadn't yet opened when Deepbriar knocked on the window round the back. Harry flung open the door. 'Hello, Mr Deepbriar. You coming in for a quick half?'

'No thanks, I'm on my way home. I just wondered if you know where Bronc went on Saturday night after he left here. He said he'd got a place to sleep, any idea where that would be?'

'No, he didn't say.' Harry's brow creased, a light appearing in his eyes. 'Actually he was a bit cagey about it, you think that means something?'

'Only that he was probably planning to stop in somebody's barn without asking permission,' Deepbriar replied gloomily.

Don Bartle arrived, peering over his son's shoulder. 'Afternoon, Thorny. What are you doing out there? Ask the man in, Harry.'

'I already have,' Harry replied, as Deepbriar shook his head. 'He just wants to know where he can find old Bronc.'

'The old man was a bit mysterious about where he was headed,' Don said. 'He stayed till nearly closing time, and he did well for drinks, one or two of the regulars sent something out for him. And Phyllis made him a sandwich.'

'Did he say any more about that black car?' Deepbriar asked.

'We were too busy to stay and chat,' Don said, 'there were quite a few strangers in as well as the regulars, I heard one of them say they'd come from the other side of Belston, just for the performance; fancy that, Minecliff's getting famous. Bronc'll turn up, don't you worry. Got a schedule he has, regular as clockwork. In the old days his next call after The Goose was always The Lodge, but he'd get no welcome there since Mrs Emerson moved in.'

'I suppose not, but I'll check.' With a sigh Deepbriar thanked him and set out for home, wondering what sort of reception he'd get from Mary, and heartily wishing he'd never heard of Mrs Emerson, or the Minecliff Amateur Operatic Society.

The week didn't improve. On Wednesday the night-time marauder visited Quinn's farm again, turning a tap on in the dairy and causing a flood that made the morning's milking so late that the milk couldn't be collected and had to be poured away. Deepbriar spent an hour investigating the crime, if crime it was, with Ferdy Quinn bellowing at him the whole time. He came away no wiser.

When a gate was left open in the early hours of Thursday morning, and a dozen bullocks strayed on to the arterial road over a mile away, the consequences could have been very serious, but luckily a couple of men heading for the early shift at the

Falbrough paint works stopped and herded the bewildered animals into a vacant paddock nearby.

Once the loss was discovered, Alan, the cowman, was despatched with old Bob to fetch the beasts home. Faced with compensating the owner of the paddock and buying the factory workers a pint, Quinn drove into Falbrough and spent an hour haranguing Sergeant Hubbard, who in turn gave Deepbriar a dressing down on the telephone. As a result the constable endured a cold and damp Thursday night riding his bicycle along the lanes surrounding Quinn's farm.

Things were bad on the home front as well. Mary seemed determined not to forgive him, and meals were eaten in silence, nor did the significance of their content escape the constable. There was cold beef, the remains of Sunday's burnt offering, on Tuesday, not the usual hot cottage pie. On Wednesday he made no comment when there was tripe for dinner, although he disliked it. Next day he sat down to a plate of pigs' trotters, which he liked even less.

On Friday morning, summoned to report to his superiors, Deepbriar cycled, yawning widely, to Falbrough, his thoughts on little but his bed. Unimpressed by his lack of progress, Sergeant Hubbard urged him to double his efforts to track down Quinn's raider.

'Maybe you ought to hide yourself on the farm,' he suggested, 'be ready for him.'

'It's too big an area,' Deepbriar protested. 'The fire wasn't even in sight from the farmhouse, nor were the gates that were left open.'

'Well, you'd better think of something. Mr Quinn's got influence. He's threatening to go to the Chief Constable if we don't get something done, and I wouldn't put it past him.'

'I'm doing my best, Sarge,' Deepbriar said, stifling another yawn. 'But a man's got to sleep sometimes.'

They were interrupted then, a constable calling for Sergeant Hubbard to help at the front desk. 'It's this woman,' he said. 'Reckons her husband's gone missing. I was looking for Sergeant Jakes, but there's nobody in the CID office.'

'Is there ever?' Hubbard grumbled, getting to his feet. 'That's all we need, another flipping Walkingham. All right, Thorny, go home and get your head down, we want you fresh as a daisy out on watch tonight.'

Detouring to the canteen for a cup of tea, hoping it would wake him up for the journey home, Deepbriar passed the interview room, where the door had been left ajar. He could hear Hubbard's voice, raised to frustration pitch. 'Look, I've told you, we can't go rushing around looking for a man who may have just decided to go AWOL for a few days holiday.'

Deepbriar paused, enjoying Hubbard's discomfort.

'I've already told you,' the woman replied, shrilly, 'my Joseph's not the sort to go away without telling me! He wouldn't—'

'Deepbriar!' Inspector Martindale came shooting out of his office as if on springs. Deepbriar jumped guiltily, thinking he'd been caught eavesdropping.

'The very man!' The inspector thumped him on the back. 'Come in here a moment, will you?'

'Yes sir,' Deepbriar said, obediently following his senior officer, his heart sinking, and the image of his welcoming bed vanishing before his eyes. 'Something I can do for you?'

'More like something I can do for you,' Martindale said cheerfully. 'Chance for a bit of overtime, not to mention being a bit more interesting than chasing poachers, or whatever it is you've been up to. They've got a crisis over at Belston, flu epidemic. Half their men are down with it. I told them I'd send some of our chaps to fill in. You'll have heard about the trouble they're having with the drivers at Rondvale's depot; that strike shows signs of turning nasty. Fact is, we're a bit pushed here as well. That's why I thought I'd pull in one or two of you village bobbies.' He laughed. 'Not as if you've got much serious crime on your hands, eh?'

'But I'm working nights, trying to catch this man who's been up to mischief on Quinn's farm,' Deepbriar objected.

'Mmm. Tell you what, I'll see if we can send one of our new patrol cars, it'll give them something to do once the pubs have turned out and it's gone quiet, taking a run round Minecliff. You never know, two pairs of eyes instead of one and all that, could be the case will be solved by the time you get back. You keep watch tonight, then I'll see they take over on Saturday.'

Martindale smiled, taking Deepbriar's arm and steering him back to the door. 'Make sure you get a rest on Sunday, there's a good chap, won't do to have you getting sick too. Report to Sergeant Parsons here at seven on Monday morning. We're arranging transport to Belston.'

An hour later Deepbriar dropped on to his bed with a groan,

and was instantly asleep. He woke, starving hungry, and went downstairs, but he was in for the cruellest blow of the week when he sat down to his dinner. Instead of the usual tasty battered cod served with a heap of hot chips, he found himself facing a pallid dish of steamed plaice and mashed potato.

Enough was enough. He pushed the meal away untasted. 'Can't seem to fancy that,' he said. 'Always makes me think of being ill when I was a boy; invalid food, my father called it. I've people to see at the pub, maybe Phyllis Bartle will have time to make me a sandwich.' Mary heard him out without comment, merely nodding as he pushed his chair back from the table. He made a last bid for her sympathy. 'I'll be out half the night again, up at Quinn's farm.'

'It's a hard life,' Mary offered, starting on her own meal. 'We all have our cross to bear. I suppose you've forgotten about what happened to Bella? She's quite upset about it. You were going to help sort through the props to see what's missing, but I suppose somebody opening gates up at Quinn's farm is more important than a robbery at the village hall.'

'A robbery?' Deepbriar snorted. 'Far as I heard there was nothing missing. Mrs Emerson left the door open, so it's her own fault if a couple of youngsters got in, and anyway there didn't seem to be any harm done. I never offered to go and help, either, I suggested she might get a few members of the Operatic Society to do it.'

'That's not what Bella says. Did you know the thief pushed her over when he escaped? Imagine if she'd confronted him! She might have been seriously hurt.'

'Not likely. I bet it was just a couple of 10-year-olds.' Deepbriar refrained from saying that it might have been a music lover hoping to put Mrs Emerson out of action before the performance of *Madame Butterfly*; relations with Mary were strained enough already.

'Always thought Bella was a funny name,' he muttered. 'Reckon it must be short for Belladonna.'

'Don't be so childish,' Mary snapped. 'So what shall I tell her? Will you go and talk to her again? It's been nearly two weeks now, shouldn't you have taken a statement?'

'Not if nothing's been stolen,' the constable said patiently. 'Tell her I'll call in when I've got time.'

'When?'

He sighed. 'Tomorrow maybe, if nothing else crops up.' Anything for a peaceful life.

Deepbriar left the house with a head full of uncharitable thoughts concerning Mrs Emerson, the uncaring cause of his marital discord. But for her, he'd have enjoyed the performance at the village hall, and foresworn the temptation of the Bartles' ale. Murdering great music ought to be a punishable offence.

Chapter Six

At the Speckled Goose, Deepbriar took refuge in the saloon bar, too embarrassed by his domestic discord to face the pub's regulars until he'd been fed. Harry Bartle brought him his sandwich and a pint of bitter.

'Mrs Deepbriar gone to see her sister?' he hazarded sympathetically. 'Mother says there's a second round if you want it.'

'Thanks, Harry, this is fine.' Deepbriar took a mouthful and tried to banish the image of a plate of cod and chips from his mind.

Harry rested his elbows on the bar, in no hurry to get back to his work. 'I hear Mr Pattridge's funeral's arranged for next Tuesday,' he said. 'Has there been any news of Tony?'

'Not a word, so far as I know,' Deepbriar replied. 'It's in the hands of the solicitor now, he'll be trying to track him down.'

'He was a bit of a wide-boy,' Harry mused, 'but he still had a soft spot for Minecliff. I'm surprised he stopped coming home. I remember him saying, one night in the bar, how his Dad always let him come back, no matter what sort of trouble he'd been in.'

'When was this?' Deepbriar asked.

'About eighteen months ago. He stayed at the farm for a couple of weeks, and he came in for drinks a few times. One night he even brought his old man with him.'

'Well, he'll have a lonely homecoming if he turns up now,' Deepbriar said. 'Folk often don't realise what they've got till it's gone, that's for sure.'

'That reminds me, did you find out what happened to Joe?' the young man asked, leaning forward conspiratorially. 'He's just come in,' he added, jerking his head towards the public bar, 'some of the lads are trying to get him to talk about it. Just like one of Dick Bland's cases, it is, a real mystery.'

'Reckon it needs Dick Bland to solve it,' Deepbriar replied. 'I'm not getting far.'

'Don't you worry, Mr Deepbriar,' Harry said, 'I bet you'll crack it. Talking of mysteries, I've been asking around about Bronc. Nobody seems to know where he's gone. Funny, he's a great one for sticking to a regular route, but he's vanished this time. After The Goose he used to go The Lodge, but that's out of bounds since Mrs Emerson moved in. His next port of call is usually Goldings. They let him sleep in the barn in return for sharpening a few tools, but I asked George Hopgood last night, and he says he's not turned up there yet.'

'It doesn't matter anyway,' Deepbriar said morosely. 'I've been told to leave it alone. The sergeant says there's no harm done, and he doesn't like missing persons's cases. They give him indigestion.'

For a second Harry looked baffled, then enlightenment dawned. 'You mean after what happened with Mr Walkingham. The local gossips had a field day on that one.' He gave a sheepish grin. 'It was a bit of a joke.'

'Oh yes, very funny. We were the laughing stock of every police force in the country.' Deepbriar bit into his sandwich again; it was ham and pickle, fairly tasty but a poor substitute for a proper dinner. He was beginning to feel very sorry for himself.

'What this village needs is a fish and chip shop,' he said. For a second he considered cycling to Falbrough, but there had been rain in the air as he left home. Bad enough that he was expected to patrol Ferdy Quinn's boundaries again; he didn't want to be wet through before he even went on duty.

For the next ten minutes Deepbriar regaled his patient listener with his opinion of irresponsible nitwits who went around opening gates and burning down barns, not to mention his superior officers who believed a single village bobby could be in ten places at once.

'How about,' Harry said, looking uncannily like the little boy Deepbriar had once clipped round the ear for playing knock down ginger, 'I'll come out tonight and give you a hand. We could cover twice as much ground. Got a new front lamp for my bike,' he offered, as an added inducement, 'a battery one. It shines all the way from our door down to the post office.'

'You know I can't let you do that, Harry,' Deepbriar said. 'It's no job of yours.'

'But if I was a gamekeeper you'd let me chase after poachers.

And there's nothing to stop a member of the public helping the police, if they just happen to be passing by when a crime's being committed,' Harry argued. 'I could just choose to take myself for a cycle ride, with or without your say so. There's no law against it.'

Constable Deepbriar sighed. Harry Bartle had been heart-broken when he failed to grow to the required height to enter the police force; it was hard that the lack of half an inch of leg bone could exact such a punishment. He still had dreams of becoming a detective, which was why he devoured vast amounts of crime fiction.

'I tell you what,' Deepbriar said at last, having taken a long pull at his beer. He wasn't given to breaking the rules, but after the week he'd had he was ready to try anything if it got the sergeant off his back. 'I'll be cycling along the Falbrough road when I leave here tonight, turning down by the wood and then over the bridge at Moody's corner, through Will Minter's and back past Quinn's gate. Suppose you just took a fancy to have a word with me, you might feel like setting off so we'd meet, come round in the other direction as it were. And if you saw anything suspicious you'd tell me, wouldn't you? No harm in that.'

Harry's face lit up as if somebody had turned on a hidden switch, his cheeks glowing pink. 'Of course, Mr Deepbriar. I've been wanting a chance to try that new lamp on a dark night, reckon now's as good a time as any.'

'Long as you don't mind the rain,' Deepbriar said gloomily. 'The way my luck's going it'll be blooming cats and dogs by midnight.'

Emotions straggled across Harry's open features as he hunted for something heartening to say. 'You've not had time to read that Mitch O'Hara mystery yet then?' he asked. 'A real good one that is. I couldn't put it down.'

'No.' Deepbriar refused to be cheered. 'Got the new Dick Bland from the library too, be due back before I even start it at this rate. Never did like working nights. I'm snowed under with flipping paper work. And next week they want me to go and help out in Belston! The Inspector says he'll send a patrol car to keep an eye on Quinn's place. Fat lot of good that'll do, couple of young lads still wet behind the ears who don't know a shorthorn bull from a five bar gate.'

'You must get some time off,' Harry suggested hopefully. 'What about the weekend?'

'Be playing the organ at St Peter and St Paul's on Sunday,' Deepbriar said, looking increasingly downcast as he picked the last crumbs of bread from his plate. 'And I suppose I'll be expected to play at the service for Colin Pattridge, since funerals don't suit Mrs Emerson's artistic temperament. That's if the Inspector will let me off duty. Just have to hope I can keep my eyes open, seeing I'm getting no sleep.'

Harry gave up on a lost cause. 'Tell you what, why don't you come into the public bar for a while? Have a bit of company.'

The regulars in the public bar of the Speckled Goose hardly noticed when the constable came in, all their attention being on the two men by the fire, one of them slumped on the only bench that sported a cushion, a pair of crutches propped beside him, the other standing by the hearth, a half pint of shandy held tight between his two hands, his cheeks flushed almost to the colour of Bert Bunyard's red neck-cloth.

'I think,' Joe Spraggs was saying, a little diffident but very dignified, 'you shouldn't go making remarks when you know nothing about it, Mr Bunyard.'

'Lot o' daft nonsense, pretendin' you'd gorn an' disappeared,' Bunyard scoffed, before burying his face in his pint mug, then emerging with a wet froth of foam on his top lip. 'Had two glasses o' that cat's piss you're drinkin' an' didn't dare go 'ome to that pretty young wife, thass what it was.'

'That's a lie, Bert,' somebody spoke up from the crowd gathered round the bar. It was George Hopgood, Emily's father. 'Young Joe's a good lad, he wouldn't go upsetting our Emily like that, and don't you go spreading no nasty rumours to the contrary.'

'Aye, watch your tongue, Bert,' Don Bartle put in, 'we'll have nobody calling names in my pub. As for folks having too much and not being fit to go home, reckon you're a right one to talk. Or maybe that wasn't how come you fell down the market steps in Belston. Maybe you broke your leg because you tripped.'

'Thass right, tripped I did,' Bunyard said indignantly. 'All uneven them steps are.'

'Aye, they tend to jump up and down a bit sometimes, too,' Hopgood said, 'especially after lunch on market day.' There was a laugh at this, and a general buzz of conversation, until a new voice broke in, one that Deepbriar didn't recognise. He eased his way forward to take a look, and saw a florid faced man in a shiny dark suit that set him apart from the countrymen around him, most of whom were in their working clothes.

'You're not taking this very seriously,' the stranger said. 'If I was you I'd be getting worried. I wasn't surprised to hear what happened to this young man last Saturday night. There've been some right peculiar goings on, and not just around here. When you get to travel the country as much as I do you hear things, you know.'

'Hear young Joe snorin' while 'e was sleepin' it off did you?' Bunyard scoffed.

'It wasn't what I heard, it was what I saw,' the man said. 'I don't suppose there's anybody else to back me up, since it was so late at night, but I tell you, it was enough to make a man's blood run cold.'

'See a few pink elephants, then?' some wag suggested.

'Who's that?' Deepbriar asked Harry quietly, under the cover of laughter at this sally.

'Agent for a farm machinery firm, Jenkins, his name is. He's staying for the week because of that big show they've got on in Falbrough market hall. Come to think of it he was very late coming in last Saturday, must've been well past midnight. He'd missed the last bus and his boss ran him back out here in his car. I had to get up and let him in. Don't think he was drunk though.'

'You can laugh,' Jenkins was saying, 'but it doesn't change what I saw.' He shuddered as he turned to speak directly to Joe Spraggs. 'What happened to you was no practical joke. You're lucky to be here. Not everyone gets away so easy.'

He had the attention of the whole room now, and he paused for effect, taking a long slow mouthful of his stout.

'Well?' Bert prompted. 'Let's 'ear it.' There was a general murmur of encouragement.

'Don't you read the newspapers? It's happening in America mostly, but they've been here too, more than once.' He nodded grimly at Joe. 'Abducted by Martians, you were, in one of those flying saucers.'

There was a stunned silence, broken by Bert's deafening guffaw. 'That's bliddy nonsense,' he said. 'Only little green man you'll see round 'ere is painted on the pub sign at the Woodsman, over by Possington.'

'I dunno,' George Hopgood said. 'I've read one or two of them stories. Sends a shiver down my back it does. There's been folk seen some funny going's on, that's for sure.'

'Yes,' the salesman said, 'there have. Like the lights I saw in the sky that night. Floating about they were, right over this very village.'

Harry Bartle turned to look at Constable Deepbriar. 'Flying saucers?' he whispered.

'About as likely as flying pigs,' Deepbriar replied. 'But if chummy there saw lights where they shouldn't be on Saturday night, it could be something to do with Ferdy Quinn's troubles.'

Once the suggestion that Joe had been abducted by Martians had been thoroughly chewed over by the regulars, and the drinkers in the bar had slipped back into their more usual somnolent state, the constable gave Harry a nudge. 'Look who's just come in,' he said, 'I'll bet that's why Joe's here tonight, he must've known Peter was coming home for the weekend. If there's anyone Joe will confide in it's young Brook.'

'Confide in?' Harry looked intrigued. 'Do you think Joe hasn't been telling the truth?'

'No, but his memory's still a bit hazy and he'd be happier letting the whole thing drop. That's all very well, but I don't like the idea that somebody can do things like this on my patch and get away with it. If it happens again somebody might get hurt. I reckon if Joe hears his friend saying the same thing he'll put his mind to sorting things out with a bit more enthusiasm.'

Harry nodded thoughtfully. 'Peter was always the clever one, too smart for the rest of us. Funny the way Joe tagged along with him.'

'Did him no harm, nice quiet pair of lads they were, not like you and your little gang,' Deepbriar said. He dug a ten shilling note out of his pocket. 'Here, fetch me another pint and tell those two I'm buying them a drink. Say I'll join them in a bit. Seeing as how Joe's not used to drinking, even another half of that shandy might loosen his tongue.'

'You're sure it wasn't a joke that went wrong? People do silly things when their friends get married,' Harry suggested. 'I mean, if it was, Peter might have been behind it. Things could have just turned out nastier than he planned.'

'No.' Deepbriar said. 'I won't deny I thought about it. Peter's clever enough, but I can't see him playing that sort of trick on Joe. And he'd have been at college. He was home for the wedding, but I didn't see him around at all last weekend.'

While Harry threaded his way across to the fire, Deepbriar

went to join Jenkins, the farm machinery salesman. 'Can I buy you another?' he offered.

'That's very civil of you constable,' Jenkins said, draining his glass. 'Thank you. Mustn't stay too long, though, I've got to put a telephone call through to my boss. He's already gone back to Manchester.'

'About done here are you then?'

'Yes, I'll be catching the early bus in the morning, we're packing up at lunch time.'

'Been a good trip, has it?'

'Not bad. Made a few sales. Our new tractor's doing really well. It's very interesting the way they've designed the gearing ...' he launched into a sales pitch, of which Deepbriar only understood about two words in twenty. When the man paused for breath the constable chipped in quickly.

'Not mechanically minded myself,' he said. 'Understand how my old bike works, and that's about it. I was interested in what you were saying about those lights though. It's my job to investigate anything strange that goes on around my patch, so if there's any more you can tell me I'd be grateful.'

'Really?' Jenkins's face flushed a deeper red. 'So many people scoff at this business, but we ought to be taking these flying saucers seriously. What we've seen so far is probably just the scouts, studying the lie of the land so to speak. There'll be more to come, you mark my words, and we ought to be ready for them.'

'You could be right,' Deepbriar agreed. 'Tell me, your boss, he was driving the car wasn't he? Did he see these lights?'

'He says he didn't,' Jenkins replied. 'Reckons he was busy driving the car, but I'm not so sure. He's the kind of man who wouldn't risk saying he'd seen anything out of the ordinary; he wouldn't like anyone telling his boss that he believed in flying saucers.'

'I see. Exactly where were they, these lights you saw? You reckon you could point out the place?'

'Indeed I could.' The salesman was enthusiastic. 'If only I wasn't leaving tomorrow! I'd really like to scout round and see if there's anything to find, they say sometimes there's signs of burning, or patterns left in the mud. Just think of it, being the one to find footprints left by misshapen little feet!'

More likely left by large wellies if he was right about Quinn's night-time visitor, Deepbriar thought, but he kept his doubts to himself. 'Tell me where you were when you first saw the lights,' he suggested. 'Maybe I'll be able to work out where it was and have a look.'

Half an hour later, having heard a long and impassioned lecture about the threat from outer space, Deepbriar finally reminded Jenkins of the time. Reluctantly the salesman left, pressing a business card into his hand.

'Call me if there's anything more you want to ask me,' he said. 'And I'd be very much obliged if you'd let me know if you find any evidence when you go looking for the spot where I saw those lights. I could come back one weekend if you like, so we could make a proper job of searching for them.'

'I'll bear it in mind,' Deepbriar promised. 'One more thing. That night, you didn't happen to see any other cars?'

'No, it was very late. As far as I recall we never saw a soul after we left town.'

When Jenkins had gone Deepbriar made his way across to the fire. Bert Bunyard was leaving too, making much of heaving himself and his plastered leg from the bench, his voice raised in complaint. Harry Bartle went to help by moving a stool out of the way, receiving nothing but an insult for his pains.

'Going home already, Bert?' Deepbriar asked. 'Bit early for you, isn't it?'

'I'm goin' home to mind my own bliddy business, Thorny Deepbriar,' Bunyard retorted, 'reckon you'd be best off doin' the same.'

'Just as long as you weren't thinking of taking any little detours,' the constable replied. 'You're pretty nimble, broken leg or no.'

'Nimble!' The old farmer swung round, his face red as his neckerchief. 'Call this nimble? Think I'm goin' off to visit that carrot-noddled neighbour of mine do you? Don't be more of a fule than you can 'elp, constable, an' keep a civil tongue in your 'ead. Defamation of character, that's what that is.'

'Mr Bunyard doesn't change,' Peter Brook said cheerfully after the door had slammed shut behind the hobbling farmer, moving over companionably to make room for the constable to join him. 'Thanks for the drink, Mr Deepbriar, it's Joe's round, if you'd care for another.'

'Don't mind if I do,' Deepbriar nodded, giving Spraggs his glass. 'Funny, rogues like Bunyard never mellow with age.'

'No,' Spraggs said. 'The local lads won't risk scrumping in his orchard. He was always a bit too ready to use that old shotgun of his. Now he's laid up he'd be shouting for you to get out there and chase them instead.'

'The worst villains are always the loudest to shout about their own rights,' Deepbriar agreed thoughtfully; Bunyard's reaction had been a little too extreme. Somehow, no matter how impossible it seemed, he had to be involved with the raids on Quinn's farm.

'How's life in Cambridge?' He asked, turning back to face the young student once Joe had gone to the bar.

'Fairly dull most of the time,' Brook replied. 'I keep my head down and get on with my work. Reckon I'm lucky to get the chance, I'm not going to waste it living the high life, I'll be doing my finals in a few months. It sounds as if Minecliff's been having a bit of excitement, though, what with kidnappings and rustling and midnight bonfires.'

Deepbriar sighed. 'As long as I don't have to start hunting for little green men from Mars, I can stand the rest, even Mrs Emerson leaving the door unlocked at the village hall then claiming it's been robbed.'

'I didn't hear about that,' Brook said. 'I suppose you're not allowed to tell me any more.'

'It's no secret, the whole village is sick of her talking about it. She was in the props store looking through the costumes and she reckoned somebody came in and pushed her over. A burglar she said, but by the time she'd picked herself up he'd gone. Calling him a burglar may not be fair to my way of thinking, seeing as he forgot to steal anything.' Deepbriar shook his head. 'As far as I'm concerned that's an end of it. I've got my hands full looking for Ferdy Quinn's unwanted caller; at least when Bunyard was mobile I knew where to look when Quinn started complaining.'

'Yes,' Brook said thoughtfully, 'opening gates and setting barns on fire, they really sound like the sort of things Bert would do. What about Joe though?' he looked at his friend who was standing at the bar. 'Are you in charge of the investigation or have the CID taken over? It's really odd, I mean, he's such a peaceable soul, he's got no enemies. Imagine how he felt, coming round to find himself locked up in the dark like that. It must have been terrifying.'

'Reckon it was,' Deepbriar agreed. But there won't be any further investigation, not even by me, let alone the plain clothes boys. I've been told it's not a case for the police.'

'Never!' Brook said indignantly.

'Some think you might be behind it,' Deepbriar said, watching the young man's face.

'You don't, though.' The young man grinned. 'There's a bloke in our hall who could do with taking down a peg, one of those arrogant types who thinks he's better than me because he went to a posh public school. Locking him up wouldn't be a bad idea, but I'd never do anything like that to Joe. I can't imagine anyone doing that to him, he's always been such a sobersides. We never even got him drunk before his wedding. So, apart from me, you don't have any suspects.'

Deepbriar sighed. 'No, but there were a few juicy clues. It's a shame there won't be any fingerprinting, because I had high hopes of the cup that was left on the bonnet of the lorry. Then there's the tyre tracks, they might have been useful. I've got drawings but no photographs, and I don't know where to go from here. As a matter of fact I was wondering whether that brilliant brain of yours might come up with anything I missed.'

'You're the professional,' Brook protested. Then he grinned. 'Actually I do have a couple of thoughts. Did it occur to you that it might be a case of mistaken identity?'

'Yes, but it would have to have been a fairly stupid mistake. The only other person who'd be driving Wriggle's lorry into his yard is the old man himself, and he's sixty if he's a day, you couldn't get the two of them mixed up. I wondered if the motive might be robbery, but nothing was taken.'

'Just like the break-in at the village hall,' Brook pointed out. 'You don't think the two things are connected?'

'Mrs Emerson getting knocked over doesn't seem in the same league as Joe getting drugged and whisked off unconscious, not to mention being locked up overnight.' Deepbriar said. 'I reckon it was just a couple of kids larking about in the village hall.'

'Joe being kidnapped could still be something to do with Wriggle.' The younger man looked thoughtful. 'He's a mean old beggar, and there's a lot of bad feeling in the building trade at the moment. Or maybe he's trodden on Sylvester Rudge's toes somehow, and this was by way of a warning. Bit drastic though, drugs and kidnapping.' He looked up as his friend returned. 'You know Joe, we can't help wondering if you really were carried off by those little green Martians.'

Joe didn't return the smile. He shook his head. 'They were human right enough,' he said.

Chapter Seven

'What hat makes you so sure the people who locked you up were human?' Peter Brook asked. 'No, seriously,' he went on, as Joe began to protest, 'I don't believe the flying saucer story, I can't see little green men putting something in your cup of tea, but your reasons could help us work out who these men were.'

Deepbriar looked at Brook with new respect. He'd always known the young man was bright, and winning a scholarship to Cambridge had proved it; that was just the sort of thing Mitch O'Hara or Dick Bland came up with.

'I don't remember much,' Joe said. 'Though I can't stop thinking about it.' He stared down into his glass, shamefaced. 'I never thought I'd be so scared, you know, not of anything. To tell the truth I've been having nightmares, and I'd far rather forget the whole thing.'

'That's not surprising,' Deepbriar said. 'It was enough to give anybody bad dreams, and that's a fact. Still, finding out who did it and why, well, I'm sure that would make you feel better.'

'But it's all over isn't it? It's not likely to happen again?' Spraggs's face looked drawn, and suddenly much older than his twenty two years.

'I honestly don't know,' Deepbriar said. 'Because we've no idea what's behind it. I'd rather get the case solved and make sure. I don't like to think we've got villains getting away with a thing like that in Minecliff.'

'You said your bosses weren't interested.' Spraggs protested.

'No, but I am.' It was frustrating, having no official backup. For some reason the snatch of conversation he'd overheard at Falbrough police station that morning came to his mind. Like Emily another woman had been driven to report her husband missing. Then a thought struck him. The man's name was the same as Joe's. 'My Joseph', she'd said. He immediately dismissed the wild idea that the man's disappearance might be somehow connected to young Spraggs, Joe was a very common name. They were dealing with fact, not fiction.

Deepbriar sighed. 'I don't know, Joe, I suppose we could just let the matter drop. The trouble is, if something similar does happen again, maybe the victim won't just turn up unhurt. Suppose the person who did it has a grudge against you? It could be your Emily they pick on next time.'

At that Joe straightened his shoulders. 'You've got me there.' He was silent for a moment, staring at nothing, looking back into the past, then he seemed to shake himself and he nodded decisively, meeting Deepbriar's eyes. 'All right then, I did see one of the men, though not very well. He looked tall, and broad too. Big all over. And I could see a sort of outline of hair around his head. I think it was a bit long, as if he was overdue to get it cut.'

'Not bald then,' Peter Brook put in. He aimed a sidelong glance at Deepbriar. 'And nothing like wireless aerials sticking out of his skull.'

With a grin, Joe Spraggs punched Brook lightly on the shoulder. 'No, and before you ask, he only had one head.'

'Did you see anything else? What he was wearing?'

Joe shook his head. 'No. I told you, he was just a dark shadow. It was really dim.'

Brook pushed his spectacles up his nose. 'It's a start. If your eyes didn't tell you anything more, what about your sense of smell?'

'Hey, there was something.' Joe's eyes widened as he turned to stare at his friend. 'Yes. When the man came in it made me think of the cottage hospital.'

'Chloroform's got a sweet smell,' Deepbriar said.

'This wasn't sweet. I do remember something sort of sickly, but that was later, just before I passed out. The stuff this man smelt of was strong, not unpleasant but not nice. I don't know, how do you describe a smell? It was just different, and it made me think of hospitals, that's all.'

'Disinfectant,' his friend suggested. 'Was that it?'

'I don't know. If it was, it's not the stuff my Mum uses for the drains.' Joe was despondent. 'I told you I wouldn't be able to tell you anything useful.'

'It's more than you told me before, and it could be a help,'

Deepbriar said encouragingly. 'We're really getting somewhere. What about this place you were in? You said it was big. How big? Like a barn?'

'It wasn't a barn,' Joe said at once, then appeared to be surprised by his own certainty.

'Why not?' Brook asked.

'Barns smell of hay, or animals, even when they're empty. And they're draughty. There was no air moving about at all. And it was really quiet. Every move I made set up a sort of echo.'

'A cellar,' said Deepbriar, looking triumphantly across at Harry Bartle. The young man was supposed to be collecting empties, but he'd come to hover at Joe's elbow, listening with obvious interest. He nodded now, obviously impressed. And so he should be, Deepbriar thought, pleased with himself; his idea was paying off. Joe's friend had persuaded him to open up, and they were getting some answers.

'That's it,' Peter Brook said, laughing. 'You've been rumbled Harry, you're the one who did it, he was locked in downstairs with your barrels.'

'Our cellar's not quiet, and it's not empty either, there's barely room to turn round without knocking yourself out on a heap of crates. Not to mention the creaking floors, even when we're closed there's people walking about over your head.' Harry shook his head. 'The boards are so old, it's a wonder we don't all end up falling through from the kitchen.'

'It wasn't like that,' Joe mused. 'It was all sort of solid and dead quiet.' He shivered. 'I felt like I was shut up in a tomb.'

'That suggests it was dug out of solid rock or built of stone then, which means it's probably underneath a big house,' Deepbriar said. 'That's got to narrow things down a bit. I think I've got a sort of lead on how they took you there, too. Old Bronc claimed he was knocked down by a big black car, though so far I've not found anyone else who saw it, but I'm pretty sure it's the same vehicle that made the tracks I discovered in Wriggle's yard. If only we knew where it went.'

'So that's why you've been looking for Bronc,' Joe said. 'The whole village has been trying to work out what he's done.'

'I just want a word, that's all. Trouble is, he got all confused with a time he got knocked into the midden in the middle of Falbrough, but that was before the War. I'm sure we could jog his memory, given the chance.'

'So, we find Bronc and get some answers,' Brook said. 'If only you hadn't been out cold when you were in this car, we might have been able to work out how far they took you. Have you got any idea how long you were locked up?'

'It felt like a week at least,' Joe said sombrely.

A sudden gust of wind blew a spatter of rain into Deepbriar's face and he lowered his head, leaning hard on the pedals to propel his bicycle up to the top of the rise. According to Jenkins the lights of the 'flying saucer' had been visible from the crest of the hill as his boss drove him back to Minecliff from Falbrough. He had claimed the strange phenomenon appeared high above the horizon, but Deepbriar was sceptical; the lie of the land, with Ferdy Quinn's fields rising steeply to the side of the village, might easily have deceived a stranger.

The salesman had given an expressive shudder as he described the lights, insisting that they had moved continually in a most unsettling and unnatural way, sometimes looking bright white then turning an unearthly blue. Only towards the end of their conversation had Jenkins admitted that he needed glasses to see anything that was further than ten yards from the end of his nose, but that drawback hadn't shaken his certainty that he'd witnessed the flight of an enormous space-ship, hovering menacingly over the slumbering citizens of Minecliff for several minutes before it vanished. Deepbriar, in his turn, was convinced that the light was clear evidence of the presence of Quinn's midnight intruder, a man not green but of the normal flesh colour, carrying a torch or lantern while he drove the heifers to their illicit date with the bull.

Warmed by his exertions, Deepbriar reached the summit and paused for a moment, looking down at the lights of Falbrough, blurred through the rain. Then he turned, freewheeling into the shelter offered by a large oak tree beside the road, leaning his bike there and turning off the battery headlamp he'd been using to supplement the dynamo. After the bright lights of the town, back the way he'd come the darkness seemed absolute, rain-clouds obscuring the sky so no glimmer of stars or moon showed.

Clapping his gauntlets together to keep the circulation moving to his hands, Deepbriar continued to scan the darkness. In time he made out a tiny pinprick of light, which he identified as the street lamp by Minecliff's post office. A long way over to the right there was another light; it hung on the side of Will Minter's barn, to illuminate the way into the farmyard. Deepbriar stamped his feet. Midnight was only moments away, and the street lamp would go out, followed by Will's, the farmer being very much a creature of habit. He'd told Deepbriar he let his dogs out for a few minutes every night, then turned off the light when he shut them in before going to his bed.

Sure enough the village lamp blinked off. As his eyes adjusted, Deepbriar made out the horizon. Between the village and the remaining light lay Ferdy Quinn's farm, shrouded in darkness. As he'd suspected, anybody in that top field could well appear to be above the horizon. A man walking behind a herd of cows, maybe shooing them along with a lantern, could account for the strange motion that Jenkins had put down to the flight of a space-ship.

The speck of brightness at Minter's farm vanished. A rising wind brought more rain and Deepbriar shrugged deeper into his cape. He decided he'd done all he could, so he fetched his bike, doing his best to dry the saddle before hoisting himself back on to the machine, ready to take up his patrol around Quinn's farm. His detour had taken over half an hour, but he thought it had been worth while. He rode without lights. Freewheeling down the hill he was travelling fast and quietly; if the prowler came back tonight there was at least some chance of taking him by surprise and catching him in the act. There wasn't likely to be any traffic, but if there were any motor vehicles out this late he'd hear them in plenty of time to turn his lights back on.

As the slope lessened Deepbriar turned into the lane through the woods that would take him to Moody's Corner, still making good speed with his lights off and his back to the wind. A brief flash of light showed somewhere ahead. It appeared only for the briefest moment then went out.

Deepbriar coasted to the side of the lane and put his feet to the ground, staring into the night, listening. There was no sound. He was sure that the man who let Quinn's heifers out had been walking across the fields just after midnight, waving a light to keep them moving. If the villain planned to make another attack then he was probably out and about already. Deepbriar pushed off again, dodging round the puddles, careful to be as quiet as he could; he had no intention of announcing his approach.

The light appeared again, almost blindingly bright as it found a space between the trees. It had to be somewhere near the bridge at Moody's Corner. The constable was elated. That light was where it had no business to be at half an hour after midnight on a Sunday morning; it looked as if the prowler was up to his old tricks again, only this time he'd have a surprise waiting for him.

Pushing on as fast as he dared, keeping one eye on the potholed surface beneath his wheels and trying to watch the light, coming and going like a will'o'the wisp, without letting it spoil his night vision, Deepbriar pursued his quarry. The man who held the light must be travelling fast; he seemed to be darting about among the trees, maybe moving from one patch of cover to the next, intent only on being unseen from the direction of the farms, and giving no thought to anyone who might be up ahead on the road.

Deepbriar put on a burst of speed, putting his head down and throwing his whole weight into it, going fast towards the sharp bend that would take him over the bridge. He thought he could hear a faint humming sound above the swish of his tyres and the splatter of rain.

As Deepbriar rounded the corner a bright light shone straight into his eyes and he swerved. He could see nothing behind the light, but he heard a cry of dismay as he careered across its path. Half-blinded, he glimpsed a dark shape that loomed up at him, sliding by and landing a glancing blow on his knee as it passed. Only when it had gone from his vision did he realise it had been another cyclist.

Frantically Deepbriar fought for control of his own machine, somehow keeping it upright and coming to a halt with the front wheel precariously close to the drop into the stream beyond the side of the bridge.

'Is that you, Mr Deepbriar?' Harry's voice sounded strained, but he too had managed to stay on his bike, and was struggling to turn round. The new headlamp that had played so distractingly among the trees as he rode along the lanes was now wavering wildly across the landscape, sending random beams in all directions.

Deepbriar turned on his battery lamp. 'Harry! I'd forgotten about you! Are you all right?'

'Bit of a shock,' Harry Bartle admitted. 'I didn't see you. I'd expected to meet you a long way back. I thought you must have gone off after somebody.'

'I was riding without lights,' Deepbriar admitted, and he explained about the information he'd gleaned from the salesman, and his theory that Jenkins had seen a light used by the man who had been targeting Quinn's farm all week.

'That sounds about right,' Harry agreed. 'I'm sorry; if the villain's out there I've just messed up your plan, coming blundering along with a light that he could see all the way from Falbrough.'

'Can't be helped,' the constable said ruefully. 'I thought it was my lucky night, seeing that lamp of yours. But it might be worth carrying on. If he's out there we could still catch him, if you don't mind doing the rounds again.'

Harry nodded eagerly. 'No, of course not. At least the rain's nearly stopped.'

'So it has. Reckon those clouds might lift in a bit.' Deepbriar shook his head gloomily. 'That's not so good, there's more than half a moon, and this villain prefers a dark night.'

'Shall I turn my lamp off?' Harry asked.

'Long as nobody sees you riding through the village,' Deepbriar replied, 'don't want you being reported, you know what a load of busybodies they are, can't trust 'em to be asleep even at this hour, so just keep your eyes peeled. Should be safe enough once you're heading up to Quinn's.'

'Right. I won't let you down this time, Mr Deepbriar, I'll see you somewhere near the farm gate,' Harry said. 'This is a right old game. And wasn't it great all that stuff Peter Brook came out with? It was like having Dick Bland or Mitch O'Hara in the bar.'

Deepbriar sniffed. It was all right for the likes of Harry Bartle to be so cheerful; he wasn't the one who would have to face Sergeant Hubbard if they'd missed another visitation at Quinn's farm.

The water had begun to seep into Deepbriar's regulation size tens, making slow but inevitable progress towards his toes, and he could feel a coldness creeping down his neck as well. The rain had stopped, although drips from trees by the roadside kept up a constant shower so it wasn't much of an improvement.

Will Minter's house and outbuildings lay shrouded in silent darkness, along with the row of four labourers' cottages that fronted the road. No dogs barked as Deepbriar pedalled stoically by, his eyes fixed on the distant shadows that hid Ferdy Quinn's farm. Too late now, but he realised he should have sent Harry this way, for if the villain was at work again tonight he was far more likely to be found between the village and Quinn's place, not out here.

As he rode Deepbriar considered who it might be. Somebody from Minecliff surely, since the attacks had been concentrated on just one local target. But what was their motive? Ferdy Quinn wasn't popular, but he wasn't the kind to make serious enemies, and he insisted that once Bunyard was discounted he could think of nobody who wished him harm.

Deepbriar's calculations always came back to Bert Bunyard. Could a man ride a bicycle with one leg in plaster? That was impossible. And he'd taken a good look at the ancient wreck of a lorry that stood forlornly on flat tyres in the yard at Hurdles Farm; it hadn't been moved in months. Bunyard had a sway-backed old draught mare too, but there had been no trace of hoof marks at any of the crime scenes.

It was no use, in this instance it would take more than the detective skills of his two heroes to find the villain by a process of deduction: he needed evidence. He needed to catch the criminal in the act. And the sooner the better, because he wanted to get back to spending his nights in bed. He had no illusions about the Inspector's patrol car which was supposed to take over while he was facing a picket line in Belston, that would be like sending a couple of lap-dogs out to catch a wily old country fox.

Deepbriar kept a constant watch for any sign of life in the dark landscape as he cycled on. Once he saw something move on the other side of a hedge, but it was only a cow. Nothing stirred as he arrived at Quinn's gate. He dismounted for a few minutes and stood straining his ears, hearing nothing but the normal after-dark sounds; the rustle of some small creature on the grass verge near his feet and the distant hoot of an owl.

Deepbriar had just set his foot to the pedal again when the scream split the night. It rose to an unbearable pitch, unearthly and utterly terrifying; it was the sound of a soul in torment, in the last desperate throes of pain or fear.

Chapter Eight

For less than a heartbeat Thorny Deepbriar hesitated, then the long years of experience took over. He almost flew down the road, legs pumping, head bent low over the handlebars, every ounce of effort concentrated on reaching the source of that terrible sound.

He had given no credence to Jenkins's wild theories, and he still didn't, but a terrifying thought drove him; suppose this had some connection to the abduction of Joe Spraggs? The mysterious car that had knocked down old Bronc could have reappeared, and not missed its victim this time, but surely he'd have heard the sound of the motor?

As he pedalled, Deepbriar was praying with all his heart that the terrible cry hadn't been uttered by Harry. He suppressed a shudder; no human should ever be driven to make such a sound. It had been a bad idea giving in to the young man's enthusiasm, he should never have agreed to let him come.

Without slackening speed, Deepbriar leant forward to turn on his lamp. The bright beam showed him the wet surface of the road, but around him the shadows deepened; field, hedge and tree passed by unseen, shrouded in darkness.

The dynamo outshone his battery lamp. At some distance it caught a glimmer of metal; as Deepbriar drew closer, the shiny speck became a reflection from the rim of Harry's new bicycle lamp, now showing no light. The machine lay in the middle of the road; there were no skid marks, no sign of a car, and no movement except the bike's back wheel slowly spinning. No Harry.

Brakes screeching, his tyres skidding on the wet surface, Deepbriar came to a halt beside the abandoned bike, reaching down to snatch Harry's new lamp from its bracket, relieved to find it unbroken. He shone the bright beam along the sodden hedgerows.

Nothing moved. There was no sound but the steady drip of water and a faint sigh of wind in the leaves. To the right of the road a gateway led into one of Ferdy Quinn's fields. Deepbriar hastily dropped his bike on the verge and dragged Harry's machine out of the road, then he stumbled across the rough grass and shone the lamp into the field.

Thin pasture poached by many cloven feet sloped away uphill, with a fence running across from left to right, about halfway up. What appeared to be a body was slumped bonelessly against the sodden wooden rails, looking as if it would fall without their support.

Deepbriar climbed over the gate and ran, his heart thumping as if it would burst with the effort. The rag doll figure didn't move as he approached, though to Deepbriar it seemed his breathing was making enough noise to waken the dead. With a feeling of unreality he recognised Harry Bartle's checked cap and knitted scarf. Gasping for breath he reached out to the sagging shoulder, afraid that the body would fall at his touch. 'Harry?'

The young man leapt as if he'd been hit, straightening up and turning, his fists coming up in a swift gesture of defence. His face was paper-white, and his eyes were like two dark holes poked in fresh snow. He stared wildly at the constable.

Deepbriar dragged in a lungful of cold damp air. 'Harry?' he said again.

Bartle shuddered, a deep involuntary spasm that shook his whole body. Gradually, as if he was coming from a deep sleep, he focused his gaze on the face of the man before him. 'Did you see it?' he asked bleakly.

'See it?' Deepbriar was confused. 'I heard it. I heard something. It wasn't you that yelled then lad? You're all right?'

'I think so. But ...' He sunk his head into his hands. 'Dear Lord!' Despite coming from a man who never entered the village church except for weddings and funerals, it sounded more like a desperate prayer than blasphemy. 'I hope I never see a thing like that again!'

'What did you see?' Deepbriar shone the lamp across the deserted field, the beam illuminating nothing but wet grass.

'Up there,' Harry said, pointing to a copse of trees that crowned the hill and straggled away down the slope towards Quinn's farmhouse. He gave another convulsive shudder. 'I don't know what it was.' His voice shook. 'I don't even know what made me look that way. Then there was that scream ... I leapt off the bike and ran up here.' He gestured at the lamp in Deepbriar's hand. 'I was an idiot, I didn't think of bringing that. There was a break in the clouds, just for a second, and that's when I saw it.'

'Saw what?'

'I'm not drunk, Mr Deepbriar, I swear. I only had a pint all evening.' The colour was coming back to Harry's face now, and he grimaced. 'You'll think I'm crazy.'

'Can't judge that unless you tell me,' Deepbriar said reasonably, playing the beam of the lamp across the line of trees.

Harry Bartle swallowed hard. 'Well, for a start it had a long head, pale coloured, coming up to a sort of blunt point. And it was big. Wide as well as high, if you know what I mean. The top of it was a good three foot above that bit of fence you can see there.' He shook his head. 'I can't describe it. It was like something out of a nightmare. It wasn't human, it couldn't have been. Its body was misshapen, lumpy just below the head, then sort of rounded. The way it moved was weird, like its legs were too short for its body.' He shook his head. 'You know me, Mr Deepbriar, I never swallowed any of that flying saucer stuff, but maybe I was wrong.'

The constable patted his shoulder. 'I reckon I'll take a look up there, see if there's anything to see. I won't believe in Martians until I've shaken one by the hand. A man's mind can play funny tricks in the dark,' he went on, reassuringly, but he couldn't help remembering that awful scream; he too might have been ready to see monsters if he'd been confronted with something out of the ordinary just at that moment.

'I'll come with you,' Harry said firmly, climbing on to the railings. 'I think I'd rather be going out of my head than believe that I saw what I thought I saw.' He paused astride the fence. 'Am I making sense?'

'Enough. Don't you fret, perhaps you got a bit overheated getting yourself up here so fast. A long time ago, when I was a lad, I had a spot of fever. And there I was, lying in bed, telling my poor mother to throw these three big dogs out of my room, because they were keeping me awake! I can still remember what they looked like, they were as real to me as you are right now. For years I thought she'd been telling me fibs when she swore they weren't there.'

'The scream was real,' Harry reminded him.

'That's why we're going up there,' Deepbriar said. 'Can you tell exactly where you saw this thing?'

'It was inside the fence,' Harry replied, his eyes following the sweep of the lamp. 'There, just by that big beech tree.'

They reached the spot and peered over the wooden rails. Just inside, the tangle of undergrowth was too thick to have allowed anyone through, but a little further into the wood a grassy track ran between the trees. Deepbriar worked his way towards it, but he couldn't make out any tracks. 'It's no good,' he said, 'I'll have to come back in daylight, we'll only trample on the evidence, if there is any. Was it going towards Quinn's farm, or away from it?'

'Away.' Harry pointed. 'Down there. And it was moving fast.'

As any midnight prowler would, Deepbriar thought, if he was afraid of being discovered. But he was at a loss to explain the thing Harry had seen, or the reason for that terrible scream.

The sun rose in a glory of red and yellow streaks splashed broadly across the eastern sky. Deepbriar breathed in deeply and forgot to care about the shortness of his night's sleep. The rain had left the world clean and fresh, and even the coldness of the air seemed invigorating rather than unpleasant; he was in a rare good mood as he cycled out towards Quinn's farm, heading for the spot where he'd found Harry Bartle the night before. Having received his assurance that he'd fit in a visit to Mrs Emerson, Mary had thawed a little over breakfast, and although she hadn't totally forgiven him yet, she'd given him a second rasher of bacon.

Another source of pleasure was the knowledge that it was Saturday, so he was only on duty until midday. He'd had four hours sleep, which was enough, and no matter what happened he was determined to spend a few hours in the company of Dick Bland that afternoon.

In daylight the little copse on the hill was a place of peaceful green solitude, in keeping with his cheerful frame of mind. Deepbriar located the beech tree and climbed over the fence, noticing the marks he and Harry had left the night before. Under the canopy of leaves the green track ran away to left and right. A little reluctantly he turned to the right, towards Quinn's farm. He didn't particularly want to see Ferdy Quinn, but if Harry's apparition had been the mischief-making prowler then he'd have to find out what he'd been up to this time. With luck he might have left some sign of his passing.

The path skirted the wood then led out through a gate to follow an old trackway between two hedges. A few yards beyond the gate Deepbriar found what he was looking for. A patch of mud in the centre of the track held a boot print. The impression was perfectly clear, and it had obviously been left since the rain stopped. Unless Ferdy or one of his farm hands had been out overnight, then it looked as if he'd finally made a breakthrough.

Deepbriar measured and sketched the imprint, which had been left by a man's right foot, in a size nine boot. If there had been more damage done at Quinn's farm then perhaps he might persuade Sergeant Hubbard to send somebody to take a cast of it. He had a momentary vision of himself giving evidence in court, while the lawyer presented exhibit 'B', and he explained how he had run the villain to ground, thanks to this vital piece of evidence. The judge was congratulating him profusely on his skill in cracking the case, before the bubble suddenly burst. Deepbriar shook his head. It was funny the effect a bright sunny morning could have on a man.

Having come this far, he decided to follow the trail all the way. He had some bread and cheese in his pocket for elevenses, and although it wasn't yet nine o'clock he fetched it out as he strode down the hill, keeping his eyes on the ground as he ate. His perseverance paid off; he found two more partial prints, one of them of the left boot, which showed signs of wear on the outside of the heel. A gleam in his eye, Deepbriar made a record of that as well. Minecliff wasn't a big place, he reckoned he'd have the case all wrapped up in a couple of days.

There was the usual morning bustle going on at Quinn's farm. Deepbriar spotted the farmer himself, just coming out of the house on the heels of old Bob.

Ferdy Quinn stared at the constable. 'Well, I suppose it proves something, you being on the way when I telephoned. But you didn't stop him last night, did you?'

'So, I was right, he was here again.' Deepbriar scanned the yard. 'What was it this time?'

'He's taken to thieving,' Quinn said grimly. 'Something's gone missing.'

'Not the heifers again?'

'No, this isn't just a matter of a gate being left open.' Quinn marched across the yard, Deepbriar and old Bob trailing in his wake. 'You were supposed to be out making sure nothing like this happened, constable. And now I've been robbed.' He came to a halt and waved a hand dramatically. 'There!'

It was a pigsty. And it was empty. Deepbriar stared at the emptiness, then looked back at Quinn, as the light dawned. So that was it! He couldn't help the smile that flickered at the corners of his mouth; it really was a good morning. The mystery of Harry's alien was solved, and he was well on the way to making an arrest.

'I don't know what you've got to be so pleased about! Where were you last night when somebody was running off with my prize sow?' Quinn demanded furiously.

'Keeping watch,' Deepbriar said. 'A man can only be in one place at a time. Your villain has all the luck, I'll say that for him. However, this time we've had a bit of luck of our own. I think he's left us some evidence. Did you or any of your men come down that path since the rain stopped last night?' He pointed at the track he'd followed from the copse on the hill.

'I certainly didn't,' Quinn replied, obviously mystified. 'I'll find out.' He hurried off and came back a couple of minutes later, shaking his head. 'No, they all came straight into the yard. What's that track got to do with anything?'

'It was used by a man in size nine boots,' Deepbriar said triumphantly. 'And I've got a good print of the pattern on the sole.'

From inside the next sty came a squeal of outrage, and a large pink pig appeared, shaking itself indignantly as it rushed out into the walled yard at the front, followed a moment later by a cluster of little pigs.

'Give Ant a hand with that feed, Bob,' Ferdy Quinn said.

'It's on its way,' the old man replied, pottering towards them bowlegged under the weight of two full buckets.

Deepbriar stared down at the sow, which had its front trotters up on the wall as it yelled for its breakfast. He'd heard plenty of pigs in the past, he should have known what had made that inhuman scream the previous night. Come to that, so should Harry. He hid another grin as he shook his head. If he let on in the Speckled Goose, young Bartle would never hear the end of it. Martians!

'Exactly how would our man go about stealing a pig?' he asked, as Bob tipped the food over the wall into a trough. 'They're not exactly easy to drive, I'd guess.'

'That they ain't,' the old man replied. 'If'n a sow don't want to go someplace then her won't, not nohow, and Matilda was a right independent-minded old biddy.'

'So it might be easier to pick her up and carry her?'

'Could be.' Bob sighed, grimacing as he straightened his back, and giving his boss a baleful glance. 'If you'm got the strength, that is. Mind you, Matilda ain't such a big 'un as this 'ere. Time was I could hoist that beast on my shoulders an' not notice her was there!'

Piggy back, Deepbriar thought. Perhaps that was where the phrase came from. Harry's monster had been a man, and the pale deformed head was a pig's snout pointing skywards. So all he had to do was find a strong man with short legs, wearing boots that fitted the print in the wood.

'Constable?' Ferdy Quinn interrupted his train of thought, and somehow also anticipating it. 'Are you sure Bert Bunyard's out of action?'

Hurdles Farm lay deserted in the bright Sunday morning sunshine. Ferdy Quinn had threatened to visit Falbrough police station again unless Deepbriar promised to question Bunyard once more. Leaving his bike down the lane Deepbriar walked the last fifty yards; he'd assure himself, once and for all, that neither the old rogue of a farmer, nor his son, had been out on the prowl the night before.

He trod carefully, weaving from one side of the track to the other as he scanned the ground for boot prints; there were plenty, but none that matched the pattern he'd seen up in Quinn's copse. Continuing his search in the yard he studied the gateway then went up to the back door. Common sense told him that Bert Bunyard couldn't be Quinn's tormentor, not this time, but at the back of his mind a nagging doubt persisted.

Deepbriar stood precariously on one leg, balancing on a narrow drain cover, while he inspected the patch of mud beneath an overflowing gutter. A loud guffaw sounded behind him and he whirled round, having to put his other foot down quickly to avoid losing his balance. Wet mud splashed on to his trouser leg.

'I saw you move,' Humphrey Bunyard said, pointing at him in childlike fashion and grinning. 'Statues,' he went on. 'We played that at school.'

'Hello, Humph. Good at playing statues were you?'

The big head nodded and the grin widened. 'I liked playtime. Got any chocolate?'

'Not today. Do you know an old man called Bronc, Humph?'

Humphrey nodded again. 'Boys used to shout at him.'

'Have you seen him lately? In the last few days?'

The young simpleton thought for a long while. 'No,' he said at last. 'I don't go to school any more.'

Deepbriar extricated himself from the mud and walked over, taking a good look at Humphrey Bunyard's boots. They were very large and well worn, almost scuffed through at the toes.

'You got any more boots, Humph?' Deepbriar asked.

The young man shook his head. 'Got some shoes,' he said proudly. 'Black ones. Me Dad gave them to me.'

Abandoning this line of questioning Deepbriar turned to look at the house. 'I came to see how your Dad's getting on. When are they going to take that plaster off his leg?'

Instead of looking blank, as Deepbriar expected, the childlike face was suddenly wary. 'Dunno.' Without another word he turned away and slouched across the yard to the cow shed.

Deepbriar went to the back door. Ducking under the low lintel as he pushed his way in, he was lost in thought. There had to be an answer here. Humphrey Bunyard couldn't possibly squeeze his feet into size nine boots, even if he could be persuaded to leave Hurdles Farm. None of the marks in the mud resembled those he'd found at Quinn's place, although it looked as if Bert's feet were a couple of sizes smaller than his son's. Only there were no right prints. How could there be, when Bunyard's right leg was in plaster? Yet again he made a mental tour around the village, trying to dredge up the guilty party, but try as he might he couldn't think of anybody else who would set out to persecute Ferdy Quinn.

Deepbriar stood in the big kitchen and shouted, receiving an answering call from somewhere above. He clumped upstairs, and found Bert Bunyard in the first room at the front of the house, lying in a huge old fashioned bed, his back against blackened brass rails. The old man was half propped up on two grubby pillows, his neck at an uncomfortable angle, and the pair of crutches lying beside him on the floor, his plastered leg a lump under the blankets. His face was damp with sweat and he was breathing heavily.

'Never thought I'd be glad to see you, Thorny Deepbriar,'

Bunyard growled. 'Got meself stuck here, can't get up nor down. Give us a heave, will yer?'

Half an hour later, having found himself brewing the invalid a pot of tea and making him some toast, Deepbriar escaped thankfully back into the fresh air. On his way out he'd inspected Bunyard's boots which lay by the kitchen door. They were size nines, almost new, and while the left was damp as well as dirty, the right one was caked hard with dry old mud, and the pattern on the sole was nothing like the one he was looking for.

As he made his last call of the morning, Deepbriar made no attempt to look for boot prints; Mrs Emerson's drive was immaculate, no mud dared show itself in her neat garden. Besides, in the year since Mrs Emerson moved to Minecliff there had been no evidence of a man in her life. An image of Mrs Emerson wearing oversize boots and rampaging around the countryside carrying a pig flitted through Deepbriar's mind. It took him a while to get his expression back under control, then he lifted the shiny brass door knocker.

'Thorny! How lovely to see you. Do come in.' A small soft hand with painted fingernails grasped his sleeve and practically hauled him over the threshold. Deepbriar gritted his teeth; only friends, or acquaintances who'd known him a very long time, were allowed to use his nickname, and Mrs Emerson didn't qualify.

'It's such a shame,' the woman gushed. 'I hardly ever see you. And Mary and I are such close friends. Let's go into the library.'

'I shan't keep you long Mrs Emerson, just a word or two about that person you found in the village hall.'

'Oh please, I've told you before, do call me Bella.'

'Not while I'm on duty if you don't mind, Mrs Emerson.' He followed her into a room where a single shelf of leather-bound classics was overwhelmed by cabinets stacked full of knickknacks and trinkets.

'Oh Thorny,' she turned on him, simpering, 'you're always so very upright and correct. As if anyone would know, when we're here all alone. Do have a seat. Would you like a cup of tea?'

'No thank you.' He took out his notebook, leafing back to find the entry he'd made the day she'd reported the incident. 'Now, when I spoke to you before, you didn't think this person had deliberately knocked you over. I recall I asked you that. Ah, here we are "... he must have been behind the door, and when I pushed it open it hit him, quite hard. I was surprised when it bounced back, and it knocked me down. Somehow I fell on my hands and knees, and I didn't see him when he ran out of the building." Is that how it happened, Mrs Emerson? Only from something my wife was saying I gather you may have changed your story.'

'Oh, no, not exactly. I'm sure I didn't. Perhaps she didn't quite understand. I was only saying how lucky it was that I hadn't been hurt. I mean, imagine, with the production so close, it would have been a disaster!'

'And you're quite sure there's nothing you can tell me about this person? He didn't say anything when the door hit him? There was nothing you heard, or saw, that might help us to identify him?'

'Well no,' She spread her well manicured hands in a helpless gesture so that the light caught on the many rings she wore. 'There was a sort of grunt, that's all. I didn't see a thing.'

'And nothing was taken.' Deepbriar was already slipping the notebook back in his pocket.

'I can't be sure of that,' she said, her tone a little sharper. 'After all, there are a great many costumes and props in the Society's store. I only moved to Minecliff a year ago.'

'So you did.' Deepbriar nodded. 'Somehow it seems much longer. That reminds me, Mrs Emerson, there's a man who used to call on Mr Plummer and do a few odd jobs. He generally spent a couple of nights in one of the sheds in the garden. Has he been here recently? Everyone knows him as Bronc—'

'That tramp!' She interrupted him indignantly. 'I found him trying to break into the gardener's bothy last year, only a few weeks after I arrived. I assure you I gave him short shrift, he's not likely to show his face on my property again.'

'You've not seen him since then.'

'I have not. And if I ever catch him in my garden I shall most certainly inform you. I have no sympathy with beggars and vagrants. My poor dear husband worked hard for his money, I have no intention of defiling his memory by wasting it.'

'Perhaps you'd allow me to take a look at this bothy, just to make sure he hasn't been there without your knowledge.' Deepbriar suggested.

'Very well. It's behind the *ligustrum ovalifolium*.' She indicated a privet hedge to one side of the lawn. 'Mr Witherby is here this morning, so it won't be locked. He doesn't usually come on a Saturday, but the dead leaves make the place look terribly untidy, so I asked him to work a few extra hours.'

'Thank you, I'll have a word with him first, then. As to the Operatic Society's property, if you find anything's missing, perhaps you'd let me know.' He nodded, turning away quickly to avoid shaking her flabby hand again. Everything about the woman rubbed him up the wrong way; her phoney friendliness; the bolster-like figure tied tightly into expensive clothes; her cut-glass accent, but most of all Mary's inability to see through her. That particular weakness seemed to be shared by half the village.

Chapter Nine

Deepbriar found Simon Witherby in the garden, the old man's round face pink with effort as he pushed a wheelbarrow full of leaves up the steep grassy track.

'Morning, Simon.'

'Mornin' Thorny,' Witherby huffed, lowering the barrow and straightening his back with a groan. 'Come to see the Duchess have you? You'll not find her out here, gardens are grubby places, she might get her hands dirty.'

'I was looking for you,' Deepbriar replied, hiding his amusement at the nickname the old gardener had bestowed on Mrs Emerson. 'I was wondering if you'd seen Bronc lately, I know this used to be one of his haunts.'

A wary look came into the faded grey eyes. 'I've never seen him in this garden, not since her Highness turfed him out last year,' Witherby said. 'What do you want him for?'

'It's all right, he's not in any trouble, I just think he might be able to help with my enquiries. He sees things, travelling about the way he does. Has he been here?'

Witherby nodded, taking a crumpled packet of tobacco and some Rizlas from his pocket to roll a cigarette before he answered, then looking over his shoulder to check that his employer hadn't come out of the house.

'Reckon he spent a couple of nights here,' he said. 'I saw him on Saturday morning, when I was fetching some bulbs from Van Hoorns for the Colonel. He was t'other side of Possington, heading this way. He said he was going to call in at Quinn's, and maybe go to the Goose. Then he asked if her ladyship was likely to be about. Said he was needing a place to get his head down, but that he'd be on his way by Monday night.' He tilted his head at the bothy. 'I told him where I hide the key. There's an old sofa in there, pretty comfy. Used to use it myself for a nap at lunch times now and then.' He put the finished cigarette, a skinny, rather crumpled looking object, into his mouth and struck a match against his apron to light it.

'Have a look if you want. Funny really, I thought he'd be back for his things.'

Apart from a rack of tools along one wall, the place didn't look much like a garden shed inside. It was furnished with an old black stove, a table, two mismatched chairs, and a large sofa, covered with several brightly coloured rugs. At one end of the sofa lay a parcel tied up with newspaper; and a Deerstalker hat.

'Cosy ain't it,' Witherby said complacently. 'Old Mr Plummer took good care of his staff, I'll say that for him. Not like her. Lucky to get time for a cuppa and a bite these days, let alone a decent sit down.'

His voice droned on, bemoaning the changes the last year had brought. Deepbriar ignored him and examined the Deerstalker. He found some longish grey hairs on it, which seemed to confirm that it was the hat Bronc had been wearing the previous Saturday night, and although one parcel might look very much like another, he thought the package was the one that had been lying under Bronc's seat in the Speckled Goose when he'd last seen him.

'I found the hat out by the compost heap this morning,' Witherby said. 'Wasn't till I brought it in here that I found the parcel. Funny, that. When I was here first thing Monday morning there wasn't a sign of him. Always carries that parcel, he does, never seen him without it.'

'I don't suppose he told you where he was heading next?' Deepbriar asked. 'You've not found anything else?'

'Like what?' Witherby stared at him, his mouth dropping open and the skinny stub of cigarette hanging down, stuck to his bottom lip. 'You sound worried. Don't tell me you think some-thing's happened to old Bronc?'

'Have you ever known him to leave his belongings behind?' Deepbriar asked.

Witherby scratched his head. 'Can't say I have. Come to that, I've never seen him take off his hat.'

On Monday morning Thorny Deepbriar struggled through the crowd of officers waiting for the arrival of the van that was to take them to Belston, and knocked on the door of the CID office, which stood open. He walked in to find a man in his late twenties, sitting yawning at an untidy desk, his fashionable shoes propped on an upturned wastepaper bin. Sergeant Jakes looked a great deal more comfortable than he had when Deepbriar last saw him, out at Oldgate Farm.

'Whatever it is will have to wait,' Jakes said, 'I'm off duty in ...' he consulted his watch, '... exactly forty-four minutes.'

'Forty-four minutes will do, Sergeant,' Deepbriar replied, pushing the door to behind him, 'seeing as you plainclothes types can get the use of a car any time you want. I need help with a spot of evidence, and Sergeant Hubbard told me to pass it on to you, said he'd clear it with Inspector Stubbs. Might already be too late, seeing that I couldn't get anyone to turn out on Saturday, but it hasn't rained, and I covered it up, so it might still be fit to use.'

'Exactly what are we talking about here?' Detective Sergeant Jakes dragged a pad of paper towards him.

'Boot print. Belongs to somebody who's been committing acts of criminal damage, robbery and arson at Quinn's Farm. A photograph would be good, but a cast would be even better.' Deepbriar handed over a map. 'I've marked the exact spot, and written directions on the back.'

Jakes sighed. 'OK, I'll get it done. Is that it?'

'I'm not sure. I'm a bit worried about an old tramp, goes by the name of Bronc. He was in the Speckled Goose last Saturday week, and I think I know where he spent the next couple of nights, but after that he seems to have gone missing.'

'That's what tramps do,' Jakes said. 'They move on.'

'Yes, but not without their belongings; people who don't have much tend to hang on to what they've got,' Deepbriar said. 'And this man's a creature of habit, he has a routine, visiting the same places according to the time of year.' He had spoken to a few more people in and around Minecliff over the weekend, but had found nobody who'd seen Bronc later than Monday the previous week. 'I just thought I'd mention it, maybe you'd ask around here, some of the older coppers will know him. He's used to living rough, but I don't like to think of him lying outside somewhere if he's been taken ill. Weather's getting a bit nippy.'

'Yes, all right. I take it you didn't mention this to Sergeant Hubbard? He won't like it.'

'Smacks too much of missing persons,' Deepbriar agreed. 'Lord knows what he'll say if I try to organise a search party.'

'Just make sure you do it when I'm off duty,' Jakes said. 'Talking of missing persons, Inspector Stubbs asked me to pass this on to you.' He produced a letter on heavy duty paper, with an impressive printed heading. 'It's from Morton and Childs,' he added unnecessarily, handing it to Deepbriar.

Stripped of legal jargon, the letter was a request for assistance in tracing the whereabouts of Anthony James Pattridge, once of Oldgate Farm, sole benefactor under the will of his father, Colin, recently deceased.

'But he's not been seen in Minecliff for a year,' Deepbriar protested, 'how am I supposed to find him?'

'Local knowledge,' Jakes replied, tapping the side of his nose. 'Though to be honest I think this business is being passed around like a hot potato, I know for a fact that Inspector Martindale had this letter on his desk yesterday. I shouldn't worry, just ask the regulars in the Speckled Goose. You could put a couple of pints down as legitimate expenses.'

'Hmph,' Deepbriar grunted, 'the solicitors can't have tried very hard, they've not even had time to put a notice in the newspapers yet. As if I haven't got enough to do.'

'It's not exactly urgent, just something to do in a quiet moment, eh? The request's probably got something to do with the Superintendent having been to school with old Archibald Childs. If he asks I'll tell him I left it in your capable hands.' Jakes grinned. 'Nothing else the CID can do for you?'

'Not unless you want to play Prince Charming once you've taken a cast of that print, and find our Cinderella.'

'I'd say that requires local knowledge too, wouldn't you, Constable?' The younger man pushed himself to his feet. 'Actually this suits me nicely, chance to get away before somebody gives me something else to do.'

Deepbriar followed him out into the corridor, to find that most of the crowd had gone. Sergeant Parsons beckoned from the door. 'Come on Thorny, you don't want to miss this. You village bobbies don't get much fun. Time to see a bit of action.'

'It's not all straying sheep and supervising the hoopla at the vicarage fête, you know,' Deepbriar said solemnly. 'Remind me to tell you how I nearly met a Martian.'

By eight o'clock Constable Deepbriar had already had enough of his new assignment. He was crouching uncomfortably in the police van, squashed between Sergeant Parsons and a youngster he didn't know, a fairly new man who was recovering from flu. Deepbriar found himself thinking longingly of nights spent patrolling the lanes around Minecliff; the young constable had a perpetual sniff, which was beginning to get on Deepbriar's nerves.

The van swerved round a corner and Deepbriar was bounced off Parsons' ample frame for the tenth time in as many minutes. 'Sorry,' he muttered.

'Cosy in here,' Parsons said. 'Shame they don't use WPCs for this kind of job.'

Deepbriar nodded gloomily, reflecting that with his luck, even if they did, he'd be posted alongside a woman like Bella Emerson.

'They reckon this'll be settled by the end of the week,' the sergeant said hopefully. 'They're a rough lot though, some of these drivers.'

'Drivers?' Deepbriar asked. He had a vague idea Martindale had told him who the strikers were, but he hadn't been paying much attention, being more concerned about the prospect of getting home to his bed. 'What's the company do then?'

'They run a fleet of lorries, nearly fifty of them. Everything from local deliveries to bloody great trucks going all the way to Scotland.'

Deepbriar recalled that Peter Brook had mentioned outbreaks of violence between drivers of different transport companies when they'd been mulling over Joe Spraggs's disappearance; perhaps old man Wriggle had upset one of the big carriers by trying to muscle in on somebody else's business, though with only one run-down old lorry it didn't seem likely.

Making conversation was a distraction from the continuous sniff on his other side. 'I'd have thought with such a lot of competition the drivers would have kept their heads down rather than scrapping with their bosses.' Deepbriar said.

Parsons shrugged. 'Trouble is, so many men came out of the army able to drive, and a lot of them thought that setting up with a couple of lorries was an easy way to make a living. They're undercutting some of the bigger firms, and when the big boys feel the pinch they try to save a bit of money on their wages bill. This lot were threatened with dismissal if they didn't take a drop in pay. They decided to fight, but there's plenty who'll do the same job for less, that's why they set up the picket line.'

The van finally lurched to a stop and Parsons opened the door.

'Come on, lads. Let's get to it, here's a chance to show these Belston cissies what the Falbrough lads can do.'

Deepbriar groaned and Parsons laughed, patting him on the shoulder. 'Never mind Thorny, at least there's no chance of meeting any little green men out there.'

For the first quarter of an hour the picket was peaceful, but the numbers around the gate of the transport yard were growing all the time, stretching the line of policemen ever thinner. Obviously the drivers had found some support, probably from men feeling the pinch as Belston's heavy industry struggled in the tide of closures following the end of the War.

'This is getting a bit warm,' Parsons said, as the human barrier wavered under the pressure. 'Still, I was glad to be getting out of the office this morning.'

'Why's that?' Deepbriar asked, thrusting out a knee to deter a spotty youth who was trying to crawl between them.

'There's this woman. Says something's happened to her husband. She's hardly left the station all weekend. You've only got to mention the name Spraggs and Hubbard's face turns purple.'

'Spraggs?' Deepbriar half turned, but at that instant the pickets lunged forward in a concerted attack, and the police line was in retreat, helpless against the sheer numbers of men heaving and shouting, intent on reaching the entrance to the depot. Two men who were trying to break the strike ran for their lives, taking refuge inside the firm's offices and barricading the door.

Deepbriar never saw what hit him. One minute he was stepping backwards as the line tried to hold the onrush, his left arm linked with Parsons' right, then his helmet was knocked over his eyes and he was falling. A flash of light lit up the darkness, and he knew no more.

He was watching Big Jim, the blacksmith, hammer a horse shoe to shape. Nothing unusual in that, the village smithy was a favourite place, and he wasn't the only youngster who came to stand in the doorway, offering to work the bellows and thus enjoy the warmth of the forge when the weather was cold. But today there was something unpleasantly loud about the ring of metal on metal. It was hurting his head, each strike thudding against his ears like a blow. The fire was uncomfortably bright too, the red and orange glow shot through with painful white lightning. He wanted to leave, but when he tried to turn away his feet wouldn't move. A small sound of frustration escaped his lips.

'Thorny?' The voice was familiar, and pleasant somehow, but it didn't fit, it didn't belong here. He tried to think why, and finally worked it out. Mary hadn't lived in Minecliff as a child, so she'd never been in the smithy, not when Big Jim was alive. With one last reverberating crash of the hammer against red hot metal, the dream burst, and he was back in the present; the pounding became the throb of the pulse in his aching head. Deepbriar screwed his eyes tighter shut against the pain.

'Mary,' he whispered. A hand took hold of his, and he squeezed it, taking comfort from the familiar feeling of the roughened skin on her fingers. From somewhere beyond the persistent hammering he heard another sound; she was crying.

'Don't, love,' he said, his voice sounding as if it was echoing from an unimaginable distance. 'I'm fine,' and with that he sank easily down into the blackness again.

By the time he came round again he was, if not fine, at least a great deal better. He opened his eyes, and although the brightness was uncomfortable it didn't hurt too much. In answer to his query a bustling nurse told him his wife would be in at visiting time that evening; relatives were only allowed in during the day under special circumstances, and once he'd regained consciousness that privilege had been withdrawn.

A screen was trundled back, giving him a view of the rest of the ward. There was a contraption of levers over the next bed, holding up a leg encased in plaster. Turning his head he saw a familiar face grinning at him.

'Sarge?' Deepbriar drew his brows together, puzzled. 'What happened?'

'Don't you remember? No, I suppose you wouldn't, you were the first to go down.' Parsons went on to describe the near riot that had followed Deepbriar's collapse, the strikers carrying the police line halfway to the yard entrance before smashing through it. He dwelt with relish on the way his leg had been broken when he was swept up against a concrete gatepost. 'Hurt like the blazes. It's a wonder there's only the two of us in here. I didn't see the last of it myself, got carted out of the way by a couple of the lads,' he finished cheerfully.

'I remember being in the van on the way to Belston,' Deepbriar said, 'it's a blank after that.'

'Not surprising,' Parsons said. 'That was a nasty knock you got, you had us all worried for a while, wondering if you'd ever come out of it.'

'How long have I been here then?'

'Work it out for yourself.' The sergeant pulled a wry face. 'They'll be cooking fish for our dinner tonight. Out cold you were, until about eight o'clock this morning.'

'You mean it's Friday?' Deepbriar sank back, digesting the magnitude of having lost three whole days. 'No wonder I'm starving,' he said.

'You'll need to be to enjoy the food in here, it's all bloody slops and gristle.' Parsons cast a guilty glance towards the door. 'Have to watch my language,' he explained. 'That sister, she said if I turned difficult she'd wash my mouth out with soap and water. Reckon she would too. A man feels so flipping helpless with his leg hoisted up in the air.'

Parsons wasn't exaggerating, the food wasn't good. Although Deepbriar ate everything they gave him, he was still very hungry when visiting time came around.

'Well, you're certainly looking a lot better,' Mary said, as she bent to kiss him. He was amazed to see that her eyes were damp with tears.

'I've got the mother and father of all headaches,' he grumbled, and she gave a quavering laugh.

'Now I know you're all right,' she said, 'if you're well enough to start complaining.'

'It was just a knock on the head, nothing for you to get upset about,' he said.

'Oh no, with you lying there like the dead, when I'd sent you off in the morning without even giving you a spot of lunch. And I'd hardly spoken a word to you in a week! I felt so guilty, and all because of that business over *Madame Butterfly*. As if it mattered, a silly little show in the village hall!' Suddenly the tears were flowing, though she made no sound, and turned her head away so nobody else would see. He reached out to take her hand.

'It mattered to you,' he said awkwardly. 'I'm sorry, love, I shouldn't have stayed for a drink with young Harry and missed hearing you sing. Even if Mrs Emerson's voice does sound as musical as a stick pounding on my old mum's tin bath.'

She gave him a wan smile, drying her eyes. 'We all know she's not very good. It's just that she puts so much into the production. Without her we'd have had no new sets or costumes at all.'

'I'd rather listen to you singing at the kitchen sink wearing your old pinny, than sit in the Albert Hall listening to her, no matter how grand the costumes and the set were,' Deepbriar said gallantly. 'It's time they let you take the lead part, your voice is better than the whole lot of them.'

'Go on with you.' She was blushing now, her tears forgotten. 'You do talk a lot of nonsense.'

Mary had arrived burdened with a large shopping bag, and, suddenly businesslike, she lifted it on to her lap. Deepbriar sat up hopefully as she delved into it.

'Clean pyjamas,' she said, taking them out, 'and I brought these two books that you left on the sideboard. At least you'll get time to read them now. Then there's this bottle of tonic that the doctor gave you when you had that cough last month, I'll leave it with the sister; I thought it might help to build your strength up. And there's a letter from Auntie May, telling us all about her new grandson. Look, she's sent a photograph.'

Deepbriar's stomach rumbled.

There was only ten minutes of visiting time left when Harry Bartle appeared at the door, peering hopefully down the ward. Mary Deepbriar rose hastily to her feet. 'You've somebody else to see you,' she said. 'Anything you'd like me to bring in tomorrow?'

'A bit of your apple pie would be nice,' Deepbriar replied longingly. 'Or some fruit cake.'

'I'm not sure if it's allowed,' she said, bending to kiss his cheek. 'I'll have to ask the nurse.' She hurried away, offering Harry a perfunctory greeting as she passed him.

'Evening, Mr Deepbriar,' Harry said, 'I hope Mrs Deepbriar's not too put out about me coming, but I wanted to bring you this.' He reached into the pocket of his overcoat and pulled out a small parcel, which turned out to be another book. '*The Alphabet Murder*. I found it in that second-hand shop in Wood Street,' he explained, 'I thought you'd be bored, lying here with nothing to do.'

The constable forbore to explain about the headache which was still thudding away behind his eyes. 'Thanks, Harry. Everything all right in the village is it? Has Bronc turned up yet?'

'Not a sign of him. He's really keeping his head down. We've asked everyone we can think of. I did find out a thing though. Bronc was in our porch again that Monday, at lunch-time. And evidently somebody was in there talking to him for a while, and whoever it was didn't come into the bar, which could be suspicious, couldn't it? A couple of people saw the man walking away down the road, and they said he was a stranger.'

Deepbriar pulled a face. 'I don't know Harry, I don't suppose there's anything in it. Maybe he offered Bronc a bit of work.'

'Could be.' Harry looked at Deepbriar anxiously. 'But I did think it was a bit odd, so I took my bike over to Possington and Cawster on Tuesday, and spoke to a few people over there, asking if Bronc had been around, and I tried describing the stranger too. I hope you don't mind, I never said it was anything to do with the police, just that I was looking for Bronc and this other chap. Nobody had seen them, anyway.'

'No harm done,' Deepbriar assured him. 'Anything else happened out at Quinn's?'

'No. Old Bob came in last night, he said they've had one of those new police cars calling in, he was moaning about it, says they wake him up, driving in and out of the yard at all hours of the night and setting the dogs off, but at least there's been no more trouble.'

'They've not caught anyone though.'

'They never get out of the car,' Harry was scornful, 'townies. Couldn't catch a cold.'

The bell went then, ringing with a prolonged jangling discord that did nothing to improve the pain in the constable's head. With the visitors gone the patients were supposed to settle down for the night, although it wasn't much past eight o'clock. Deepbriar opened the book Harry had left, but he couldn't read; the letters swam in front of his eyes and refused to make any sense.

'What's that you've got?' Parsons asked, lifting his head awkwardly to see what Deepbriar was looking at.

'I've got a thumping headache and all they brought me was books,' Deepbriar complained. 'And I'm lying here starving. My belly thinks my throat's been cut.'

'I'll swap,' Parsons said eagerly. 'Look at this great heap of fruit. I couldn't eat all that in a month of Sundays.'

'You sure?' Deepbriar looked hungrily at the basket on Parson's locker.

'If you can reach it, it's yours, Thorny,' the sergeant said, gesturing ruefully at his leg. 'Sorry I can't bring it over to you.'

He had been forbidden to leave his bed without the assistance of a nurse, since he felt dizzy as soon as he stood upright, but hunger drove him, and after a few false starts he made it to his feet and across the narrow gap to Parsons' bed, where the exchange was duly made. He had barely clambered back under the covers when the sister arrived, tutting about the untidy state of his sheets. Deepbriar, with a mouthful of grapes and more clutched in his fist, didn't attempt to reply.

The night seemed endlessly long as Deepbriar tossed and turned, wide awake. His mind refused to give him any peace, as if he had a touch of fever, and his thoughts kept ranging over the exploits of his two fictional heroes. Dick Bland wouldn't have wasted time lying in a hospital bed. He would have got up as soon as he regained consciousness, and returned to the job, probably with the solution to his latest investigation already hatching in his mind. As for Mitch O'Hara, the blunt instrument wasn't yet invented that could lay the American low; he had a skull like solid rock.

Deepbriar stared up at the ceiling. The answers were there, swimming around in the feverish confusion, tantalisingly close. If he could just get his mind to focus, maybe he'd think of something useful. He went over and over the attacks on Quinn's farm until his aching head was spinning with the effort, and still he came up with nothing. What use was a solitary boot print, even if Sergeant Jakes had succeeded in making a cast of it? He couldn't prove it belonged to the midnight marauder.

Then there was the matter of old Bronc; had he vanished by choice, or was there something more sinister behind his disappearance? At his age it was quite possible he'd been taken ill, or died even. And there was Harry's news. Who had been talking to Bronc? Was it anything to do with the black car, and had that been the vehicle which carried Joe Spraggs off?

Spraggs. The name woke something in his memory; where had he heard it? His pulse thudded like a drumbeat in his head, beating out the name. Spraggs, Spraggs ... Then it came to him. Just before the police line had broken and he'd got a crack on the head, Parsons had mentioned a woman who was plaguing Sergeant Hubbard, insisting that her husband had gone missing. Her name was Spraggs!

He delved deeper, rooting around in his memory; seeking for another connection, knowing it was there, turning the incident over and over, his body tossing and turning as he tried to pummel his unruly brain into submission. At last it came to him. He'd stopped outside the interview room, amused by Sergeant Hubbard's predicament when he was faced with a woman reporting her husband missing. It had been the day Martindale had called him in to tell him about the picket duty.

The woman Hubbard was talking to had said something must have happened to her husband. 'My Joseph'. That was it! If it was the same woman then the missing man was another Joseph Spraggs! It couldn't be a coincidence.

Deepbriar forgot the pain in his head as he stared unseeingly into the darkness. He'd thought of it when he was talking to young Peter Brook, but he'd let the incident slip out of his mind. Just the name Joseph hadn't been enough to link the two men; if only Martindale hadn't appeared he'd have heard the surname as well.

As it was, he'd wasted a whole week. It couldn't be down to chance that two men with the same name had vanished within a few days of each other. But had the second Joe Spraggs ever come back?

Chapter Ten

Finally, at six o'clock, Constable Deepbriar fell asleep, only to be awakened half an hour later by a staff nurse, brightly assuring him that it was morning, despite the darkness still shrouding the world outside the windows. He felt drained. The fever had left him, but so too had the conviction that he had solved the puzzle of Joe's abduction and Bronc's subsequent disappearance. As dawn crept into the bleakness of the ward, Deepbriar decided that his over-active mind had endowed his nocturnal ramblings with a verity they didn't deserve. In the grey reality of early morning they looked more like the wanderings of a mind still suffering the after-effects of concussion.

Having eaten his meagre breakfast, Deepbriar had to endure those indignities routinely visited upon the bedridden, grumbling intermittently at the two young nurses who conversed over his head about the Robert Ryan film they'd seen the night before. Then, with the pulse in his temples drumming, he was folded tightly between his sheets and warned not to disturb the bed with its neat 'hospital corners' before the doctor made his rounds.

The case of the second Joe Spraggs was once more revolving around Deepbriar's brain. He concluded that there had been some sense in his meanderings during the night, after all, and he tried to get things straight in his mind.

Falling asleep wasn't on his agenda, but his head was muzzy and it was restful to close his eyes against the glare of the lights; hours later he woke up to find the dragon-like Sister Hunt by his side, grasping his wrist with one hand while the other held up the watch she wore pinned above her ample bosom.

'You had a nice nap,' she said complacently, releasing him then thrusting a thermometer between his lips. 'Doctor will be here in a few minutes, then you can have some lunch.'

Deepbriar's mouth was dry and his stomach growled with hunger, but the headache had almost left him. 'I gotha phone Falbrough folithe thtathion,' he said indistinctly, holding the thermometer down with his tongue. 'Fleathe can I go to the thelethone?'

She snorted. 'You most certainly cannot! I told you, the Doctor is on his way. And I very much doubt if he'll allow you out of bed today.'

'Thomebody could thake a methage?' he pleaded. 'It'th urgent.'

'Nothing is urgent on my ward except the care of the patients,' she retorted, removing the thermometer and looking sternly at it. 'I hope you're not going to be difficult, Mr Deepbriar. The last patient I had from Minecliff was difficult. Fortunately *he* was only with us for a few hours.' With that she marched away.

From the next bed Parsons chuckled. 'You'll not pull rank with that one. What's the trouble?'

'I remembered something that happened on Monday. I've only just realised what it might mean. I really need to talk to one of the officers at Falbrough. Hubbard would do, or the Inspector.'

'It's a shame you were asleep all morning, then,' Parsons said. 'Inspector Martindale popped in a couple of hours ago to see how we're getting on. I'm not sure how he got past the dragon. Perhaps he went over her head and used his sweet-talk on the matron.'

'Martindale was here?' Deepbriar blew out his lips in frustration. 'Dammit, it might even be his case.'

'Watch your language,' the sergeant cautioned, 'she's got ears like a fox that woman, and eyes like a hawk. What are you on about? What case?'

Deepbriar explained about Joe's abduction and his subsequent return, and how he was sure it must be connected to the disappearance of Joseph Spraggs, a case Sergeant Hubbard had refused to take seriously. 'But he'd have to listen now. A thing like that can't be a coincidence,' he said.

Parsons was dismissive. 'I bet this missing man turned up, probably within minutes of his old woman getting back from the station. It happens all the time. Some chap goes out and has a few more drinks than's good for him, then he ends up sleeping it off somewhere and wanders home the next day with his tail between his legs.'

'But at least the Inspector might have known if he didn't. I wish he'd woken me up,' Deepbriar said.

'I think he was feeling a wee bit guilty about getting you involved, you being a village bobby,' Parsons confided. 'You don't get much practice at crowd control out at Minecliff, though to be fair nobody expected that picket line to turn into a riot. Dunno what things are coming to.'

Before Deepbriar could reply the double doors to the ward were swung open and the doctor arrived, advancing in procession with matron and three nurses who danced attendance on them; no more talking was allowed on the ward until the ritual was over. Deepbriar gritted his teeth and waited. It wasn't until lunch time that he found a chance to try again, this time asking the nurse who brought him his dinner if she could escort him to the telephone.

'You're not allowed up yet,' she replied. 'And as soon as you've eaten you're to rest. You need your sleep.'

'I slept all morning,' he pointed out.

'You see? That proves you need it,' she replied. 'Just do as you're told and you'll be out of here all the sooner. Eat up, you won't get your strength back if you don't.'

'I'm not likely to get much strength out of this,' he grumbled, scooping thin soup on to a spoon. 'A man needs a bit of decent food in him. Ham and eggs, that's what I call a proper meal.'

She laughed. 'That's funny, the last man we had here from Minecliff said the same thing, but he wanted it for breakfast. He was really rude; you should have heard the things he said to sister! I told him he was lucky to get anything at all; he'd already had a nice bit of boiled fish, and some toast. We were glad to see the back of him, I can tell you; if he'd been here any longer there'd have been sparks flying. Sister Hunt won't stand for any nonsense on her wards, and she doesn't like difficult patients, so you'd better mind your p's and q's.' With that warning she whisked away.

Deepbriar ate what she'd left him, then made a further attack on Parsons' basket of fruit, now sadly depleted. He pondered briefly over the identity of the other patient from Minecliff, and realised it must have been Bert Bunyard. Deepbriar was indignant; it was a fine thing when a police constable found himself spoken of in the same breath as a man like that. And all because he was trying to do his duty.

The evening brought Mary, but although their reconciliation was complete, she refused to call Falbrough police station for him.

'You'll be back at work quite soon enough,' she retorted, then distracted him from his bad temper by unpacking a fruit cake from her bag, hiding it, along with a sharp knife, behind the winter dressing-gown she'd put in his locker. 'I'm not sure you're supposed to have it,' she said, 'but you can share it around, I expect all you poor men miss a bit of home-cooked food.'

It was after midnight and he was on his second slice of cake when the night sister caught him. She scolded him as if he were a naughty child, and the remains of the cake were confiscated. 'I'll ask the doctor,' she said, when he protested. 'You're lucky Sister Hunt's not on duty, it would have gone straight in the pig-bin. I'll see it's taken care of, maybe you can have a piece after your dinner tomorrow, since it's Sunday.'

'If I don't die of hunger before then,' Deepbriar muttered sullenly.

Despite his gloomy speculation, Constable Deepbriar survived until midday on Tuesday, when an ambulance delivered him back to the police house in Minecliff. Mary fussed over him, insisting that he should lie on the settee with a blanket over his legs, since he refused point blank to go to bed. Deepbriar declared himself to be in no need of mollycoddling, hiding the fact that he still felt dizzy whenever he walked more than a few steps, and as soon as he could get a word in, he demanded to be allowed to use the telephone.

'There's a young constable in the office taking care of everything,' Mary said. 'Inspector Martindale sent him out so you wouldn't be tempted to start work again until you're better, he came to see me himself to tell me so. I'll ask Constable Giddens to come in and see you once you've had your dinner, and you can tell him all about this man you're worrying over. If he thinks there's any need, he can phone the sergeant for you.'

With the meal out of the way, and compliments made to Mary concerning the quality of her cooking, which tasted even better than usual after several days of hospital fare, Deepbriar pushed to his feet. 'I'm going to make that phone call,' he said, when his wife tried to dissuade him. 'It will only take a few minutes, and I'm not going to faint, or fall over, I promise.'

But Hubbard, when Deepbriar got through to him, was totally unhelpful. 'Glad you're back home, Thorny,' he said, 'we were all sorry to hear about that knock on the head, though we should have known your skull was made of pretty solid stuff. As for that Spraggs woman, you're officially off-duty for the rest of the week, that's what I've been told. I can't talk to you about ongoing cases, can I? Have a good rest and get yourself fit again. Now put Constable Giddens on the line.'

There followed several minutes with Giddens standing rigidly at attention and saying 'yes, Sergeant,' and 'no, Sergeant,' at regular intervals. Having heard a few of Hubbard's lectures himself over the years, Deepbriar gave the young man a sympathetic pat on the shoulder, sighed expressively and returned to the settee.

Shortly after that Doctor Smythe arrived, adding the full weight of his medical authority to that of Sergeant Hubbard and Mary Deepbriar. 'You've been sent home to rest, Thorny,' he said. 'Though to my mind you'd have been wiser to accept the offer of a week at the convalescent home. You had a serious concussion, and it takes a man time to recover from a knock as hard as that. But since you're here you have to do as you're told; you can read for an hour or two each day if your head isn't aching, but no work and no telephone calls. Visitors mustn't stay more than half an hour, and you don't leave the house.'

'I'll die of boredom,' Deepbriar grumbled.

'You can listen to the wireless,' the doctor suggested. 'There are some good educational programmes on the Home Service during the day. And if that's not enough to keep you quiet then maybe Mrs Deepbriar could teach you to knit. By the end of the week you could have made yourself a nice woolly scarf!' With that he left, laughing uproariously at his own joke.

By Thursday morning Thorny Deepbriar was seriously considering Doctor Smythe's suggestion. He was so bored he didn't even mind when Mrs Emerson came to call.

'Poor dear man,' she gushed, when he assured her he was feeling quite well. 'So courageous. And you were injured in the line of duty by those awful ruffians. I read all about it in the local paper, you're quite famous.' She fluttered her eyelashes at him. 'Oh yes, you can't deny it. Now where else did I hear your name? It can't have been more than a couple of days ago.'

'Don't worry about it,' Deepbriar said, as a frown creased her brow.

'Got it,' she said, ignoring him. 'It was Mr Witherby. He said he'd come to see you once you were recovered. I'm not sure why, it all sounded rather strange. I believe he was worried about something he'd found in the garden, or was it in the bothy? He interrupted me when I was busy with my voice exercises, and that's not a good time.'

She gave a tinkling laugh. 'We artistes have to look after our instruments. That reminds me, I must have a word with Mary, the Society still haven't made a decision about our next production. Do you know, some of our members actually want to perform Gilbert and Sullivan! Such a waste of our talents. And of course the lead roles are totally unsuitable for me. We have a meeting on Friday, I'm sure Mary will give me her support. You'll excuse me, I'll just pop into the kitchen.'

Deepbriar pulled a face at her retreating back; he'd heard the same story from Mary, and was encouraging her to take the side of the operetta fans; if they won Mrs Emerson might take umbrage and decide to resign. Then he turned his thoughts to Simon Witherby, wondering if Bronc had returned to claim his belongings. It would be good to know that the old man was all right.

Despite his wife's vigilance and Hubbard's strictures, Deepbriar had twice managed to have a quick chat with Constable Giddens, who assured him he was continuing to enquire into the where-abouts of the missing tramp. Unfortunately there was no news, but he promised to keep trying. He also reported that Quinn's farm remained quiet, and that as far as he knew, no major search for a missing man had been started in Falbrough, but whether that was because Joseph Spraggs had turned up, or because of Sergeant Hubbard's prejudice against missing person's cases, Deepbriar had no way of knowing.

The eight day clock on the mantel shelf struck ten, marking off another tediously long hour. Deepbriar rose and picked the clock up, suppressing an overwhelming desire to throw it out of the window; it had been a wedding present and Mary was fond of it. Instead he turned off the strike; with luck she wouldn't notice.

There was a tentative knock at the parlour door, then Constable Giddens's head appeared in the gap. 'Just heard there's been an accident on the arterial road,' he said. 'The fog's really thick out there. Can you ask Mrs Deepbriar to pass any calls on to Falbrough for me, please?'

Deepbriar glanced out of the window. He could see nothing but a swirl of white. 'Mind you don't get lost,' he said, only half joking, as Giddens withdrew, 'and keep your ears open once you're out of the village, drivers always take that road too fast in this kind of weather.'

The young man had only been gone a few minutes when the outside bell rang. Deepbriar was halfway to the office before he remembered he wasn't supposed to go in there, but Mary didn't appear from the kitchen, obviously still deep in conversation with Mrs Emerson, so he carried on and opened the door.

Two people stood on the step, their clothes spangled with shining droplets of dew from the fog. 'Morning, Thorny,' Colonel Brightman said, sweeping his hat from his head. 'I heard you were still on the sick list. Don't often see you in mufti.'

'Good morning, Colonel,' Deepbriar replied, opening the door wide and ushering him inside. 'I'm not officially back on duty, but Constable Giddens was called out.' At nearly eighty Brightman was still spry, but the years had worn him down to a thin stick of a man. Behind him came the bent figure of Simon Witherby.

'It's Simon's day for working at the Manor,' the Colonel explained, 'and there's something he was telling me that I thought you should know. In fact I got the Humber out p.d.q. and drove him in, although in this weather we'd have been as quick on our feet.'

Deepbriar got them both seated and gently closed the door that led into the rest of the house, satisfied to hear the faint murmur of female voices from the kitchen, before settling himself at his desk and picking up a notebook and pencil. 'Well?'

'Don't rightly know where to start,' Witherby mumbled.

'It's probably quicker if I explain,' Brightman said, 'military mind and all that. The thing is, when Simon was working in Mrs Emerson's garden on Monday he found some clothes. He thinks they belong to Bronc.'

'Found them? Where?' Deepbriar asked.

'Pushed into the bottom of the bonfire. It sounded a bit fishy to me, so when Simon told me about it I thought we'd better come and report. I've known Bronc a good few years, and I can't see him throwing away a serviceable coat, not without a very good reason. And since I'd heard you'd been looking for the old boy I thought you'd better hear about it.'

'You said clothes, it wasn't just his coat?' Deepbriar turned to Witherby. The gardener shook his head.

'There's two coats. One of them looks near new. I don't know where that might have come from, but I've seen Bronc wearing the other one many a time.'

The old car crept through the fog, the light from the head lamps barely showing the side of the road. Deepbriar sat beside the Colonel, keeping a watch for the telltale dips in the verge where there was a gateway. Mary's protests were still ringing in his ears; only the Colonel's assurance that he would personally escort the constable to Mrs Emerson's house, and bring him back again, had finally dissuaded her from telephoning Sergeant Hubbard. And Mrs Emerson had approved the scheme, enjoying the drama of the occasion, and eager to avail herself of a ride home in the Colonel's car.

'This is quite exciting,' Mrs Emerson said, leaning forward to tap the constable on the shoulder. 'Do you really think Mr Witherby has found something suspicious? I didn't think that awful old tramp would dare come into my garden, these people have such a nerve.'

Deepbriar didn't bother to answer; the woman had been saying the same thing in a dozen different ways ever since Colonel Brightman explained why they wanted to take a look at her bonfire. The big car crawled into the gateway at The Lodge and stopped in the drive. Deepbriar took a deep breath before he got out, fighting down the dizziness that struck him. Following the Colonel, who in turn was following Simon Witherby, he made it safely along the gravel path to the end of the garden, glad that they were walking slowly. Mrs Emerson twittered along behind, occasionally treading on his heels.

'Here we are,' Simon Witherby declared, arriving beside a heap of garden rubbish nearly five feet high. 'Getting a bit out of hand, it was, with all the wet weather we've had. I decided to have a go at burning it anyway, I thought it'd go well enough if I once got it alight. T'other side had caught before I noticed these and pulled them out. When I saw what they were I put the fire out again, just in case there was anything else. I had a bit of a poke with my pitchfork, but I couldn't see owt.'

The two coats were draped across the ruins of a wheelbarrow. Deepbriar recognised them both, the ancient Burberry with the ragged tear where a strip had been torn off, and the nearly new tweed overcoat Harry Bartle had given to old Bronc less than three weeks ago. He picked the latter up gingerly in a gloved hand, holding it high so the garment unfolded.

'Oh my goodness!' Mrs Emerson's voice squeaked with excitement. Along one side of the collar, and splashing the breast, was a large rusty coloured stain.

'Couldn't be helped, Sarge,' Deepbriar said, standing stolid and unmoving under Hubbard's glare. 'With Giddens called to that accident on the arterial, I had to go and take a look.'

Hubbard grunted. 'You were on sick leave. You should have called it in to us, not gone traipsing about in the fog like a flipping boy scout.'

Ignoring this gibe, Deepbriar asked the question that had been on his mind ever since the previous day, when he'd entrusted the coats to Giddens for delivery. 'Has the analysis been done, Sarge?'

'You're to see Inspector Martindale, he'll tell you.' He jerked his head in the direction of the Inspector's office. 'Missing blooming Spraggs, now missing blooming tramps,' he muttered, just loud enough to be heard, as Deepbriar turned away. 'Missing a few screws if you ask me.'

'Constable,' Martindale waved him to a chair. 'Good to see you back on your feet. Are you fully recovered?'

'Dr Smythe had nothing to say against me coming in,' Deepbriar said, side-stepping the fact that he hadn't actually seen the doctor, who'd therefore had no chance to comment. 'I'm feeling much better.'

'Good. Sorry that duty in Belston turned into such a roughhouse. So, this strange business of the missing tramp. I understand you'd been looking for him?'

'Yes, sir, I thought he might help with my enquiries, although it wasn't actually official.' Deepbriar hesitated. He could see no alternative, he had to tell him about Joe Spraggs's disappearance, and that he'd continued his investigation in defiance of Sergeant Hubbard's orders, since that was what had led him to search for Bronc in the first place.

'So you see, sir,' he finished, 'I was hoping Bronc might have remembered something about the black car, because I'm fairly sure it must have been used to kidnap Joe Spraggs. I explained all this to Sergeant Hubbard, but since Joe turned up again, and he hadn't come to any harm, he didn't think the case was worth pursuing. That was before this business with the other Joseph Spraggs, but maybe that's been cleared up by now. I – er – I haven't been able to ascertain whether he turned up again, since I'm not officially back on duty as yet.'

Martindale turned the start of a grin into a grimace of sympathy. He had joined the county force only a few months before, moving out from an inner city area. 'I've heard about the sergeant's dislike of missing person cases,' he said. 'However, in your shoes I think I'd have wanted to know how and why your Joseph Spraggs was kidnapped. I can't blame you for looking into it. As for the other Joseph Spraggs, I gather Sergeant Hubbard has satisfied himself that there's nothing suspicious about his disappearance. It's not that unusual, men often decide to walk out on their wives without any warning.'

'Yes sir, but considering what happened to the local lad, it seems a mighty big coincidence, them having the same name....'

'Strange things do happen, Constable. Anyway, perhaps we can go into that later. You'd better tell me a bit more about this tramp. Bronc is it?'

'Yes. There's not a lot. Nobody seems to know his full name for a start, he's always been known as just Bronc. I was wondering if anyone had gone to pick up that parcel he left in the garden shed at The Lodge, there could be something in it that would help.'

'That's being dealt with,' Martindale said. 'And we'll be raking through the rest of that bonfire, too. Stick to the point, constable. Any idea of the man's age?'

'Definitely over seventy, maybe close to eighty,' Deepbriar replied. 'I'd have said he was still pretty fit though.' He shook his head slowly. 'He's been around as long as I can remember, always coming through Minecliff at the same time of year, heading south in autumn, north in spring. Like the birds, he used to say. And he always stopped at the same places, mostly where they'd let him do a few odd jobs in exchange for a place to sleep, but with some it was purely charity, especially as he got older. He's a harmless old soul.'

'But I gather this Mrs Emerson didn't care for him. And she didn't know he'd been sleeping in her garden shed?'

'No. Mrs Emerson has only been in the village about fifteen months. She turned Bronc out this time last year, and she thought he didn't turn up in spring, but I wouldn't be surprised if Simon Witherby didn't let him in and make him welcome, which probably explains how Bronc's things turned up there this time, I'd guess he moved into the bothy after dark on the Saturday.'

Martindale looked down at the papers on his desk, sorting through them. 'Witherby's the one who found the coats, isn't he. But he wasn't in any hurry to report it.'

'He knew I'd been looking for Bronc, and although I told him the old man wasn't in any trouble he probably thought he was doing him a favour by keeping quiet.' He shrugged. 'Even law-abiding citizens prefer to keep us at arm's length sometimes.'

'Is Bronc likely to have made any enemies in the village? Other than Mrs Emerson?'

'As far as I know he's been travelling over the same route for more than forty years without any trouble. He's always been pretty predictable, if anybody meant to do him harm they'd find him easily enough.'

Deepbriar stared at the piece of paper Martindale had picked up from the desk; it was a laboratory report.

'I take it that's not good news, sir.'

'No.' Martindale paused. 'The stain on both coats was human blood. There was a lot of it. In fact, according to the police surgeon, that amount of bleeding suggests a mortal wound.' He looked solemnly across at Deepbriar. 'Since we don't have a body and the man wouldn't have been able to move very far after sustaining such a serious injury, I think we can rule out an accident or suicide. It looks very much as if Minecliff may be harbouring a murderer.'

Chapter Eleven

To his disgust, Deepbriar was excluded from the search of Mrs Emerson's garden and the surrounding area. While Martindale was sympathetic to the constable's pleas, he claimed he could do nothing to help.

'The case is being turned over to the CID,' the inspector explained. 'You could try asking Inspector Stubbs, but until the doctor has signed you off I doubt if you'll be allowed back on duty. If I were you I'd maintain a low profile, keep an eye on things from your end as it were. If that tramp doesn't turn up soon, or there's some innocent explanation as to how all that blood came to be spilt, they'll be into a full-blown murder enquiry. Then you'll be the man on the ground, the one with the local knowledge the plainclothes boys are going to need.'

A little later Deepbriar left the station and walked to the bus stop. He'd only been there a minute when a decrepit lorry pulled up alongside, belching smoke.

'Can I offer you a lift, Mr Deepbriar?' Joe Spraggs called, 'I'm going back to the yard, but I can drop you in the village first.'

'Thanks, Joe,' Deepbriar said, heaving himself into the cab, and doing his best to get comfortable on the heap of sacks which served as a cushion.

'I heard that knock on the head you got was a bit nasty. Are you fit and well now, Mr Deepbriar?' the young man asked, selecting a gear and pulling away from the kerb with an ease the constable couldn't help but admire.

'I'm fine. You know what these doctors are like, making a lot of fuss. They won't let me ride my bike yet, that's why I was waiting for the bus. How about you? No more nightmares?'

'Well, not so many,' Joe replied. He gave a slightly embarrassed laugh. 'Still jump when I hear somebody behind me, and I gave up making tea at the yard.' He patted a bulky canvas bag at his side. 'Emily makes me a flask. And to give Mr Wriggle his due, he's letting me take the lorry home when I'm late back.'

Deepbriar nodded and sat silent for a while, grabbing hold of the door handle as they swung round a bend at twenty miles an hour. The modern pace of life took a bit of getting used to; he supposed youngsters like Joe took it for granted.

'Joe, do you happen to know another man by the name of Joseph Spraggs?' He said at last. 'You remember, when we were talking to Peter Brook about what happened to you, he suggested that it might have been a case of mistaken identity. Something's happened that makes me think he wasn't so far off the mark. You don't have a cousin with the same name I suppose?'

'Not a cousin, but there is another Joseph Spraggs. He lives the other side of Belston somewhere, he's my Dad's cousin's son, though he's closer to Dad's age than mine. We don't have much to do with that side of the family, my Mum doesn't approve of them. They spend too much time and money in the pub for her liking.' He grinned. 'She was never too keen on me going into the Goose for a shandy, it's lucky Emily's not inclined the same way. Did I get nabbed instead of this Joseph?'

'Just a thought,' Deepbriar said. 'What else do you know about him?'

'He was the black sheep of the family, got into all sorts of mischief when he was a boy, I remember my Dad talking about him, though they didn't meet up much. I don't think he's changed either, I heard there was some trouble over forged ration books just after the War. Do you think he's been up to something more serious?'

'Maybe. I heard that he might have left his wife. And that it was all a bit sudden.'

Joe's chin came up suddenly, and he stared fixedly out of the windscreen. 'Are you saying he's gone missing? Like I did?'

'I don't know.' Deepbriar ran a hand over his hair. He'd been unable to get anything more out of either Hubbard or Martindale regarding Joseph Spraggs's possible disappearance, only that they were satisfied the man had left of his own free will, so there was no need for an investigation by the police. He probably shouldn't be talking to Joe about it, but the lack of information was frustrating. Two weeks had gone by since he'd first heard Mrs Spraggs report her husband's disappearance; if she was right and he hadn't gone voluntarily, then somebody ought to be looking for the man, even if he was a villain.

'Fact is, I was wondering if he'd turned up again, and I thought you might have heard something, with you being family.'

'We're not exactly close,' Joe grinned. 'They did come to our wedding though, you might have seen them; he's nearly six foot tall, and going bald. He was wearing a very sharp suit. His wife was dressed up to the nines, too, reckon he made a fair bit of money during the War.' He was silent for a moment.

'Mum still sees a few of Dad's relatives when she goes to town on a Saturday,' he said at last. 'She hasn't mentioned Joseph recently, but I'll ask her if you want.'

'Thanks, lad, I'd be grateful.' Deepbriar sighed. When he returned to duty he'd have plenty to do, without risking Martindale's displeasure by pursuing the Spraggs affair. The business at Quinn's yard didn't have the same urgency as a suspected murder, but it needed sorting out, he really didn't have time to investigate a possible kidnapping as well.

Come to think of it, the hunt for Bronc had become another missing person case, except that this time they had evidence in the shape of two bloodstained coats. That certainly made it look like a matter of foul play, yet Bronc as a murder victim seemed unlikely, it was hard to imagine why anyone would want to kill the old tramp. Joseph Spraggs, on the other hand, might have made many enemies, since he was involved with the criminal fraternity. Deepbriar was very much afraid that Falbrough CID were about to start investigating the wrong crime.

By doing as Martindale advised and keeping his head down, Deepbriar found he was far better informed than if he'd been out with the poor unfortunates combing through Minecliff's fields and gardens. He was also a great deal more comfortable, since a relentless drizzle fell all weekend, leaving the searchers damp and discouraged. The police house became the centre of operations, and the pungent odour of wet wool mingled with the pleasanter smells that issued from the kitchen as Mary prepared countless mugs of hot soup for the hapless officers. Deepbriar was much in demand for his knowledge of the people and places involved in the search, all pretence that he was still on sick leave being abandoned by Sunday morning.

'We'll need to make an early start again tomorrow,' Inspector

Stubbs said, glowering out of the door at the fast-approaching darkness, then turning back to face Deepbriar, stifling a yawn. 'I'm going home to get some sleep. You're lucky, your bed's nice and handy.'

Deepbriar grinned. 'Yes sir. But I'm afraid I shan't be available first thing in the morning, I've got to go to the hospital. I'm seeing the doctor there; once he's signed me off I'll be officially back on duty.'

Stubbs grunted. 'I suppose you have to go then. We'll put Constable Giddens in here for the morning. But get back as soon as you can, I need you.'

'I'm not supposed to ride my bike yet. I'll be back all the quicker if I get a lift,' Deepbriar hinted.

'I'll see what I can do. Call at the station once the quacks have finished with you, I expect there'll be people coming and going all day,' Stubbs said, lifting his battered felt hat off the stand and heading back to the door, 'can't get far without our local man, not in a case like this.'

The drizzle finally relented, but next morning the fog returned. A grumbling clutch of policemen were huddled outside the house in the cold when Deepbriar went out to catch the bus. Mary kissed him goodbye at the door, to his great embarrassment, before handing him a big square tin. 'That's for Sister Hunt, she enjoyed the little piece of fruit cake you gave her, you really should have shared it. Anyway, I said I'd send one for the nurses.'

Deepbriar tried to tell her that he'd only eaten two slices before his contraband was confiscated, but she was busy counting heads, and thinking of cups of tea. 'I hope I've got enough milk,' she said absently, ignoring his protest. 'I'll need to borrow another kettle.' With that she bustled away.

The fog was thick on Falbrough High Street, and Deepbriar almost bumped into the little man who shot out of the hospital entrance just as he turned in.

'Sorry.' They both spoke simultaneously, then recognised each other in the same instant.

'Mr Crimmon.'

'Constable Deepbriar.' The organist's hand was wrapped in an even larger bandage than before.

'Still not fit to play, I see,' Deepbriar commiserated.

'I'm not even able to give lessons,' Cyril Crimmon replied, 'the wound turned septic. I was sorry not to see you in church yesterday, we were left at the mercy of Nicky Wilkins.' He pulled a sour face. 'It was most unsatisfactory.'

'I'll hope to be there next Sunday,' Deepbriar said, 'but only if I'm not on duty. We're a bit stretched for manpower just at present.'

'Perhaps you'd be good enough to let Miss Lightfall know if you're not coming, we may be able to find somebody else. There has even been talk of Mrs Emerson playing for us.'

'And leaving Minecliff in the lurch?' Deepbriar was indignant. He'd heard that in his absence she had refused to play the organ at Colin Pattridge's funeral, but luckily a friend of the vicar's had been persuaded to come from Belston.

Crimmon's smile was almost a smirk. 'Well, given the chance to play a far superior instrument, you can understand the temptation for a musician of her calibre ...'

There was the sound of an engine, muffled a little by the fog, and a large dark shape, dimly seen, slowed by the kerb on the opposite side of the road. As the mist swirled and thinned for a second, Deepbriar realised it was a hearse, its polished black paint work dulled by a sheen of damp. The car rolled to a standstill, its engine purring, and Aubrey Crimmon looked across at them from the driver's seat, lifting a hand in greeting.

The organist returned the salute. 'Ah, I was hoping my brother wouldn't be long. You'll excuse me, constable.'

Deepbriar's brows lifted, he'd forgotten about their connection; it was an unlikely relationship, the two men were physical opposites. Cyril Crimmon looked far more like an undertaker than the rosy-cheeked Aubrey, nearly always wearing a suitably sombre expression. 'Of course, we're always quite happy with your playing,' Crimmon condescended as he turned away, 'when you're free. Excuse me, I mustn't keep Aubrey waiting. Good day.'

'And a good day to you too,' Deepbriar muttered as the man climbed into the sleek black car and vanished into the fog. 'And as for Mrs Emerson, as far as I'm concerned Possington is welcome to her.'

Once he'd seen the doctor and been given a clean bill of health, Deepbriar sought out Sister Hunt. She looked no less formidable, and Deepbriar, feeling about two feet tall, wished he'd worn his uniform. However, the cake having been duly inspected and approved, she unbent enough to grant that Deepbriar almost redeemed the citizens of Minecliff in her estimation.

'I'm glad you don't still see me in the same light as Bert Bunyard,' the constable replied.

Sister Hunt gave a brief decisive nod. 'A totally unpleasant man. I was very grateful that he only stayed one night. If it had been up to me I wouldn't have admitted him in the first place, the state he was in. A man has no business being inebriated at that time of day, it's a disgrace. There's not much we can do about bruising anyway.'

'Bruising?' Deepbriar stared at her. 'Didn't he have a broken leg?'

'Of course not!' She was shocked. 'No matter what kind of man he was, I'd hardly suggest sending a patient away with broken bones!'

'We are talking about the same person here?' the constable asked. 'Thickset and untidy, always wears a red neck cloth. He fell down the market steps.'

'That's the one. And it's no wonder he fell, the amount of alcohol he must have consumed. He positively reeked of it.'

'Bert Bunyard, you old rogue!' Deepbriar breathed. 'Well, I hope the nurses enjoy their cake. Thank you again, Sister.'

'Only doing my job.' She glanced at her watch. 'You'll have to excuse me now, constable, it's nearly time for matron's rounds.'

Deepbriar sat beside the young driver as the police car nosed its way towards Minecliff through the fog. He was hardly able to believe his luck. Falbrough's finest might be no nearer to finding Bronc, but thanks to Sister Hunt he'd solved a case. Or, to be more precise, he'd solved two, for he now knew exactly what had been taken from the Operatic Society's store in the village hall, and why.

A rare smile curved Deepbriar's lips as he remembered Minecliff's one attempt at farce. Most of the biggest laughs had come at the wrong times. In those days Mary had been responsible for props; it must be ten years since she'd persuaded Doctor Smythe to help her make that mock plaster cast.

Ferdy Quinn had been right all along, and although it would bring Deepbriar great satisfaction to confront Bert Bunyard, it would be no fun admitting his mistake to his neighbour. Deepbriar decided he must soften the blow. Perhaps if he found a way of returning the missing pig ... That thought stopped him dead. Last time he visited Hurdles Farm, the day after the animal disappeared, Humphrey Bunyard had proudly, and quite inno-

cently, shown the constable every one of his four legged charges.
There were no pigs.

'Deepbriar, thank heavens you're back,' Stubbs met him at the
door of the police house and ushered him into the office. 'We've
got a problem. Man by the name of Bunyard, doesn't want us
searching his farm. I don't want to bring in the heavy mob, we're
still short-handed anyway, but it could turn nasty if he's not
handled right.'

'Bert?' Deepbriar rubbed his hands together. 'I'll deal with him
inspector, there's a little matter of a stolen pig to answer for, not
to mention arson and criminal damage. I was planning to go out
there anyway, it's time him and me had a word.'

'No, the name's not Bert,' Stubbs interrupted, consulting the
piece of paper he held. 'The man we've come up against is
Humphrey Bunyard. According to this report he's built like a
brick privy and is just about as unmovable.'

'Humphrey?' Deepbriar was taken aback. 'He's just a lad, I
can't imagine him being much trouble, though you have to know
how to talk to him,' he conceded.

'Then let's get out there,' Stubbs ordered. 'The car that brought
you from town can take us, it's waiting outside.'

'Right. Only we'll have to stop at the village shop on the way,
there's something I need.'

'This is no time for you to be buying your groceries, constable.'
Stubbs said, climbing into the car.

'It's not for me, sir, it's for Humphrey. Unless you happen to
have a bar of chocolate handy?'

On the short journey, detouring via the shop, Deepbriar told
Inspector Stubbs about Bert Bunyard and the phoney plaster cast,
and about the night-time raids at Quinn's farm.

'This is all very interesting constable, but I don't see any
connection between this and our missing man,' Stubbs said. 'And
right now all I want to do is locate this Bronc. Unless the tramp
got on the wrong side of Bunyard. Maybe he found out what he'd
been up to. It's a bit strange, the son trying to stop us searching
the farm.'

'I can't see Bert getting violent, not beyond swinging the odd
punch when he's had a few,' Deepbriar replied. 'I doubt if
Humphrey stopping your men from searching the farm is relevant
to our case, it's more likely that Bert is in hiding, and he's told the

lad to be on his guard.' He shook his head thoughtfully. 'Bert's gone too far this time, it's not a case of giving him a caution. I reckon the magistrate's likely to put him behind bars for a while.'

'It's your patch,' Stubbs said, 'None of my business as long as you're right and it doesn't involve our missing person. You're sure you've got enough evidence to prove he's behind the arson and so on? Pretending to have a broken leg isn't a crime.'

'Maybe not, but I'll nail him,' Deepbriar replied. 'Because if I don't I'll have a full scale war on my hands, once Ferdy Quinn finds out what's been going on.'

Humphrey Bunyard stood in the gateway at Hurdles Farm, his feet spread wide and a fixed expression on his lumpy features. When Deepbriar climbed out of the car the young man's face brightened for a moment, then returned to its former look of stubborn incomprehension.

'Hello, Humph,' Deepbriar said, strolling up to him. 'Can I have a word with your Dad?'

'He said not to let anyone in,' the young man said, shifting his feet uneasily.

'Yes, but he didn't mean old friends like me. Where is he? Inside?'

The large head moved slowly from side to side. 'Gone.'

'Gone? There's no market today, Humph. Are you sure he's not indoors? Maybe he told you to say he wasn't home.'

'Gone,' the answer came again.

'When did he go then? This morning was it?'

Humphrey's face creased with the effort of working this out. 'No.'

'Was he here yesterday?' Deepbriar was getting an uncomfortable feeling in his belly.

'No.'

'Tell you what, Humphrey,' Deepbriar said, taking a large bar of Whole Nut from his pocket, 'why don't we go indoors and talk about it. We can have a cup of tea, that'll go down well with a bit of this chocolate, won't it.'

Humphrey's eyes widened at the sight of the purple wrapper. 'He said nobody was allowed in.'

'Yes, but he meant villains, people who might want to steal things. You and me are pals, and these people with me are my friends. Look, they're policemen, just like me. There's a man missing, Humph, we're worried about him. He's maybe lost somewhere. Think about how that feels, Humph, you wouldn't like to be lost, would you? You'd hate being all alone in a place you didn't know.'

There was a short silence then the simpleton reached out to take the chocolate. 'He won't be very happy, will he,' he said, leading the way to the house.

'No,' Deepbriar agreed, giving Inspector Stubbs a quick nod as he followed. 'So while we have our tea we'll let our friends look for him, shall we?'

The inside of the house looked no worse for Bert's absence, in fact Deepbriar thought it had improved a little, though it took him a while to work out that this was because there were no dirty cups or plates lying about. It seemed Humphrey had been doing some washing up.

'So, when did your Dad go?' Deepbriar asked, once Humphrey had eaten his first mouthful of chocolate. Getting nothing but a puzzled look in response he tried again. 'You say your Dad wasn't here yesterday. Are you sure?'

Humphrey nodded.

'How about the day before yesterday. Was he here then?'

Humphrey's face took on its habitual vacant expression and Deepbriar sighed. Then he remembered something.

'Was your Dad here on Saturday? He brings you a packet of crisps doesn't he, when he goes to the Speckled Goose. Do you remember that?'

'Yes,' Humphrey said decidedly. 'There was ...' he paused then held up two fingers. 'Two lots of salt,' he said, grinning. 'I got a free one. In blue paper. I remember.'

'He brought you some crisps and the packet had some extra salt inside,' Deepbriar nodded. 'And when he came back, did he go to bed for the night?'

The big head shook slowly. 'No.'

'He didn't go to bed. So he went off somewhere instead. Did he go to Ferdy Quinn's? Was he going to steal another pig?'

Humphrey looked blank. 'I like pigs,' he said, 'But Dad won't let me have one.'

Deepbriar sighed. It was going to be a long day.

'So, all we know is, this Bunyard came back from the pub on Saturday night, then nothing.' Stubbs frowned. The fog had lifted a little and he could see about a hundred yards across the fields, where a couple of uniformed men were inspecting a ditch. 'I hope it's only a coincidence that he's gone missing exactly three weeks after the old tramp disappeared.'

'I doubt if there's any connection, sir. Unlike Bronc, Bert went under his own steam,' Deepbriar said. 'As far as I can make out he packed a spare pair of socks and a bit of food, then walked out. I'd guess he got scared and decided to skip until the heat died down. Not that I was on to him, not then, something else must have put the wind up him. He'll be hiding out somewhere. Bert Bunyard's a wily old bird though, he might not be too easy to find.'

'And this Humphrey, you're sure he's not going to turn violent? It'll take us another hour to finish the search, I never saw such a rabbit warren.'

'He won't cause you any trouble. He's a bit simple, but he's not a bad lad. As a matter of fact it looks like he's got more nouse than I thought, he's cooking for himself, and he's even cleaning the place up.'

'Doesn't show,' Stubbs said sceptically.

'It was worse when Bert was home,' Deepbriar assured him.

'If you say so. Well, we'll finish the search, but I don't think we're likely to find any sign of this missing man ever having been here. A man who was bleeding to death couldn't have walked this far, and I can't see anyone carrying a body dripping with gore for nearly a mile.'

'Nothing's turned up near The Lodge?'

'Not a darned thing. And if we don't find a body, or at least a bit more evidence, we can't take the case any further,' Stubbs said gloomily. 'Not to mention we still don't even have a proper name for our victim. We'll go on asking questions of course, but it's not looking too hopeful.'

A distant rattle became a hum and a clatter, and a bicycle turned in at the gateway, skidding as it hit the mud. Constable Giddens, his fresh young face flushed with the cold and the exercise, came to a halt beside them and leapt off the machine. 'Sir! We've found something.' He paused to take a breath, then plunged on. 'It was the bothy, sir, the garden shed at The Lodge. I thought about how all that rain would have washed away any evidence, but when I scouted around I found there's this big over-hang at the back, where the roof sticks out at least a foot, and with the prevailing wind coming from the west, it keeps the ground pretty dry there. And I realised the stuff lying around, leaves and twigs and so on, well, it looked as if it had been disturbed. I had a bit of a poke about, and I found a huge great stain. Something red and sticky seeped down into the ground behind that shed. I bet that's where it happened, sir, you can see it's blood, even now.'

Chapter Twelve

'Oh, Inspector, isn't it just dreadful!' Bella Emerson's eyes were bright with excitement, and she twisted a tiny lace-trimmed handkerchief between her fingers as if recreating her performance as the tragic Cio Cio San. 'All that blood! It quite makes me shudder to think of the poor man.'

Deepbriar wondered cynically at the process that had transformed Bronc from a dirty old tramp into an object of pity, and decided that for the likes of Mrs Emerson it had a lot to do with his being dead. Not to mention that a murder being committed in her garden would give her a certain standing among the village gossips.

'When I saw it I felt quite faint,' she went on, 'in fact I'm still feeling a little strange. Imagine, a murderer, here!' Her eyes rolled as she swayed ominously towards the constable, but he stepped aside without apparently noticing her, as if in a hurry to follow the inspector. Mrs Emerson recovered her balance, and with a glare at the constable's back she fell into step behind the three men as if fainting had never been further from her mind.

Inspector Stubbs paused briefly. 'I don't know that we're dealing with a grave, Mrs Emerson. Constable Giddens, why didn't you tell Mrs Emerson to keep away from the garden shed?'

'I did advise her it wasn't a suitable sight for a lady, inspector,' Giddens protested.

'I'm not thinking about her sensibilities, man,' he gave the woman an unconvincing smile. 'Mrs Emerson is not a child. What I'm concerned with is the evidence. We've precious little, and now you've found some we don't want half of Minecliff tramping about on it!'

'Sorry, sir.' Giddens was downcast, but he brightened as they approached the bothy. 'I did put a couple of tools across, before

Mrs Emerson came to see what I was doing, so I doubt if she's actually done any damage.'

'Hmm. All right constable, I think you'd better escort the lady back to the house. If she's of a nervous disposition we don't want to expose her to any more shocks. We'll be in to have a word with you shortly, Mrs Emerson,' he added, turning to her, 'and we'll need to talk to your gardener again. I take it he's here somewhere?'

'He's in the conservatory,' she said. 'Since your men wouldn't allow him to get on with his usual work, I had to find him something to do in there. It's almost time for his lunch, and I think he was going into the village. I'll warn him to wait until he's seen you, shall I?'

'Yes, thank you. You can tell him we shan't keep him long. Come on, Deepbriar.' Stubbs led the way to the bothy, glancing back over his shoulder. 'That woman gives me the pip,' he said. 'Sorry, I shouldn't say that. I gather she's a friend of yours.'

'Not mine, sir,' Deepbriar hastened to assure him. 'My wife's. I can't say I've exactly taken to her.'

'Not the type to have committed bloody murder though,' Stubbs mused, sighing regretfully. 'Women are capable of killing, constable, but in my experience they prefer to keep it clean. Poison, perhaps, or maybe a blunt instrument, in the heat of the moment, but not knives, and I'd say that's what the evidence points to in this case.'

'What about a gun?' Deepbriar suggested, as he peered over the Inspector's shoulder into the space behind the bothy. Giddens had protected his find with a rake and a broom propped across some upturned flower pots. 'A man could bleed to death from a gunshot wound.' A heap of leaves and twigs had been swept to one side to expose the bare ground beneath; the young constable was right, the projecting roof had kept the surface dry, and the dark moist area, almost three feet across, certainly looked like a blood stain.

'That's true, I'll keep it in mind, though we've found no cartridge, and there weren't any powder burns on the coats. Still, I think I'd better get this area searched again. If this was missed, maybe there's something else we haven't found.'

'If we're looking for a sharp instrument, there's a lot of tools inside,' Deepbriar suggested. 'And Simon keeps a good edge on them.'

Stubbs grimaced. 'Sergeant Jakes and the fingerprint chappy were supposed to have checked those, the first day we were here, but I suppose it won't hurt to take another look.'

At first sight the task was daunting, but many of the tools obviously hadn't been moved for several months. In half an hour they were down to three possible weapons; a pruning knife, a scythe, and a spade. All of them had been cleaned recently, and were extremely sharp. 'Doesn't bear thinking about,' Deepbriar mused, inspecting the spade without touching it, and with an uncomfortable image in his head of old Bronc's scrawny neck beneath its many layers of clothing. 'This would be lethal, slashed across a man's throat.'

'Everything was checked for fingerprints, you can pick it up,' Stubbs said, lifting the knife gingerly between finger and thumb, 'I'll send these to County headquarters. I've heard they can find traces of blood, left in dents or scratches in the metal or in the joint with the handle, even when a weapon's been cleaned.'

'Yes sir, I've heard that. Pretty clever these scientific types,' Deepbriar agreed, stopping short of admitting that his knowledge came from one of Dick Bland's recent adventures.

'Go and fetch Giddens,' Stubbs said. 'We'll give him a treat, seeing as he found that bloodstain; these young lads love to get behind the wheel of a car, he'll enjoy a trip to the big city. And we'll send them a sample of that earth, too, just to make sure we're not getting excited over a spilt can of paint!'

Mrs Emerson was inclined to be a little sulky when they returned to the house, but when Stubbs sat her down and informed her that they needed to take a formal statement, with Deepbriar ordered to take down her every word, she recovered her good humour. 'Oh, my,' she said archly. 'I do hope I'm not a suspect, inspector.'

'Not at the moment, madam,' Stubbs replied, straight faced. 'But we do need to clarify a few things.' He started by asking her about the events of the weekend before Bronc's disappearance, and had some difficulty persuading her not to give a repeat performance of her leading role on the Saturday evening.

'We know the man only arrived in Minecliff after most of the villagers were gathered in the hall to see *Madame Butterfly*,' the inspector told her, holding up a hand to interrupt her in full flow, 'so let's start when you returned home, shall we?'

Deepbriar's fingers were cramped by the time they reached the details of what happened on Monday evening; nothing of any interest had come to light, despite a minute by minute account of Mrs Emerson's life. Of one thing she was certain; she would have heard a gunshot if a weapon had been fired in her garden.

'I can hear the guns clearly when the Colonel has people shooting on his land,' she said, 'and since I mentioned the noise to him he makes sure they don't come too close, but I still find it quite deafening. And I am a very light sleeper, the least sound awakens me. It's a price one pays for having an artistic temperament. In spring I'm always awake at dawn, the birds make such a noise. At this time of year I'm quite grateful for the longer nights, although occasionally an owl disturbs me, screeching the way they do.'

'Just one more thing then,' Stubbs said. 'Are there any firearms in the house, Mrs Emerson? Perhaps your husband had a shotgun to keep the rabbits down? Or some people brought weapons home from the War, as a keepsake.'

She shuddered. 'On no, nothing like that. I wouldn't allow anything so dangerous under my roof. And my poor dear Edgar was in the pay corps, as far as I know he was never given a gun.'

'How about the tools in the garden shed? Do you ever use any of them?'

She looked shocked, as if he had said something indecent. 'Oh no. I have a little fork and trowel, and some scissors for cut flowers, that sort of thing. I keep those in the conservatory. The bothy is entirely Witherby's responsibility.'

It was as they were leaving that Mrs Emerson suddenly remembered that she had something to tell Constable Deepbriar. 'I'm so sorry, Thorny, all this excitement, it quite drove the other matter from my mind,' she said. 'That kind Mr Harvey gave up his bridge evening to help me check through the property store at the village hall on Friday. Do you know, it's the strangest thing, but only one item was missing, and I can't imagine why anyone would want to steal it.'

'Let me guess,' Deepbriar said. 'It was a plaster cast.'

'Why yes!' She clasped her hands together as if in amazement, though there was a touch of disappointed resentment in her eyes. 'How clever of you!'

'And,' Deepbriar added, not without a touch of asperity in his voice, 'I suspect you told a few other people about it. Maybe on Saturday?'

'I believe I may have mentioned it, yes.' She sighed and fluttered her eyelids at him. 'Was that naughty of me? I went into church to see how the flower ladies were getting on, and then I had to call at the shop. Everyone in the village is so very friendly, don't you think, all these rustic types, they are so rural and homely, and always ready to stop for a chat.'

Which cleared up the mystery of Bert Bunyard's abrupt exit, Deepbriar thought glumly, as he extricated himself from the woman's clutches and followed Stubbs to the conservatory.

Simon Witherby was muttering to himself as he scattered DDT over some begonias. He gave the two police officers a baleful look as they came in, closing the door behind them.

'I'm almost out of baccy,' he grumbled, when Stubbs invited him to sit down so they could talk, 'I was going to the shop. She'll be closed for lunch by the time I get there.'

'Have one of mine,' the inspector offered, holding out a pack of Players. 'If you don't mind smoking ready-made.'

'They'll do,' Witherby said. 'But I don't know what you're after now. I told that young copper everything. Took it all down in writing he did.'

'Yes, I know. And we're grateful for your help, but there are just a few more things I need to ask you. That spot behind the shed. You didn't notice that there was something strange about it?'

'I've not been round there in months, not since I slashed the nettles down, back in summer. Would have got round to raking off the leaves in a week or two, other than that I've no call to go rooting about in corners, there's more than enough to be done in a garden this size, specially when I'm only here Mondays and Fridays.'

'And you haven't dropped anything out there, no paint or oil or anything?'

Witherby looked at him scornfully. 'You trying to tell me what that young chap found isn't blood? I was on the Somme. I've seen a pint or two spilt in my time, and the smell's enough to tell you, even if it has been there a fair old time. And before you ask, no, I didn't notice that neither, not till your bobby started digging around in it.'

'Fair enough. We'll be taking away some of your tools. They'll be returned as soon as we've finished with them.'

'And how am I supposed to do my job without my blooming tools?' Witherby demanded.

'We're only taking three items, and you seem to have plenty more hanging up in the shed, quite an arsenal in fact. Lots of good sharp blades.'

'You really think old Bronc was killed with something out of my shed?' The gardener seemed to shrink visibly at the thought.

'It's a long shot, Simon,' Deepbriar consoled him, 'but we have to check.'

'Well, I don't think we need to keep you any longer,' Stubbs said, getting to his feet, 'unless you've got anything you'd like to ask, constable?'

'There is one thing, sir,' Deepbriar said, pleasantly surprised by the inspector's invitation. 'Do you remember what Bronc was wearing when you met him that Saturday morning?'

'Aye.' Witherby gathered himself together, his face resuming its usual rather jaundiced expression. 'He had on that silly hat, the one I found by the compost heap. And the mac, that was in the bonfire. The same one he were wearing last year, and the year before that too I reckon. I already told you that, Thorny.'

'I know. You didn't happen to notice if the coat was torn, did you?'

'It was a bit tattered,' Witherby said. 'But I don't know as it were any worse than usual. What's that to do with owt?'

'I see what you're getting at, Deepbriar,' Inspector Stubbs's eyes narrowed. 'The older coat was badly torn when it was found. You think that happened when he was attacked.'

'No, I think it happened when a car knocked him into the ditch on the way to Minecliff,' Deepbriar said, 'though what that's got to do with him disappearing I honestly don't know. Where do you think Bronc might have gone on the Monday, Simon? He wouldn't be tramping the roads just for the fun of it, not at this time of year.'

The gardener shook his head. 'I don't know, and that's a fact. I thought he'd moved on to Goldings, but George swears he never went there.'

'George?' Stubbs asked.

'Hopgood,' Deepbriar said. 'He's foreman at Goldings. I checked with him myself, and spoke to a couple of his men. Bronc hasn't been seen there since the spring.'

Stubbs gave Witherby two more cigarettes before they left, and the old gardener stuck them behind his ear with a nod of thanks. The inspector led the way to the police car that was waiting to carry him back to Falbrough.

'Unless there was some jiggery pokery with the hat and the parcel, Bronc was out and about on Monday, which means somebody must have seen him,' Stubbs said. 'I don't see much point widening our search for the moment, we've covered the whole of the village.'

'Hold on, I think I've been missing something here,' Deepbriar said, stopping in his tracks. 'Bronc was in the pub!'

'What? When?'

'Monday lunch-time. I'm sorry inspector, Harry Bartle told me, but it had slipped my mind. He came visiting when I was in hospital, and my head wasn't too clear at the time. He said Bronc had been in the porch at the Speckled Goose, and there'd been a man in there talking to him. A stranger.'

'Yes, I knew there was somebody in there, I heard them talking.' Don Bartle was thinking hard, his brows furrowed with the effort. 'But I didn't see who it was with Bronc. And it's no use asking Phyllis, she was in Belston visiting her cousin.'

'Harry didn't see him either,' Deepbriar said. It was frustrating. He'd found three people who swore old Bronc was talking to somebody in the pub that Monday lunch-time, but the most he could discover about the stranger was that he wore a pale coat and dark hat, that he wasn't very short, nor very tall, and that when he left the pub he had hurried out of the village on foot, in the direction of Gadwell, a village some four miles away.

'Sorry, Thorny,' Don said. 'We were a bit busy. We had a barrel sprung a leak, and Harry was down in the cellar dealing with it for the best part of an hour.'

'Not to worry,' the constable sighed. 'It's back to knocking on doors for me, see if anyone else saw this man, but I can't say I'm hopeful.'

He started with the three houses between the pub and the open road that led to Gadwell. As he expected, nobody had seen the stranger. It was a Monday, which meant Minecliff's housewives were all occupied with their laundry, just as they had been three weeks before.

It was a quarter to three, and he'd only had a sandwich for his lunch. Deepbriar headed back towards the police house, thinking he had time to snatch a cup of tea and a slice of Mary's cake, if those vultures from Falbrough hadn't eaten it all. As he turned in at the gate he heard the hand bell being rung in the school yard, announcing the end of afternoon play time. The sound brought him to a stop. He swung round and hurried back down the road, and was just in time to see the last pupil, a boy in a tattered jumper, overlong shorts and with woolly socks gathered at the ankles, dashing across the yard from the outdoor privy to the Victorian brick building that had been Minecliff's school for over a hundred years.

'I hope none of our pupils have been misbehaving themselves,' Mrs Harris said, once the normal pleasantries were out of the way, and the constable was settled in the visitor's chair with a cup of tea and a plate of ginger biscuits before him. 'Nobody trying to climb on to Mr Coe's shed from our roof?' She added innocently.

Deepbriar had been caught attempting that feat in answer to a dare, during Mrs Harris's very first year as headmistress. He swallowed hastily and nearly choked on a ginger crumb.

'Another old pupil of mine came to mind this morning,' Mrs Harris said, giving the constable a chance to recover, 'when I cycled past Oldgate Farm. Poor Mr Pattridge, he was devastated by John's death, and I'm afraid Tony had spent so long in the shadow of his brother that he had no hope of redeeming himself. People tended to think of him as a rogue, even as a child, but I think most of it was merely an attempt to be noticed. He had a good brain.'

'His father never rejected him,' Deepbriar said, 'but he took it hard when Tony didn't even get in touch with him over Christmas.'

'Did he not?' Mrs Harris's eyebrows lifted in surprise. 'That's strange. I met Tony in Belston last year, about the middle of December. He was out with little Barbara Baker. They were friends at school, before her mother died and she went to live with her grandparents in Belston. That was during the War of course, her father was in the army.' She smiled. 'They made a good-looking couple, I confess I hoped I might soon be hearing of an engagement. I gathered the pair of them had been shopping, and I'm sure Barbara said she'd helped Tony choose a present for old Mr Pattridge.'

'If she did I'm afraid he never received it,' Deepbriar said.

The headmistress shook her head sadly. 'A shame, I always thought Tony might have turned out well, given time. Well, Thorny, it's nice to sit and chat but I have got work to do. How can I help you?'

'I'm looking for information. I was wondering if there were

any lads out of school on Monday the third. I know one or two of them are inclined to play hooky, especially on a Monday.'

Mrs Harris sighed. 'That's unfortunately true. It's a perennial problem. Why are you interested in that particular day?'

Deepbriar explained about Bronc's disappearance, and the stranger who had been seen talking to him. 'In my experience, young lads are pretty observant. If one of them happened to be hanging around outside the village there's just a chance they might have seen something.'

'I'll check the registers,' Mrs Harris said, rising from behind her desk. She smiled, taking a packet of biscuits from a drawer to replenish the nearly empty plate. 'You seem hungry, Constable, do have another ginger nut.'

'It was about something that happened three weeks ago, Mrs Pratt,' Deepbriar said, standing outside a council house three doors up from Honeysuckle Cottage where Joe and Emily Spraggs lived. 'It's all right, he's not in trouble.'

'That makes a change,' the woman said harshly, rubbing her damp and wrinkled hands together. 'Young beggar. And now he's got the measles if you please, as if I 'aven't enough to do without running up and down stairs all day! You'd best come in.' She nodded at the stairs. 'First door on the right. I got me washin' to finish.'

Kenny Pratt lay on a narrow bed under a couple of blankets, with an old rug and his school coat spread on top. He looked up in alarm as the large uniformed figure loomed in the doorway.

'It's all right, Kenny,' the constable assured him. 'Whatever it is you've been up to, we'll wait till you're better before we run you off to gaol. Can't have all the prisoners catching the measles, can we?'

The boy grinned, only a little uneasy. 'Ain't done nothin',' he said.

'How about playing hooky three weeks ago?' Deepbriar lowered himself warily on to the room's only available seat, a rather rickety three legged stool.

'You ain't lockin' me up for that, Mr Deepbriar,' Kenny replied, his confidence returning.

'Not this time. Not if you do something for me.'

'Like what?'

'Help me if you can. See, we're looking for somebody, and

there's just a chance you might have seen him.' He described the stranger, and how he'd left the Speckled Goose at about one-thirty on the day Kenny had decided to skip school.

Kenny shook his head. 'Didn't see 'im,' he said. 'Saw somebody else though.'

'Who was that?'

'Old Bunyard.'

'That's Mr Bunyard to you,' Deepbriar reproved him. 'When was this?'

'Bell 'ad just gone arter lunch, 'bout 'alf past one. 'E was on them crutch things, goin' up the 'ill towards the old aerodrome. Cussin' an' swearin' 'e was, but 'e was gettin' along all right. I kept me 'ead down, didn't want 'im seein' me.'

'You didn't see anyone else? Somebody you might recognise even if he didn't live in the village?'

'Old Bronc you mean?' The boy shook his head. 'Everyone knows 'e's gone missin', I'd 'a' said if I'd seen 'im.'

'And you didn't see anything else out of the ordinary that day?' Deepbriar was disappointed, it had been a long shot but he had great faith in the inquisitive nature of small boys.

'I saw a car parked up the lane. A sports car it was. Ol' Bunyard, I mean Mr Bunyard, 'e 'ad to squeeze past it.'

'The lane to the aerodrome?'

Kenny nodded.

'So, it was parked where nobody could see it from the village,' Deepbriar said thoughtfully. 'I don't suppose you took down the number?'

'Nah. Give up takin' numbers, that's kid's stuff. Know what it was though, one o' them new Austin-Healeys. Bright red it was, just like on one o' them cards you get in tea packets.'

'Like collecting the cards do you?'

'Yeah.' Kenny's pale eyes lit up. 'I like the cars, but them new sports stars are best. I already got Len Hutton, an' Roger Bannister an' Gordon Richards.'

Deepbriar fished in a pocket and pulled out four cards, only slightly crumpled. 'Mrs Deepbriar's been getting through a lot of tea lately. Let's see. I appear to have Stanley Matthews, Alec Bedser, Denis Compton and Billy Wright.'

'Wanna swap one of 'em?' Kenny asked eagerly. 'I got two Len Huttons.'

'Tell you what Kenny,' Deepbriar said. 'If you promise not to play hooky any more, you can have these.' He paused, looking the boy sternly in the eyes. 'But you'd better mean it.'

'I promise,' the boy said at once.

Deepbriar handed over the cards. 'You break your word and you'll catch something worse than measles,' he warned.

The search for Bronc went on for two more days, but nothing new came to light. On Wednesday evening Inspector Stubbs returned with Constable Deepbriar to the Minecliff police house, shutting the office door behind the two of them.

'I'm out of ideas,' the inspector said despondently. 'It doesn't look as if we'll ever find out what happened to the old man. The case isn't closed, but until some new evidence turns up there's nothing left to be done. I'm off to look into some burglaries the other side of Falbrough. Minecliff's all yours again, constable. Sergeant Jakes is taking care of the paperwork and tying up what loose ends he can, have a word with him if you get anything new.'

'I'll do that, sir.' Deepbriar hesitated. 'Nothing came up about that car I suppose, the one young Kenny saw in the lane off the Gadwell Road?'

'No. We tracked down three Austin-Healeys, and one of them belongs to a minor villain in Belston, so I sent a man to have a word with him. Turns out he had a cast iron alibi for that day, which is what I'd expect if he'd been up to something, but we've got no grounds to dig any deeper. It was a bit of a flimsy connection.'

'Right. I'll get on with the case of the missing pig then,' Deepbriar said. 'I don't think Bert Bunyard will stay away from home much longer, not with the winter coming on. I'll go and have another word with Humphrey in the morning.'

'Good luck.' Stubbs held out a hand. 'Thanks for your help, constable, it's been good working with you. If you ever decide to move over to plain clothes, let me know, I reckon we could use you in CID.'

As Thorny Deepbriar cycled out to Hurdles Farm next morning he pondered the inspector's words. He'd often dreamed of becoming a detective, yet now the chance had come he wasn't sure what to do. Minecliff was his home, and as a village bobby it had been his patch for ten years. He knew every man, woman and child who lived there, and he'd never given any serious thought to leaving.

Deepbriar rounded a bend in the road, and saw one of those individuals who made up his little world; whether this one was man or child, he wasn't quite sure. Humphrey Bunyard stood in the gateway of Hurdles Farm, his puddingy face red and screwed up as if he'd been crying. Seeing the constable he hopped from one foot to the other, remaining always inside his invisible boundary, but clearly very agitated. 'Gone!' he shouted. 'All gone!'

Chapter Thirteen

'Who's gone, Humphrey? Your Dad? But he's been missing for a few days, why get so upset now?'

Humphrey Bunyard shook his big head, his mouth gobbling frantically. 'Gone!' He was so distressed that he seemed to have mislaid the rest of his limited vocabulary, and as soon as Deepbriar was within reach he grabbed the sleeve of the blue tunic and pulled the constable towards the house.

Humphrey took Deepbriar indoors, not releasing him until they were in the kitchen. He pointed at the old black stove, where a crumpled piece of greaseproof paper lay beside a frying pan. 'It's gone,' he said. 'I'm hungry.'

Deepbriar looked around, seeking the reason for the young man's agitation. He was puzzled. Clearly Humphrey wasn't referring to food, for there were three thick rashers of bacon on a plate, and a basket of eggs on the table, along with half a loaf of bread, which looked edible, if rather stale. Nor was the stove itself the cause of the problem, for a comfortable heat could be felt radiating from it.

The simpleton picked up the greaseproof wrapping and waved it under the constable's nose. 'Gone!' He shouted, impatient at the policeman's stupidity.

'Ohhh.' Deepbriar exhaled mightily in relief and understanding. 'You've run out of dripping! That doesn't matter, Humph, you can cook without it. That bacon's got plenty of fat. Look.' He moved the frying pan on to the hot plate. Within minutes there was a delicious scent wafting through the old farmhouse. Smiling, his distress forgotten, Humphrey went into the larder at the other side of the kitchen and returned with three more rashers. 'Three for you, three for me, and two eggs each,' he chanted, as if reciting well-learned lines. He selected four large eggs from the basket, then cut thick slices of bread from the loaf.

They sat companionably on either side of the big scrubbed table and Deepbriar did full justice to the breakfast, even though it was his second in as many hours. 'You've been busy, Humphrey,' he said, as, comfortably full, he leant back and looked around him, sipping at a mug of earthy brown tea. The kitchen was noticeably cleaner and tidier than on his last visit. 'The place looks very smart.'

'Like my mum, she made it nice,' Humphrey said, his brow creasing as he sought for words to explain. 'I used to help her.'

'That's very good. Your mum would be proud of you. But what are you going to do when you run out of more things? Will you walk to the shop?'

Humphrey shook his head vigorously. 'I can get bread,' he said, 'from the baker.'

'Yes, but the baker won't bring you sugar, or salt, or tea. And what about money? You'll have to pay him. Besides, who's going to take your beasts to market? You can't cope for long without your Dad. Do you know where he went?'

'No.' Humphrey stared at his empty plate.

Deepbriar persisted. The youngster might not be able to say exactly where his father was, but he knew something. 'The longer he stays away the more trouble he'll be in. Do you understand? I have to find him.'

He changed tack, seeing Humphrey had his obstinate expression firmly in place. It was the only time he looked like his father. 'You know he never needed that plaster on his leg, don't you?'

Humphrey guffawed. 'He took it off when he came indoors. It was our secret. Me and Dad laughed.' He nodded vigorously. 'That was funny.'

'But the joke's over now. You and me are friends aren't we, Humph? I need you to help me. Do you know where he is?'

The big head shook again. 'No,' he said, giving Deepbriar a sidelong look, evidently torn. 'He went up the hill.'

Up the hill. There were plenty of hills around Minecliff, but he thought he knew which one Humphrey was talking about. Bert Bunyard had been going up one of them when young Kenny saw him, and that particular lane would take him to the old aerodrome.

Deepbriar leant across the table and patted Humphrey on the

shoulder. 'Good lad,' he said, convinced that he had his answer. The airbase was securely fenced, with great rolls of barbed wire put up before it was abandoned, because of the risk from all the unexploded munitions left behind after the War. Apart from the possibility of blowing himself up, it was the perfect place for a man on the run. If Bert was foolhardy enough to find a way in, there'd be plenty of places for him to hide, and room enough for a whole herd of pigs, come to that.

Thorny Deepbriar stared through the tangles of wire at the line of defensive works and gun emplacements, many of them barely visible under mounds of brambles. As he worked his way round the perimeter of the old wartime airbase, one building was nearly always in plain view, providing a point of reference in the jumble of abandoned huts and unrecognisable bastions of concrete. This was a grandiose stone structure, solid and square, which looked very much out of place amid the detritus left behind by the air force.

The mausoleum was over a hundred years old, the site chosen because the plateau above Minecliff commanded a wide view of the surrounding countryside. This monument to the dead had almost outlived the Abney-Hughes family who built it; there were only a couple of ancient female cousins left now, who would presumably join their ancestors in the impressive tomb when their time came. The last funeral had taken place there in nineteen thirty two; as a child Deepbriar had seen the procession go by, and he had a clear memory of the magnificent hearse pulled by four horses, plumes of black feathers nodding as they walked slowly up the hill towards the mausoleum. In those days it had stood alone amidst a sea of grass; somehow the building had survived the War untouched, despite being stranded in the middle of an airfield.

Beyond the mausoleum Deepbriar glimpsed the remains of a runway. Grass was coming up through cracks in the concrete; the servicemen had moved out six years ago, it didn't take long for nature to take over.

He'd walked nearly the whole way round the perimeter, fighting his way through hedges and ditches, sometimes up to his ankles in mud. It looked as if his guess had been wrong, and yet the more he thought about it, the more certain he became. There were air-raid shelters all over the site. Any one of them could hide a pig, and no sound would reach the village if it was being kept underground.

If it hadn't been for the badger tracks, he'd have missed it. He was walking on rough grass alongside a ploughed field when he noticed the narrow path worn in the headland, and going straight across his path. The track appeared to vanish under the remnants of a dead tree, but when he bent down to investigate he realised that a couple of the branches had been carefully propped up against the fence. Once he moved them he could see the neat tunnel cut through the brambles, and the wire. A man could pass through easily, hardly even needing to bend down.

On the other side of the fence the badgers obviously went straight on, heading for some destination of their own, but there was another track, this one with several clear imprints left by size nine boots. Bert must have been careful on the approach, presumably taking a long stride from the ploughed land, but here he had made no attempt at concealment.

The trail led Deepbriar to a Nissen hut, one of half a dozen lined up on a large concreted area. A thin wisp of smoke spiralled out of a tin chimney at one end. Peering through a window, partly obscured by a protective metal mesh, the constable could see inside. Bert Bunyard was reclining in an ancient armchair alongside a pot-bellied stove, open at the front to display a red glow. He was surrounded by a scatter of rusting food tins, screwed up brown paper bags and empty bottles. More tins, evidently full, stood on a shelf, along with a crate of beer and several packets of tobacco, and below them lay a discarded plaster cast, split open to display the hidden hinges down one side. A blue haze of cigarette smoke hung over the scene.

Stepping quietly, Deepbriar retraced his steps, following a trail of loose splodges of mud and some other darker wetter substance, smeared with imprints from the now familiar boots. The smell, also familiar, grew stronger as he progressed. He found Ferdy Quinn's prize sow, as he had expected, in an underground shelter.

The animal looked up at him, grunting a welcome and pushing against the makeshift barrier of upturned trestle tables Bunyard had erected to keep her away from the entrance. She looked well enough, with a thick bed of straw under her feet, although it was in need of cleaning. There were scraps of food in a wooden trough alongside a bucket of water.

'I reckon you'll be glad to get home, eh?' Deepbriar said,

leaning down to scratch the sow's back. 'Won't be long now, but I'll deal with Bert first, if you don't mind.'

Using the ever-visible mausoleum as a marker, Deepbriar found his way back to the hut where he'd seen Bunyard. A faded sign on the door announced that this had been the N.C.O.'s mess.

The hinges squeaked a little as Deepbriar went in. Bert Bunyard jerked round and stared up at the intruder, his ruddy face blanching, his jaw dropping open to reveal two rows of broken and nicotine stained teeth. Behind him on the wall a poster shouted that 'Careless talk costs lives!'

'Morning, Bert,' Deepbriar said cheerfully. 'Looks like you've made yourself pretty comfortable. Almost seems a shame to disturb you.'

Deepbriar used the telephone box on the edge of the village to summon a police car so he could take Bert Bunyard to Falbrough for questioning. Leaving his prisoner in one of the cells to reflect on his crimes, he spent nearly an hour on the necessary paper-work, then he had to wait for Sergeant Jakes to return from lunch, as it would be the sergeant's job to conduct the interrogation.

Bert was uncooperative, insisting that he was innocent, despite the smell of pig on his clothes and the clear trail from the sow's makeshift sty to his own bolt hole. 'Found 'er I did,' he said, when Jakes pressed him on this point. 'Couldn't leave the beast to get knocked down on the road, could I?'

'Then why not keep her at Hurdles Farm until the owner was traced?' Jakes asked.

'Ain't got a pig sty,' Bert growled, 'use your 'ead, sergeant.'

'So, lacking a pig-sty, you immediately thought the ideal place to accommodate a pig would be an air-raid shelter, on land belonging to the Air Ministry.' Jakes said sarcastically.

Bunyard glowered at him and clamped his mouth shut.

'We'll have another go in the morning,' Jakes told Deepbriar, once Bert had been removed to the cells again. 'And in the mean-time I'll sort out exactly what we're going to charge him with. I reckon we can get the theft of the pig to stick, but I'm not so hopeful about the arson or the criminal damage.'

'He stole that plaster cast from the village hall,' Deepbriar pointed out. He'd brought the prop back with him, and it stood in the corner of the CID room, filthy and slightly dented.

'Petty theft,' Jakes said gloomily. 'We'd better go up to the airbase, and see if he's been up to any more mischief.' He brightened. 'If he's been poking around and digging up unexploded bombs maybe we could get him on something really serious. How about suspected treason?'

Deepbriar gave one of his rare chuckles. 'If only you could. Old Bert's been running rings round the law all his life, I'd love to see him taught a bit of respect. Though I wouldn't go so far as wanting to see him hang,' he added considerately.

Jakes nodded. 'He might just have made a mistake choosing to break in through that wire fence. It needs a bit of thought, but I'd say we'll be able to put the wind up him a bit. Come on, let's go and take a look at the evidence.'

A telephone call to Quinn's farm established that Ferdy had gone to market and wouldn't be back until late, so, thinking it best to get the animal home, Jakes and Deepbriar escorted old Bob to the aerodrome to identify the pig formally. They were joined a little later by young Alan, pushing a hand cart.

Since getting permission to enter the airfield by the gate, and then waiting for the key holder to be contacted and persuaded to come and let them in would have taken too long, they decided to manhandle the sow out through the gap in the fence. Having presumably grown fond of her temporary home, the pig proved reluctant to be moved, and the constable's uniform was in a sorry state by the time she was off Ministry property and secured in the handcart.

Jakes had stood at a safe distance yelling advice, careful to keep his shiny shoes out of the muck, but then Matilda, squealing indignantly as young Alan held desperately to one hind leg, managed to flick out the other in a hefty kick. A large gobbet of mud was flung off her trotter to hit the detective sergeant squarely between the eyes and drip messily on to his coat, which gave Deepbriar a feeling of intense satisfaction.

It was nearly five o'clock when Deepbriar returned home. 'Thorny, at last!' Mary greeted him at the door, glancing anxiously back towards the living room as she spoke. 'Somebody's here to talk to you.'

'I can't see anyone now,' he protested, taking off his boots and brushing ineffectually at the smears of pig muck on his trouser legs. 'Lord knows how I'll get this blooming stuff off. Careful love, don't come to close or you'll end up smelling like a farmyard too.'

'Give me that tunic and go up and change. Bring the rest of your things down and put them in the scullery so I can deal with them. Do hurry, she's been waiting for hours.' She bustled away without further explanation, taking his tunic with her, and Deepbriar went obediently upstairs, grumbling under his breath. If it was that wretched Emerson woman ...

Ten minutes later the constable appeared at the living room door, accompanied by a strong waft of carbolic, which failed to completely suppress the smell of pig; the odour was amazingly persistent. A woman was sitting in his favourite armchair, her bleached hair arranged in a fancy knot at the back of her head, her heavy make-up failing to disguise her years; at least fifty five of them, Deepbriar guessed.

'This is Mrs Spraggs,' Mary Deepbriar announced, bringing him a cup of tea. 'She's been waiting for you since two o'clock.'

'Mrs Joseph Spraggs,' the woman elaborated, and Deepbriar recognised the voice he'd heard in Falbrough police station, arguing with Sergeant Hubbard some three weeks before. 'I was told you might be able to help me. I must have spoken to a dozen different policemen about my Joseph, but nobody will listen.'

'It's not really my ...' Deepbriar began, but she plunged on.

'They say it's not their business if a man decides to leave home without telling his wife. I know what they think, they think he's run off, chasing after some other woman. But Joseph wouldn't do that. As if I don't know my own husband!'

As sudden and unexpected as a summer storm, her emotions overcame her and she began to cry, words spilling out between her sobs. 'I told them, even if he didn't care that much about me, he wouldn't leave his precious car ... He hadn't had it long and he never would have left it....'

Deepbriar looked an appeal at his wife and she moved in, her ample bosom heaving in sympathy. 'You poor dear. Now, don't you worry. My husband will sort things out, won't you, Thorny?'

'I'll do what I can,' he said gruffly.

Mrs Spraggs looked up at him, her eyes ringed by smears of make-up. 'I was so relieved when young Joe told me you'd been asking about Joseph. I went to the city police first, but Joseph has made a lot of enemies in Belston. When I told them he'd gone to Falbrough the day he disappeared they sent me there, but it was no better. Those wretches just wouldn't listen.' She dried her tears, spreading her eye make-up even further until she looked grotesquely like a panda. 'They weren't prepared to lift a finger to help look for him. Just because he's been in trouble a couple of times.'

'Joe mentioned that,' Deepbriar said, sounding more sympathetic than he felt. He needed the woman's co-operation, and he wouldn't get it by taking the high moral ground. 'I'm sure it wasn't his fault. He got into bad company, I dare say.'

'Yes, that's it,' she said fiercely. 'It was that Rudge. Everyone knows he's a villain, but he never gets caught. It's always somebody like my Joseph who gets dragged off to court.'

Sylvester Rudge was well known in Belston, an apparently respectable business man with a finger in every kind of criminal pie. His name had been connected with everything from receiving stolen goods to organised brothels and counterfeit money, but, as Mrs Spraggs said, whenever the police investigated these matters there was never any proof of his involvement. Deepbriar tried to think where he had heard Rudge's name mentioned recently, but although the memory was not far from the surface of his mind, he couldn't recall the details. He let it go for the present, reaching for his notebook and pencil.

'But Joseph's not in trouble with the law this time, is he Mrs Spraggs? The police aren't looking for him. So why would he decide to do a vanishing act?'

'He didn't!' She was indignant. 'Oh, he's gone right enough, but it wasn't of his own accord! He got on the wrong side of that conniving bastard, that's what it was.' Catching sight of Mary Deepbriar's disapproval at her language Mrs Spraggs muttered an apology. 'That's what Sylvester flippin' Rudge is, though,' she muttered, 'and I don't care who hears me say so.'

'You're making a very serious accusation,' Deepbriar said. 'If you're blaming Rudge for your husband's disappearance.'

'It was him or some of his muscle men,' Mrs Spraggs replied. She slumped, collapsing back into the armchair. 'I think they killed him,' she said, her voice suddenly quiet. 'That's what I think.'

Having escorted Mrs Spraggs to the bus stop and seen her safely on to the last bus to Belston, Deepbriar returned home for his belated tea. It had been a long day.

'That poor woman,' Mary said, coming out of the scullery with her hands full of his uniform. It seemed she had worked her magic, for it smelt of nothing worse than damp wool. 'You will help her, won't you?'

'Like I said, I'll do what I can,' he replied. 'With what she told me and the statement I took from young Joe Spraggs, I think I should be able to get Inspector Stubbs interested, but I'm willing to bet there'll be trouble from the Sarge. He won't like me going over his head.'

Mary hardly seemed to be listening. 'Imagine,' she murmured, 'knowing your husband's been murdered!'

'She doesn't know anything of the kind,' Deepbriar replied. 'And mind you don't go talking about any of this, or I'll be in even more hot water!'

'As if I would. So what will happen now?'

'It'll be a CID job. And if they track the man down and he's just keeping out of sight for reasons of his own then there'll be hell to pay. For Mrs Spraggs too. She'll be facing a charge of wasting police time.'

'But you don't think that's going to happen, do you?'

'No,' Deepbriar said sombrely, 'I don't. Not after that business with young Joe. I'm not sure how, call it instinct if you like, but I've got a nasty feeling this is all somehow tied up with what happened to Bronc.'

Mary Deepbriar shook out her husband's uniform and draped it over a chair. 'Well, there's nothing more you can do tonight. You must be hungry.' She wrinkled her nose. 'But before you sit down you'd better try and get rid of that smell. I'm fairly sure I've got it out of your clothes; I think it must be in your hair.'

By opening time the whole village knew the story of Bert Bunyard's capture, and the return of the missing pig. The Speckled Goose was buzzing when Thorny Deepbriar poked his head round the back door.

'Thorny!' Don Bartle greeted him with a grin. 'The hero of the hour! Are you coming in for a pint? Don't reckon you'd be paying for your own tonight. In fact the first one's on the house.'

'Thanks, Don, but not now,' the constable replied. 'I just wanted a word with Harry. Can you tell him I'm here without letting on to the rest of them? Only I promised Mary I wouldn't be long. Hardly seem to have seen her the last couple of weeks.'

'He's just putting a new barrel on tap, he'll not be long. Make yourself at home in the kitchen and I'll send him in.'

From somewhere below their feet a voice was bellowing tunelessly; by concentrating hard Deepbriar could just make out the words. Harry evidently thought he was singing *Blue Moon*, but as usual it sounded more like a cow in labour. With a pained expression Don shrugged, 'sorry, but we haven't the heart to stop him, and it's only when he's in the cellar.'

'Perhaps you could have his voice trained,' Deepbriar suggested.

'What as?' The publican shook his head in mock sorrow as he went back to his work. 'There's no call for air raid sirens any more.'

Harry Bartle arrived a couple of minutes later, rolling down his sleeves. 'Hello, Mr Deepbriar. Dad said you didn't want to come into the bar.'

'No, I just need a quick word, Harry. I'm trying to remember something and I thought you might be able to help me. Was it you who mentioned the name of Sylvester Rudge?'

'To do with what?' Harry asked. 'I don't recall him coming up in conversation recently.' He scratched his head, thinking. 'There was some talk of him whipping up a bit of that bad feeling on the picket line. Not that he was there himself of course, but one or two of his sidekicks were supposed to have been involved.'

'No, that wasn't it. Nothing else? That stranger who was seen talking to Bronc, I don't suppose that could have been Rudge?'

'I thought everyone who saw that man agreed he was about average height.'

Deepbriar nodded. 'That's true. So unless Rudge has taken to wearing high heeled boots it wasn't him. But I have definitely heard his name somewhere. Oh well, never mind, it'll come to me.' He sighed. 'Only one more call to make before I take the weight off my feet.'

Emily Spraggs opened the door, smiling when she saw who her visitor was. 'I've just made a fresh pot of tea,' she said, stepping back to welcome the constable inside. 'Would you like a cup?'

'Better not,' Deepbriar said, 'I promised Mrs Deepbriar I'd only be out a few minutes. I just wanted to speak to Joe.'

When asked about Sylvester Rudge, Joe shook his head decisively. 'No, it wasn't me who mentioned him Mr Deepbriar. He's a really bad lot, isn't he?'

'Yes, probably, but the police have never been able to gather a single shred of evidence to connect him to any crime, so don't you go telling anyone I said so.'

Joe nodded. 'Peter's cousin works for the insurance company that had to pay out over that robbery at the jewellery shop in Falbrough. He told Peter the police reckoned Rudge was behind that. It seemed like everybody knew but nobody could do anything about it.'

'That's it!' Deepbriar clapped his hands together in triumph and stared at the bemused Spraggs. 'It was your friend Peter, in the Speckled Goose. That's where I heard the name.' He shook his head. 'Doesn't do me any good, though, he was just joking, saying maybe your boss had somehow upset him, and Rudge had you kidnapped as a warning to him to keep his nose clean in the future.'

'Mr Wriggle would never have anything to do with Rudge,' Joe said decisively, 'he'd be too scared!'

'Wise man,' Deepbriar said. 'You don't know of any connection between the other Joseph Spraggs and Sylvester Rudge I suppose?'

'No. You don't really think Rudge was involved in what happened to me, do you?'

'It's not likely.' Deepbriar hesitated, then decided to go on. 'Mrs Spraggs seems to think he might be responsible for her husband going missing, though I doubt if he'd have made the mistake of having the wrong Joe Spraggs kidnapped! None of it makes much sense, and that's a fact.'

'Maybe it's one of those mysteries that we'll never get to the bottom of,' Emily put in. 'Like the *Marie Celeste*.'

'Maybe,' Deepbriar agreed, 'but in the meantime keep your door locked, just in case.'

Chapter Fourteen

'It ain't exactly a capital offence,' Bert Bunyard protested, 'stealin' a bleedin' pig!'

'No,' Sergeant Jakes agreed, 'but that's not why you're here. You were found on Air Ministry property, Mr Bunyard. You've been making free with a lot more than Ferdy Quinn's pig, and the government aren't likely to be happy about that.'

'Air Ministry property? That ol' place is all closed down. Went off an' left it they did, so what's it to them if I go up an' take a look around?'

'You did more than take a look around,' Jakes said sternly.

'Dunno what you're talkin' about,' the old farmer said dismissively. 'Lot o' bliddy fules you coppers, ain't got more nor 'alf a brain between the lot of you. If I did 'elp meself to a pig it ain't no more than I'm due, you got no call to go arrestin' me. Anyways, I'd 'a' thought you'd got somethin' better to do than pesterin' a 'ard workin' man. But then you was runnin' all over the village like 'eadless chickens lookin' for that tramp, when you 'adn't got a clue where 'e'd bin, nor yet where 'e's gorn. I was laughin' so much I got a stitch in me side.'

'Like you laughed about that little trick with the plaster cast,' Jakes nodded. 'Which reminds me, you stole that from the village hall, so we can add breaking and entering to the list on the charge sheet.'

'There wasn't no breakin' an' enterin', that Emerson woman left the doors wide open, good as a proper invite it was. There ain't no 'arm in a bit of a joke, an' that's all I done. You can't keep me 'ere like this for 'avin' a laugh. I got my rights.'

'Your rights!' Jakes hissed, leaning over the desk to bring his face close to Bunyard's. 'You'll be lucky if you don't finish up on the end of a rope, Mr Bunyard, so don't you go talking about your rights to me!'

'You what?' For the first time Bert's assurance cracked. He swivelled nervously to look at Deepbriar, who stood back against the wall as if at attention. The constable kept his face expressionless, refusing to meet Bunyard's eyes.

Jakes opened a fat folder that lay before him, careful not to let the man at the opposite side of the desk see what was inside. 'You made pretty free with government property, didn't you? Those half dozen tins of corned beef were only the tip of the iceberg.'

'I found 'em under the floorboards,' Bert protested. 'Must've bin hidden there since the War an' forgotten. Wasn't like anyone wanted 'em.'

'We've only got your word for that. But I'm more concerned about other things going missing. Maybe it's time we talked about high explosives.'

'High explosives?' This time Bert was really shaken, his jaw sagging as he gawped at the detective.

Jakes leant back in his chair. 'Come on, Bunyard, don't play the innocent with me. We've been keeping an eye on that aerodrome for quite a time. I know you weren't the only one involved, so if you want to give us the names of your associates, then maybe I'll put a good word in for you at the trial. You'd best come clean. Treason's still a hanging offence, you know.'

The air came out of Bert's lungs in a kind of strangled gasp. 'Wha ... treas ...' He was thoroughly jittery now, flinging another imploring look at the impassive Deepbriar. Seeing nothing there to reassure him he rose to his feet, taking refuge in the kind of bullying bluster that had always served him in the past. 'You're not pinnin' anythin' on me. I don't deny I made meself comfortable in that ol' hut, but I ain't done nothin' else—'

He was interrupted by a knock at the door. Jakes made an impatient noise. 'Come in,' he shouted.

Sergeant Hubbard entered and bent to whisper in Jakes's ear.

'Oh, all right,' Jakes said, getting up from his chair. 'Sit down,' he ordered, pointing a peremptory finger at Bunyard, who immediately subsided. With some ostentation Jakes closed the folder and tucked it under his arm in such a way that the impressive crest on the front was plainly visible. 'Keep an eye on him, constable,' he ordered, as he left.

There was a long silence. Deepbriar kept his gaze fixed on the closed door behind Bunyard, as if willing Jakes to return.

'Hey, Deepbriar,' the prisoner said at last. 'What the 'ell's goin' on?'

The constable said nothing, refusing even to meet the man's eyes.

'Come on, Thorny,' Bunyard said, his voice taking on a wheedling tone. 'Don't you go gettin' all official with me. I remember when you was no more'n a bit of a lad fishin' for tiddlers in the duck pond. What's this all about?'

'I'm under orders,' Deepbriar said woodenly. 'I'm not supposed to talk to you.'

'Blimey ...' the man fidgeted in his chair. 'You're 'avin' me on, you an that sergeant. It's a joke, right?'

'I wish it was,' Deepbriar said quietly, his expression sombre. He was enjoying himself; maybe he ought to join Mary in her amateur dramatics. 'I can't help feeling sorry for that boy of yours, left to cope on his own, poor lad.'

'Christ!' Bunyard was seriously worried by now. 'I don't get it. I ain't been up to nothin' bad. Least ways, nothin' like ... 'ell's teeth, Thorny, I don't even know what I'm supposed to 'ave done!'

'You aren't doing yourself any favours refusing to talk to Sergeant Jakes,' Deepbriar said, pitching his voice low as if afraid somebody in the corridor outside might hear. 'He's sure you've got something to hide, so he reckons you're tied in with this gang that Scotland Yard are after.'

'Scotland Yard?' Bunyard rubbed a hand over his chin, the bristles making a brittle rasping noise.

'Shh!' Deepbriar lowered his voice still further, glancing at the door. 'You'd have done better making a confession straight off. I mean, as far as I was concerned it was just a bit of criminal damage, not all that serious, even if you take account of setting a fire and stealing a pig.'

'But that's it!' Bert protested. 'There ain't no more. I don't know nothin' about no gang. What would I do with explosives, eh? I was just gettin' my own back on Ferdy Quinn!'

'I'm sorry, Bert,' Deepbriar looked at his victim sorrowfully, 'I wish I could help you, but it's out of my hands. The word is, the men from London will be here in a couple of hours. That's why Jakes is in such a hurry.'

'London?' Bunyard's voice rose to a squeak. 'What's flippin'
London got to do with it?'

'I told you, Scotland Yard. State security. The Air Ministry
have turned the matter over to them. Be better for us local bobbies
if the case was all wrapped up before they get here, but I don't see
much hope of that.'

'What if I was to tell that detective all I done?' Bert was almost
begging now. 'Maybe 'e ain't so stupid as 'e looks, eh? I thought
'e was still wet be'ind the ears, that's why I didn't want to tell 'im
nothin'. Go on, Thorny, be a mate an' call 'im back.'

'Thank you, constable,' Jakes said, taking the two pages of Bert
Bunyard's confession from Deepbriar's hand. 'There's more than
enough here to get us a conviction, and in the meantime a few
days behind bars won't do our Mr Bunyard any harm. It might
teach him to have a little respect for the law.'

'Thank *you*, sergeant,' Deepbriar replied. 'That's the first time
I've ever got the better of Bert Bunyard, and it'll probably be the
last, but I shall cherish the memory for the rest of my days. What's
in there?' he asked, looking down at the folder that now lay in
front of the detective. 'It looks pretty important.'

'Information leaflets issued by the powers that be,' Jakes told
him, 'relating to such vital items as uniform regulations and the
proper way to carry and wield your truncheon. I'm surprised you
didn't recognise it, it's been in the staff room for as long as I can
remember, for the general edification of all ranks.' He opened it
and drew out a sheet of paper at random. 'This one's fairly new,
it's a proposal for a decrease in the regulation height of police officers, which the county is taking under consideration. A whole
inch and a half. It won't matter if you start to shrink in your old
age, constable.'

'Very useful,' Deepbriar said. 'One more thing, though, can we
let Bunyard sweat about Scotland Yard? Just for an hour or two?'

'Do you know,' Jakes said, sitting at his desk and leaning back
with his hands behind his head. 'I think Mr Bunyard's got an
overactive imagination, not to mention a guilty conscience. You'd
have thought he'd realise we were just playing a little joke on
him.' He grinned. 'It was quite a good one too, almost as good as
his trick with the plaster cast. He kept that up for weeks, didn't
he, but I suppose we'll have to own up.'

'You want me to go and set him straight?' Deepbriar asked.

'Well, yes, but since he's had such a bad morning, maybe we should leave him in peace for a while.' He glanced up at the clock. 'Let's be civilised and offer him some lunch at twelve thirty, shall we?'

'I'll take it to him myself,' Deepbriar promised.

Jakes sighed. 'I wish our other case could be as easily dealt with. We're no nearer finding old Bronc than we were the first day we started looking.'

'It's strange the way Bert mentioned that. He can't resist any chance to rub our noses in our mistakes, but I couldn't help thinking he knows something.'

'It's possible,' Jakes agreed. 'Perhaps you'd better ask him. Before you let him in on our little joke.'

'I'll do that.' Deepbriar reached into his pocket and pulled out some papers. 'I'm afraid I've got another matter I need to talk to you about. I was going to see Inspector Stubbs, but I gather he's not likely to get back today.'

'No, nor tomorrow. It seems these burglaries have been linked to a gang working up north.' Jakes sighed again. 'So, if you want to talk to CID, then I'm your man.'

'It's about Joseph Spraggs.'

'Oh, not that again. Somebody looked into it, and there's nothing suspicious about the man's disappearance. He left his wife.'

'I don't think so. If you'd just take a look at these statements I think you'll agree that there's cause for concern. There's one from Mrs Spraggs, and another from her husband's friend, a man called Halliwell. I spoke to him before I came here this morning. He met Spraggs at the Queen's Head in Falbrough on Wednesday the 5th, which is the day before his wife last saw him. Spraggs was boasting about his new car, and mapping out the route he and Mrs Spraggs were planning to take that weekend when they drove up north to see one of her relations.

'Halliwell has known Spraggs pretty much all his life. He's convinced that the man had no intention of deserting his wife, and even if he had, he agrees with her that Spraggs wouldn't have left his car behind.' He leafed through the papers and extracted another. 'I thought I'd better check as much as I could of his story before I brought this report in. The barman at the Queen's Head has confirmed that the two men were there, and he says he heard enough of their conversation to confirm what Halliwell told me.'

Deepbriar put the documents down on the desk. 'Add this to the abduction of Joe Spraggs, of Honeysuckle Cottage, Minecliff, just a few days before Joseph Spraggs went missing, and at the very least I think we are looking at a case of kidnapping. Joe was dumped back at the yard where he works the next day. His statement is there too. I've added my own notes on the evidence that a car, almost certainly the same one that knocked Bronc into the ditch on the evening of the 1st, was driven in and out of Wriggle's yard shortly before Joe Spraggs was returned there. It was because I wanted to question Bronc further about this matter that I was trying to locate him. Something which, as you know, I was unable to do, until we found some of his clothes and an awful lot of blood.'

Jakes was silent for almost ten minutes as he read through the documents, his face growing increasingly sombre. At last he looked up at Deepbriar and sighed. 'That's a rare mess you've landed us all in, constable. It's too hot for me to handle without authority, with Inspector Stubbs away I'll have to talk to Inspector Martindale. We haven't managed to locate one corpse and if you're right we're probably looking for two. How on earth are we going to explain that it's taken us three weeks to investigate what could very well be murder?'

'You believe Mrs Spraggs then? You think her husband was kidnapped?'

'Put it this way. I don't think he walked out on her.' He tapped a finger on the woman's statement. 'People do sometimes go missing with only the clothes they stand up in, but you're right, there's something very wrong here.'

'All right, Bert?' Deepbriar asked, going sideways into the cell with a tray in his hands. 'You're lucky today, boiled beef and carrots, it's one of the things the canteen does best, and for pudding I fancied you're more of a plum duff man than fruit and custard. I put three spoons of sugar in the tea, hope that's right.'

'When do I get out of 'ere?' Bunyard said, looking nervously past the constable into the empty corridor. 'Are them cops from London still on their way? I thought they'd be 'ere by now.'

'They must have got held up. Don't worry, Sergeant Jakes will do his best to convince them you're not part of the gang they're after. Here, tuck in.' Deepbriar handed him the tray and leant back against the wall as the man began his meal.

'Reckon you had a good laugh, watching us chasing our tails when we were looking for Bronc,' the constable said after a while.

'An' what if I did?' Bert spoke round a mouthful of beef.

'Oh, nothing. We don't hold grudges. Only bear in mind that you'll be up in front of the magistrate tomorrow. You'll probably be let out on bail, so long as you go on co-operating. Talking of which, Bert, there's a couple of questions we didn't ask.'

'I already told you what I done,' Bunyard said, forking meat into his mouth and chewing vigorously. 'If this is your idea of a good dinner then I dunno what the bad ones are like.'

'Looks all right to me,' Deepbriar replied. 'Come on, Bert, you can help us.' Even as he said the words he knew he'd made a mistake; Bunyard had never helped anyone but himself in his entire life. He hurried on, hoping the man wouldn't have noticed the appeal to his non-existent better nature. 'Nearly a month ago, a few days before you stole Quinn's pig, somebody saw you going up the lane off the Gadwell road.'

'So what?' Bunyard's belligerent manner was returning, along with his confidence.

'Well, if you want us to forget we ever found you up at the aerodrome, then you'd best tell me what happened that day. We need to know if you met up with Bronc. And we've got an idea there was a car parked up the lane, a red sports car. You might have seen who left it there.'

'Mebbe I did, an' mebbe I didn't,' Bunyard replied, shovelling up the last mouthful of beef from the tin plate. 'I will tell you somethin' though, seein' you're askin'. It's a wonder you coppers can find your 'eads to put your 'ats on, an' that's a fact. There's more folk than me know about that 'ole in the fence, an' there's others what don't need to use it. Any more than that I ain't sayin'.'

'You don't want Sergeant Jakes changing his mind,' Deepbriar warned. 'Be sensible, Bert, you know something about Bronc. Why do you want to keep it to yourself? What good's it doing you?'

Bunyard pulled the pudding to him and spooned up a mouthful of plum duff. 'This ain't bad,' he said, spraying custard. He ate in silence for a while, then looked up at Deepbriar, his small eyes suddenly mean. 'You fooled me. You an' that young fancy pants detective. There wasn't no missin' bombs, an' there ain't no Scotland Yard men comin' from London. It was all a trick.'

Deepbriar shook his head. 'It's a serious business trespassing on government land.'

'That's as maybe, but I say there weren't no stolen bombs.' He glared at the constable. 'An' that bein' the case, you ain't gettin' no more outa me.'

'We can still make things hot for you, Bert, by the time we add up all the charges I reckon you might get six months, or even a year. You don't want to leave that boy of yours on his own all through the winter, do you now?'

'What I want or don't want is my business.' He dropped the spoon into the empty bowl with a clatter, then drained the mug at one go. 'How about another cup?'

Deepbriar retreated, bitterly disappointed. Outside the cell he stopped and took out his notebook, writing down what Bert had said, as close as he could recall. More people than him knew the way into the aerodrome. And there were some who didn't need to use the gap in the fence. But what did that mean?

'We'll take another look at the aerodrome,' Jakes said, once Deepbriar had reported Bunyard's words. 'But we can't keep creeping in like we did to fetch Bunyard and the pig, we'll have to go through the proper channels this time. That means approaching the Air Ministry, and heaven alone knows how long it will take.'

'It sounds as if somebody with a key uses it now and then,' Deepbriar said, looking at the notes he'd made when he spoke to Bert. 'Unless there's some other entrance we haven't found.'

'Only other way in I can think of is by air,' Jakes said. 'Most of those old runways are still fit to use in an emergency, but surely somebody in the village would notice if there were planes coming and going.'

'You don't think all that rubbish we invented about a gang using the airbase could turn out to be true?' Deepbriar asked.

Jakes groaned. 'I hope not, we're in enough trouble already. I'll try to get Inspector Stubbs on the telephone, and see if he'll help us get hold of the key.'

'There's one more thing we could try,' Deepbriar mused.

'What's that?'

'Get some lad with a sharp suit and a posh accent to act as a Scotland Yard man and put the fear of God into Bert Bunyard.'

Jakes shook his head, grinning. 'Tempting I admit, but it

wouldn't work, not now he's got wise to us. We'll just have to manage without his information. That's if he's got any, I wouldn't be surprised if he's having us on.'

'That's possible,' Deepbriar agreed gloomily, 'Bert's a great one for getting his own back. He's still paying off Ferdy Quinn for something that happened twenty years and more ago; nobody else can even remember what it was.'

'What we need is a new plan of attack,' Jakes said. 'If you're right then Bronc was killed because of what he saw when Joe Spraggs was abducted, and Joe was abducted by mistake, instead of his second cousin once removed or whatever this other man is. Since we've drawn a blank with Bronc maybe we'd better start talking to Joseph's friends, and see if we can turn anything up that way.'

'I know where I'd start,' Deepbriar offered. 'Sylvester Rudge.'

Jakes looked back at him doubtfully. 'Mr Rudge is a slippery character. We have to be careful or he'll be writing nasty letters to the chief constable. It's no job for a lowly detective sergeant, anyway. No, I'll start by having a word with Mrs Spraggs and this man Halliwell, and see where that gets us.'

'This isn't really anything to do with me,' Deepbriar reminded him. 'I was only supposed to be helping you look for Bronc because he vanished on my patch. Shouldn't I get back to my own beat?'

Jakes looked a little flustered. 'Sorry, that was something I meant to talk to you about. With Constable Tidyman helping Inspector Stubbs I'm all on my own here. While you were taking Bunyard his lunch I had a word with the inspector and he agreed to open a file on Spraggs. When I pointed out there was nobody to give me a hand he spoke to Martindale. You've been officially seconded to the CID for the duration of this case.'

Deepbriar stared at him, saying nothing. It had always been his secret dream, to be involved in the detection of a serious crime, but his requests for transfer to the plain clothes branch had always been turned down. After eighteen years in the service he had given up hope.

'Well?' Jakes looked up at him. 'I hope you don't mind working with me, constable?'

'No sir,' Deepbriar said quickly. 'As long as you and the inspector have squared it with Sergeant Hubbard.'

'Don't worry about that, even Hubbard doesn't argue when

Stubbs and Martindale form an alliance. Like it or not, we've got a missing person's case, and he'll just have to grin and bear it. Which reminds me, the superintendent asked if you've made any progress in locating Tony Pattridge. He must have had lunch with his old friend Childs last night.'

'I haven't given it a thought,' Deepbriar admitted, 'but as it happens there is somebody who might be able to help.'

'Finding Bronc has priority,' Jakes said, 'until I've had a chance to work through this properly.' He tapped the statements Deepbriar had given him. 'Finding that young lad who saw the car was a good start, it's about the only lead we've got. Isn't there anyone else who might have been close by on that Monday?'

'Not close by,' Deepbriar said thoughtfully, 'but thinking about young Kenny Pratt has given me an idea.'

A knock on the door interrupted him, and a young uniformed constable came in. 'Urgent message for you, sergeant,' he said, handing over a piece of paper.

Jakes read quickly, his mouth compressing into a narrow line.

'Well?' Deepbriar prompted.

'It looks like we've got a murder weapon,' he said. 'There were traces of blood on that pruning knife, identical to what was found on the ground behind the bothy and on Bronc's clothes.'

Chapter Fifteen

A lone cyclist coasted down the hill from Falbrough. Thanks to the heavy rain the road was otherwise deserted, and there was nobody to see Thorny Deepbriar heading homeward, his feet precariously balanced on the handlebars and his mouth open in joyous song. His rumbling bass, improbably attempting the flower duet from *Madame Butterfly*, echoed off the bare trees.

Approaching the crossroads he recovered his decorum, but he was still in a cheerful mood, as, soaked to the skin, he made a sudden detour and pedalled up the slope to a solitary farmhouse occupying an elevated site just outside the village.

'Constable Deepbriar!' Mrs Rose welcomed him with a smile. 'Oh my goodness, you're drenched! Take that coat off and hang it by the fire, while I put the kettle on.'

'I don't want to drip all over your floor,' the constable protested, hovering on the doorstep. 'But I did hope to have a quick word with young Oliver.'

'Then you'll have to come in, because he's up in his room. He hardly ever sits in the parlour, even when he's got a visitor, but I don't like to force him if he's comfortable where he is. I'll make some tea and bring it up. It's a good job I don't mind the stairs, I've only just come down.' Her smile broadened. 'He told me a minute ago he'd seen you coming.'

Deepbriar was suddenly very busy wiping his boots vigorously on the doormat, removing his bicycle clips and shaking the rain off his coat, hiding his blushes as he recalled his unorthodox ride down the hill.

'You know the way,' Mrs Rose said, once he was inside. 'There's a fire in Oliver's room, he does love sitting up there with that little spyglass of his.'

'It's lucky the lad's so good at keeping himself occupied,' Deepbriar said. 'How's he getting on?'

'The doctor was quite pleased with him last week, though there are times when the poor boy finds some of the exercises hard.' The smile faltered a little. 'He's off to hospital to get callipers fitted next month. They say he might be walking in a year, but we'll have to wait and see. It seems it's hard to tell with polio, some of them do better than others.' She turned away, busying herself with the kettle. 'Go on up,' she ordered, her habitually cheerful voice a little muffled. 'Tea won't be long.'

At the top of the stairs a door stood open and the warm glow of firelight illuminated the landing.

'Hello, Mr Deepbriar.' Oliver Rose sat in an armchair by the window, his wasted legs covered by a colourful knitted blanket, his pale pinched face beaming as brightly as his mother's. 'I'm going to ride a bike like that one day. I bet it's fun.' The boy laughed as Deepbriar pulled a comically rueful face. 'It's all right, I don't think anyone else saw you.'

'Then make sure you don't go telling tales,' Deepbriar said, 'I'd be in trouble wouldn't I, playing tricks like that when I'm on duty.'

'Are you on duty now?' Oliver asked, his eyes sparkling. 'Really?'

Deepbriar nodded. 'I'm looking for a witness,' he said, 'for an important case I'm working on. With the CID,' he added portentously. 'That makes me a detective, just for the time being. And there's a chance that a certain young man might be able to help me with my enquiries.'

'Me?' the boy's voice rose to an excited squeak. 'Honest?'

'Do you still keep a list of all the cars you see? I know how good you are at spotting number plates through that spyglass of yours.'

By way of answer the youngster picked up an exercise book from the table by his side, opening it to show pages of writing, surprisingly neat for a boy of eight. 'I put the date down when I get up in the morning,' he said, 'so I don't make any mistakes. Mummy doesn't always know what day it is,' he added conspiratorially.

Deepbriar took out his notebook and consulted it. 'Let's start with Monday 3rd,' he said. For the next few minutes the two heads, one blond, the other with dark hair showing the first signs of grey, were bent together over the boy's notebook. The Austin Healey that Kenny Pratt claimed to have noticed did indeed appear, on the Monday when Bronc was last seen, but Oliver hadn't been able to get the number.

Mrs Rose came in then, carrying a loaded tray. 'You look busy,' she said.

'I'm helping the police with their enquiries,' Oliver said importantly.

'Are you indeed.' She sat down and poured the tea. 'And what about me, can I help too?'

'You might,' Deepbriar replied, 'if you remember seeing a tramp called Bronc around the village, nearly four weeks ago?'

She shook her head. 'No, I heard you were looking for him.' She handed Deepbriar a cup of tea. 'He's been around a long time, hasn't he? I remember he used to sit on that seat by the school gate sometimes when I was a child, he must have been tramping the roads for thirty years.'

'At least that long,' Deepbriar agreed. 'How about it, Oliver, have you seen him?'

'I know the man you mean,' Oliver said. 'He wears lots of coats and a very old hat. Before I was ill, when we used to go blackberrying, he came and helped us sometimes.'

'So he did!' Mrs Rose exclaimed. 'I'd forgotten. He's a funny old chap, but harmless.'

'Would you have written it in your book if you saw him, Oliver?'

Oliver tilted his head on one side, considering the question. 'I might,' he said, 'I put down all sorts of things.'

'See what you wrote about on the first and second of November. As well as Bronc, I'd be interested in anything that happened over at Wriggle's yard.' He stared out at the rain-drenched countryside. 'You can't see the entrance from here. That's a shame.'

The boy studied his book, but once he'd turned back to the right page he suddenly seemed to lose interest. His head was bent as if he was reading, but when he looked up the animated look he'd worn since Deepbriar's arrival had gone from his face. 'I didn't write much on those days,' he said, his voice suddenly toneless and his pale face ashen. He let the book fall shut on his lap and was silent.

'I was hoping you might have seen a black car,' Deepbriar said.

'A big one. We don't think it belongs to anyone in Minecliff or Possington. Bronc told me about it, because it nearly knocked him into the ditch, but I can't find anyone else who saw it.'

Oliver shook his head. He refused the tea his mother offered him, turning his face away. 'I've got a headache. Mummy. Can I go back to bed?'

Deepbriar drained his cup and stood up. 'I shouldn't have stayed so long.' He bent down to the boy, offering his hand. 'Thanks, Oliver, you were very helpful.'

The youngster shook hands without meeting the constable's eyes.

Deepbriar went downstairs with Mrs Rose at his heels. 'I'm sorry, I over-tired him.'

'Oh no, don't worry.' The woman handed Deepbriar his coat. 'He has these funny turns sometimes.' A little frown appeared on her brows. 'I mentioned it to the doctor and he told me to keep a record of them, to see how often they happen. The last one ...' she turned to a calendar that hung on the kitchen wall. 'That's it, just over two weeks, the day of Mr Pattridge's funeral. Jim and I went, and the nurse stayed a bit longer than usual to keep an eye on Oliver for us, she's almost like one of the family, he's very fond of her, but when we came home he'd gone all quiet and washed out, like he did just now. The one before that ... Well, that is strange. It was the weekend you were asking him about, at the beginning of November.'

'I'm sorry, sergeant, until I can start searching the aerodrome I'm at a dead end as far as Bronc's concerned,' Deepbriar said, unconscious of his apt but morbid pun.

'Never mind, can you join me in Belston this afternoon?' Jakes's voice at the other end of the line sounded harassed. 'I'll be calling on Mrs Spraggs at about 3 p.m., you'd better meet me at the corner of West Street.'

'If I've got to travel to Belston is it all right if I look into the whereabouts of Tony Pattridge first? I've been given the address of somebody who might know where he is.'

'What have you got?' Jakes asked.

'His childhood sweetheart. Evidently they met up again, they were seen together about a year ago,' Deepbriar told him. 'If I catch the bus that leaves Minecliff in twenty minutes I should still be able to join you by 3.'

'Go ahead,' Jakes said. 'I'll wait for you outside the Swan Hotel. Anything you can do to get on the right side of the superintendent has got to be worth a try, all hell's going to break loose if this Spraggs turns out to have been murdered. Sergeant Hubbard's problem with missing persons could get the whole force into trouble. Try not to be late.'

Deepbriar had no intention of being late, not for his first official interview as part of the county CID, though he almost missed the bus, having taken time making up his mind what to wear. In the end Mary advised against the blazer with the silver buttons, suggesting that his blue serge suit was more suitable.

He jumped off the bus in the centre of Belston with the city map open and ready in his hand, negotiating his way swiftly to the little terrace house where he'd been told Barbara Blake still lived with her aged grandparents.

A woman in a brightly flowered pinafore answered his knock at the door, and for a moment he thought he must have come to the wrong address; she didn't look old enough to be anybody's granny. 'Yes?' She looked puzzled when he didn't immediately state his business. 'If you're selling something ...'

'No,' Deepbriar said hurriedly; he'd completely forgotten that he wasn't in uniform. 'I'm Constable Deepbriar, County Police. Have I got the right house? I'm looking for a Miss Barbara Blake.'

'Whatever for?' She demanded sharply. 'I'm her grandmother,' she added, 'I'll thank you to explain yourself, young man.'

'We're making enquiries into the whereabouts of an old school friend of Miss Blake,' Deepbriar said, not sure whether to be amused, flattered or insulted at being addressed as a young man, especially as he'd assumed the woman was only a few years older than himself. 'I need to ask her a few questions, that's all.'

'Then you'd better go and see her at the library. That's where she works.' The door was unceremoniously shut in his face, and Deepbriar stood nonplussed for a few seconds. Was that the sort of reception he could expect as a plain clothes policeman? Recovering his composure along with his wits, he turned and headed back towards the city centre.

As he pushed open the door of the library and stepped into the slightly stale-smelling hush, the clock on the town hall was reading two twenty; not a great deal of time if he was to meet Jakes at three. Unwilling to risk being mistaken for a travelling salesman again, he showed the young assistant his identification.

'You'd better see Mr Falkener,' she whispered, ushering him into a tiny room which contained a desk, a single hard wooden chair for a visitor and two filing cabinets.

Mr Falkener looked far older than Miss Blake's granny, and nearly as forbidding, but once Deepbriar had explained his mission the librarian volunteered the use of his room, and invited the policemen to sit in his comfortable chair. He left, assuring the constable that Miss Blake would be with him shortly. Nearly ten minutes later she arrived, a thin girl with brown hair pulled back in a bun and a pair of dark rimmed spectacles slipping down her nose. Despite this attempt at severity she was exceptionally pretty.

'I'm sorry,' the young woman looked flustered, pushing her glasses back into place. 'The deputy librarian had sent me to buy some more tea.'

'Without telling the librarian?' Deepbriar suggested, his eyes twinkling.

She sighed. 'How did you guess? I'll be lucky if he doesn't make me work an extra half hour tonight. What did you want to see me about?' She looked alarmed. 'It's not gran or gramps, is it? There hasn't been an accident ...'

'No, nothing like that. It's about an old friend of yours, a Mr Tony Pattridge.'

'Tony?' She was suddenly still. 'You're here to tell me something happened to him. I knew there had to be a reason ...'

'Nothing's happened to him as far as we know,' Deepbriar broke in. 'On the contrary, there's a firm of solicitors with news which may be of some advantage to him.'

'His father.' She nodded in understanding. 'I saw it in the paper. But I'm afraid I can't help you, I haven't seen Tony for nearly a year.' Unshed tears were threatening to spill from her eyes, and she dropped her gaze to stare at the worn lino on the floor.

'That would be about the time Mrs Harris met you both in town,' Deepbriar hazarded.

'Yes.' Barbara Blake looked surprised. 'How did you know about that? I was allowed to leave two hours early because I'd had to work an extra evening, so we went shopping for Christmas presents. Then Tony bought us some fish and chips and we went to the pictures. We saw Sabrina Fair, you know, with Audrey Hepburn and Humphrey Bogart. It was lovely, we had such a nice time. Tony took me home, the same as he always did, but after that I never saw him again.' She broke off, blinking rapidly to prevent more tears from falling.

'I'm sorry,' she said a moment later. 'That's all I can tell you.'

'You don't know where Mr Pattridge lives?'

'I knew where he lived then,' she said. 'When he didn't meet me from work on the following Saturday, like he'd promised, I went round to his lodgings, in case he'd been taken ill.'

Deepbriar took out his notebook and jotted down the address she gave him. 'I gather he wasn't there.'

'No, but I didn't find out then. His landlady refused to let me in. She wouldn't even talk to me.' The young woman took a handkerchief from the pocket of her overall and blew her nose. 'I don't want you to think I'm the kind of girl who'd normally do that sort of thing, but I was worried about him. I stood at the bus stop on the other side of the road for quite a while, watching people going in. Mrs Newman had other lodgers, and it was time for their evening meal, I could smell cooking when I went to the door. In the end a young man came out, and I plucked up courage to go and ask if Tony was there. He said he hadn't seen him, not for a couple of days.'

'Which day did you go to the pictures?'

'That was on the Tuesday. I didn't know what to do. The next time I went to Minecliff I walked over to Oldgate Farm, thinking I might ask his father if Tony was home, but when I got there I lost my nerve.' She shrugged. 'In the end I decided that Tony simply didn't want to see me any more. A girl can't go chasing around after a man, can she?'

'I'm sure in your case there are plenty of young men prepared to do the chasing,' Deepbriar said, uncharacteristically gallant. 'Thank you Miss Blake, you've been very helpful.'

He was afraid he might be late for his appointment with Jakes, but Deepbriar hurried off in the opposite direction, seeking out number 5, Alma Villas. It was a large four storey house in the middle of a row. Outside, a privet hedge had been pruned to within an inch of its life. A glimmer of sun, peeping through the clouds that had shredded away since the rain stopped, reflected painfully off the polished brass door-knocker and beneath the knocker a sign forbade entry to gypsies and hawkers.

When he saw the woman who opened the door, Deepbriar was glad he had again taken the precaution of having his identification ready, he felt sure she would otherwise have directed him to the tradesman's entrance at the back.

'Well?' She glared at him, sharp nose, sharp chin and sharp eyes all pointing ferociously in his direction.

'I'd like a word with you, Mrs Newman. About one of your lodgers.'

'My guests, you mean,' she said, every word a reprimand. She gave the street behind him a disapproving glance. 'I suppose you'd better come in.'

The room she showed him into was as unwelcoming as its owner, with hard chairs pushed back against the walls and a tiny rug in the centre of the brown linoleum. A single shelf on one wall held a meagre selection of books, most of them apparently religious tracts. 'This is the guests' sitting-room,' Mrs Newman said complacently. 'I do like people to be comfortable when they stay with me. Now, what can I do for you?'

'I'm looking for a man by the name of Tony Pattridge. I understand he used to lodge here.'

'Yes.' She snapped her mouth shut on the word and volunteered no more.

'But he isn't here now?'

'No.'

Deepbriar was losing his patience. 'So when did he leave?'

'The Thursday before Christmas, last year.' Again Mrs Newman snapped her lips shut to prevent any more words escaping.

'Did he give notice?'

'No.'

It was like drawing teeth. 'So he packed up his belongings and left,' Deepbriar persisted.

'No. He didn't take anything with him.'

The constable stared at her, his pulse quickening. Surely they hadn't got another mysterious disappearance on their hands. 'Didn't you think that his sudden departure was strange?'

'His behaviour struck me as very inconsiderate at the time,' Mrs Newman said, 'but then his friends came. They packed up his possessions and paid me two weeks rent, in lieu of notice. As far as I was concerned that was the end of the matter.'

'His friends? Were they people you knew? Had they visited him while he lived here?'

'I don't encourage visitors.'

'So you didn't know them?'

She shook her head.

'What day did they come?' Deepbriar asked.

'On the Saturday.'

Deepbriar scribbled hastily in his notebook. 'And you've never seen them again?'

Mrs Newman shook her head again.

'Then perhaps you could describe them to me,' Deepbriar suggested.

'One of them was quite tall. He was the younger man, about thirty perhaps. The other one had grey hair.'

'There's nothing else you can tell me about them?'

'No.'

'And they took all Mr Pattridge's possessions with them.'

'Not all.' The answer came reluctantly, as if against her will.

'And these things they left behind,' Deepbriar said, 'did Mr Pattridge ever come to claim them?'

'He did not.'

'Then you still have them?'

'There is a small bag in the loft,' Mrs Newman admitted. 'The rest I disposed of. He owed me for his laundry. Then there was a broken tooth glass, and damage to the top of the dresser.'

Deepbriar stared down into the hard dark eyes, saying nothing. The Belston town hall would get up and dance the tango before this woman let a chance to make money slip past her. 'You'll have written receipts for the goods you sold, naturally,' he said, glad to see her composure disturbed a little by the suggestion, 'but we'll leave that for the moment. I'd like to see his room, and the bag he left behind.'

At exactly three minutes past three Deepbriar arrived breathlessly at Sergeant Jakes's side, a battered old carpet bag in his hand.

'Off somewhere for the weekend?' Jakes jested.

'Evidence. Once the property of Tony Pattridge,' Deepbriar puffed, following the detective up the road. 'He left his lodgings unexpectedly on the Thursday before Christmas last year, and as far as I can make out he hasn't been seen in Belston since.'

'Did he leave without paying his bill?'

'If you'd seen the landlady you wouldn't ask that question. Rent in advance, I'd stake my life on it.'

Mrs Joseph Spraggs was waiting for them, the door opening a second after Jakes knocked. The make-up was back in place, immaculate, if rather thickly applied; Deepbriar found himself hoping she would keep control of herself this time. At least she had the comfort of knowing her husband's disappearance was finally being investigated.

The constable sat in silence while Jakes questioned the woman, his pencil poised ready to take notes. Very little that was new emerged from the interview. Joseph Spraggs had left his home at eleven o'clock on Thursday 6th November and gone to Falbrough, for reasons unstated, and had simply failed to return. He had travelled by bus, telling his wife that he was expecting to 'have a few' with his lunch. Since he'd scraped the paintwork on his beloved car by misjudging the distance to a gatepost a couple of weeks before, he wouldn't risk causing more damage to his pride and joy by driving when under the influence.

'And you were home all that day? There's no chance he might have returned without your knowledge?'

'He could have done,' Mrs Spraggs admitted. 'I had my hair done. That was at four, and I got home about six.'

'But you saw nothing to suggest he'd been in the house?'

She shook her head. 'No. I'd have known if he'd made himself a cup of tea.'

'And none of his belongings had gone?'

Mrs Spraggs hesitated. 'There was a small bag missing. And one or two things from the wardrobe.'

The two policemen exchanged glances. 'Can you be more precise, please Mrs Spraggs? This bag ...'

'It was an old thing he used to take when he played cricket. He hadn't been for at least ten years though. It wasn't the sort of thing he'd use if he was going away.'

'And what else was gone?' Jakes asked.

'A suit. And two shirts. But none of them fitted him.'

Jakes stared at her. 'They didn't fit?'

'I'd been meaning to throw them away. He'd put on a bit of weight.' Mrs Spraggs reached suddenly for her handkerchief and dabbed at her eyes. 'Two pairs of socks and some underwear had gone too, but I'm certain he would never have packed them himself.'

'What makes you so sure?'

Deepbriar looked up from his note-taking, watching the woman's reaction, half expecting her to be angry, but instead she looked sad.

'Because the socks were green. He never wore green, he

thought it was unlucky. As for the spare underwear, when we went away it never occurred to him to pack that sort of thing, I always had to remind him.'

'Sergeant,' Deepbriar put in, seeing that Jakes had run out of questions. 'There's something that occurs to me.'

'Well?' Jakes prompted.

'Where was the bag kept? The one Mr Spraggs used for his cricket gear?'

'It was in the cupboard under the stairs,' Mrs Spraggs replied. 'We keep the suitcases in the loft. They take up so much room.'

'And you hadn't started packing for your driving holiday.'

'No.' Mrs Spraggs gave a shrug. 'I'm a bit of a last minute person when it comes to packing.'

The sergeant stood up. 'I wonder if we might take a look at your husband's car, Mrs Spraggs?'

'It's in the garage.' She rose and led the way through the kitchen and out of the house, pausing to take a bunch of keys from a hook inside the larder. The garage was at the end of the garden, the entrance for the car being off a back alleyway.

'It's just possible he planned to leave by car but there was something wrong with it,' Jakes muttered to Deepbriar, as the woman swung the garage doors open.

The Rover was highly polished, and nearly new. Jakes puffed out a breath of admiration. 'I take it you don't drive, Mrs Spraggs? May we check that it starts?'

Wordlessly she handed him the keys, and Jakes reverently opened the car, staring round at the interior with obvious delight. 'I'd love one of these,' he said, pressing the starter. The car roared into life at the first attempt, the sound fading to a purr before Jakes reluctantly turned the engine off again and climbed out. Deepbriar meanwhile had walked round to check that none of the tyres were flat.

'You see?' Mrs Spraggs shut her husband's prized possession away again. 'Joseph spent hours polishing it, and dusting the inside. He never would have gone away and left it.'

'You mentioned Sylvester Rudge when I first spoke to you,' Deepbriar said. 'Exactly what connection did your husband have with him?'

'That man!' Her voice was full of venom. 'They worked together once, but that was years ago, before Joseph and I met. Since then Rudge has never missed a chance to do Joseph a bad turn. He lost him a job at the furniture factory once, just after the war. I know Joseph stepped outside the law now and then, but he never did anything really bad. Not like Rudge; he's got half the city thinking he's some kind of saint, giving money to the hospital for the children, paying to have the town hall clock repaired. And all the time he's got those women in Pier Street, everybody knows what they're up to, and who they work for, but you lot don't do a thing about it.'

'We can't act without proof, Mrs Spraggs,' Jakes replied. 'We have to stay within the law. Your husband's disappearance for example, do you have any evidence at all that Rudge might be involved?'

She narrowed her eyes, thinking. 'We saw him about two months ago. It was the day we went to collect the new car. Joseph was so happy, I think he'd have wished the devil himself a good morning. But when he greeted Rudge all he got was a glare for his trouble, and then the man said something under his breath. I've been trying to remember the exact words, but I can't. It was something like, "Enjoy it while you can" or "make the most of it", and there was so much hate in his voice. Joseph laughed it off, but it scared me.'

'Nobody else was close enough to hear what he said?'

'No. I told you, I barely heard it myself. But it was definitely a threat.'

'One that nobody else heard, and therefore no use as evidence,' Jakes said with a sigh. 'Thanks for your time, Mrs Spraggs. If you think of anything else that might be of use, telephone to the station at Falbrough and ask for me or Constable Deepbriar.'

Outside the house Jakes turned to the constable. 'Those questions about the bag he used. You're suggesting he was in too much of a hurry to fetch a suitcase from the loft, or sort out the right clothes to take.'

'No,' Deepbriar said bleakly. 'It's a bit too much like what happened in the case of Tony Pattridge. I think somebody else came and threw a few things into the first bag they could find. I'm afraid Mrs Spraggs is right, I doubt if she'll ever see her Joseph alive again.'

Chapter Sixteen

'So, constable,' Sergeant Jakes stared at Deepbriar over the rim of his teacup, 'you believe there's a link between Tony Pattridge and Joseph Spraggs.'

'It's one heck of a coincidence if there isn't,' Deepbriar replied. 'Think about it. Two men who both disappeared unexpectedly. Somebody collected Pattridge's belongings a few days after he left, though they didn't bother to take them all.' He gestured at the bag that occupied another of the Cosy Nook Tearoom's chairs. 'And somebody who didn't know which clothes fitted Joseph Spraggs, or where his suitcase was kept, packed a few of his belongings to make it look as if he'd left home, not realising that the one thing he'd never have left behind was his car.'

'It's possible,' Jakes conceded, 'though it's a bit far-fetched, don't you think? This is Belston, not Chicago. What with the tramp as well, we've got three missing men, which would mean we're looking for a mass murderer. I ask you, is it likely?' He drained his cup and sighed resignedly. 'All right, what's in the bag?'

'I haven't looked yet,' Deepbriar said, 'I thought we'd better do it together and make it official.'

Jakes looked round at the two elderly ladies at the next table. Another, white-haired and even more ancient, stood behind the counter. 'Better not empty it in here, you never know what we might find. We'll go and borrow a room at the station. I want to go and see an old pal there anyway, I think he might be able to help us. This Barbara Blake, did she have any ideas about why Pattridge might have vanished?'

'She didn't say.' Deepbriar wriggled uncomfortably on his seat. 'I didn't ask,' he amended. 'I should have questioned her about his work and his friends too, shouldn't I? My first day as a detective and I'm not doing too well.'

'You were only supposed to be tracking him down for the solicitors,' Jakes said consolingly, 'not investigating another suspicious
disappearance. In fact, so far Tony Pattridge is no concern of ours,
not officially.' He looked at his watch. 'We've just got time to get
back to the library before it shuts.'

Faced with two policemen this time, the elderly librarian looked
flustered, and he scowled disapprovingly at the unfortunate
Barbara Blake as she was summoned into his room for the second
time. 'Really Miss Blake, if you are mixing with unsavoury characters....'

'There's no suggestion of that,' Sergeant Jakes interrupted him.
'You can hardly hold this young lady responsible for the behaviour of people who happened to be at school with her. She's
already given us valuable help with our enquiries. I apologise for
the disruption we're causing you, Mr Falkener, we do appreciate
your assistance. The Superintendent often remarks on the amount
of support he gets from other local government departments.'

Mollified by this compliment, if such it was, the man withdrew.
Jakes smiled at the woman and offered her Falkener's chair, the
only comfortable one in the room; Deepbriar perched himself on
a set of library steps in a corner, with notebook and pencil poised.

'Now, Miss Blake,' Jakes said, 'I'm sorry about this, but
Constable Deepbriar's visit to Mrs Newman threw up a few more
questions and we're hoping you might be able to help us answer
them.'

She nodded, her eyes wide. 'I've been thinking about it ever
since the constable left. Something has happened to Tony, hasn't
it? I wasn't imagining things. He really did mean what he said ...'
With a sudden sob she dropped her head into her hands. 'I should
have known.' The words came out in fits and starts, muffled by
her crying. 'We were going to tell everyone that weekend. We'd
agreed to get engaged at Christmas. Tony was talking about
buying me a ring. I was so happy when he asked me to marry him.
But then when he went off ... I thought he'd changed his mind.
Oh, poor Tony. If only I'd guessed, if I'd told somebody....'

Jakes got up and leant across the desk, taking a large white
handkerchief, neatly folded, from his top pocket and giving it to
the girl, then patting her gently on the shoulder. Deepbriar was
impressed; it was the sort of thing Dick Bland would have done.

'It's all right, Miss Blake,' Jakes said, 'take your time. We'll go on when you've had a minute to compose yourself.' He looked at Deepbriar and jerked his head towards the door. 'Come on, constable.'

In the narrow corridor outside the reading-room Jakes whispered in Deepbriar's ear. 'I'm getting a nasty feeling about this, you could be right. She's a bit of a corker isn't she? If he'd just walked out, taken his stuff and quit his lodgings in the normal way, I might believe he'd had second thoughts about getting married, but it doesn't look that way, does it?'

'No,' Deepbriar said. 'You know, I saw his father's suicide note. There was something in it that suggested he'd been expecting Tony to call and see him at Christmas. Those presents they were buying, you reckon Miss Blake would know if the boy bought one for his old man?'

'We'll ask. You were right, constable, there are too many coincidences, it's a lot like what happened to Spraggs almost a year later. Somebody must have wanted both these men out of the way.'

Deepbriar ran his hand over his short-cropped hair. 'But it's crazy. Like you said, this is England. We don't have gangsters going around disposing of their enemies at the drop of a hat.'

'Maybe we do, but we don't know it,' Jakes said reasonably. 'Either way, it's our job to find the answer. So far, that's the only theory that fits the small amount of evidence we've got.' Jakes hesitated for a second. 'Look, Thorny ... You don't mind if I call you Thorny?'

Deepbriar shook his head, and Jakes went on. 'I admit I could be wrong. I may have the rank but you're older than me, with a lot more years in the force behind you. This is the first time I've been allowed to investigate anything this serious on my own, and it's only because of the flu epidemic. Two heads are better than one, and I can do with all the help you can give me. I promise I'll give you due credit if we get it sorted out. Well?'

'Agreed,' Deepbriar said.

Jakes looked relieved. 'Any time you think I'm getting it wrong then go ahead and tell me. Though not in front of a pretty girl like Miss Blake, if you don't mind,' he added with a grin. 'And if there's any questions you want answered when I'm conducting an interview, I don't see why you shouldn't ask them. Come on, let's see what else she can tell us.'

The young woman was sitting straight shouldered and dry-eyed when they returned. Deepbriar was pleased to note that there was no smudged make-up on her face; unlike Mrs Spraggs her colour was all her own.

'I'm sorry,' she said. 'It was a bit of a shock, you coming to see me after all this time. I'd thought about it you see. For months I've gone over and over those last few days in my mind. I was never sure which was worse, Tony leaving me because he'd been lying and he didn't love me after all, or something dreadful happening to him. It sounds awful saying that now. I should have known. I should have trusted him.'

Jakes shook his head. 'I'm sure there's no blame to you, Miss Blake. None of this was your fault. Tell me, when you and Mr Pattridge did your Christmas shopping, do you know if he bought a present for his father?'

'Yes, he did. We spent a long time over it, too. He bought him a pair of gloves, really nice leather ones, with a furry lining.' She smiled at the memory. 'They were quite expensive. Tony stood at the counter doing sums on a piece of paper, making sure he'd still have enough to take me to the pictures and buy me an ice cream. He laughed about it, and he said he'd never be that hard up again.'

'So, he was expecting to come into some money very soon. Do you know where he was working?'

'He didn't have a regular job. Now and then he'd help out one of his friends with his stall at the market, selling material and haberdashery, and sometimes he drove a car for a company in Falbrough.'

'Do you know if he ever worked for somebody called Rudge?' Jakes asked.

'I don't know,' she replied. 'He didn't talk about work very often.'

'What about his friend at the market?' Deepbriar put in. 'Did you ever hear what he was called?'

'Charlie,' she replied. 'That's all I know. I met him once. He's not very tall, only about five foot three, with very pale blond hair. But Tony said he wouldn't be doing that job much longer anyway, because he'd got something better lined up.'

Barbara Blake flushed and Jakes nodded at her encouragingly. 'Go on.'

'Well, I think that's why he finally asked me to marry him. He was going to have enough money to get us a little place to live.'

She smiled, her eyes distant as she stared back into the past. 'It was supposed to be a surprise, he wouldn't tell me any details, but he was full of his plans.'

'You think he'd been offered a job. But he didn't give you any hint of what it might be?'

'It was something to do with driving,' she replied. 'He loved cars. He said it was the only good thing he got out of doing his National Service, learning to drive. It's funny, because I never thought drivers earned very much.'

'They don't, as a rule,' Jakes said, exchanging a significant glance with Deepbriar.

The bag swinging from Deepbriar's hand wasn't heavy, yet he felt it an increasing weight as he followed Jakes out of the library. 'Are we going back to the station now, sarge? There could be something important in here.'

'Yes, but there's somebody else we could talk to,' Jakes said, checking his watch.

'Charlie,' Deepbriar hazarded.

'Yes, Charlie who has a market stall.' They crossed the High Street, walking fast. 'He'll be clearing up by now, but we might catch him.'

Jakes asked the first stall holder they found, a wiry old man throwing tired-looking cabbages into a sack. He directed them to a stall a few yards further on, where a young man with silver blond hair was taking down a display of linen and curtain materials and loading it into an ancient van.

'Would you be Charlie?' Jakes asked, showing his identification.

'That's me,' the youth said cheerfully, completely untroubled by the presence of two police officers. 'What can I do for you?'

'You know a man by the name of Tony Pattridge.'

'Yes, I know Tony. He worked for me sometimes, just the odd day. Haven't seen him in ages.' He stowed some towels in the van then turned to face them. 'Can't say I'm sorry, to be honest.'

'Why's that?' Jakes prompted.

'Well, we went about together a lot for a while, just after we'd done our National Service, you know, a pair of lads out for a good time. But Tony was getting up to a few things I didn't like, mixing with a bad crowd.' He smiled. 'I'd met my Janice by then, and I was thinking about settling down. I didn't want to be getting into trouble, or her dad would have been after me.'

'This bad crowd, do you know any of their names?' Deepbriar
asked.

Charlie hesitated for a moment. 'Yes, there was one called
Wilky. Shifty looking bloke. He came to the races with us once.
Once was enough for me, but I think Tony saw quite a lot of him.
There was even a rumour that Tony was getting caught up with
Sylvester Rudge, but I wouldn't know about that, I don't move in
those sort of circles.'

The two policemen exchanged glances.

'You don't mind if I get on?' The young man folded up a heap
of tea towels, and added them to the stock gradually filling his
van. 'So, what's Tony been up to? I thought he'd moved away, he
often talked about heading for The Smoke. Last time we met he
touched me for a couple of quid, about a week before Christmas
that was. I knew at the time I'd never see the money again, but
you know how it is, old mates and that. Is he in trouble?'

Jakes didn't answer him, merely thanking the man for his help.
'Does all right, does it, selling this stuff?' he asked, pointing to the
goods Charlie was packing away.

'Not bad. Janice wants me to go into dress materials, there's
more call for that now, seeing there's some good cloth coming in
from the Far East. The ladies are always keen to get their hands
on something colourful.'

They left him to his work and headed back towards the police
station. 'So,' Jakes said, 'Pattridge was getting into mischief and
Charlie didn't want to know? Did you believe him?'

'No reason not to,' Deepbriar said. 'If he was lying he's very
good at it. Didn't get the feeling he was two-faced.'

'No, me neither,' Jakes said. Then he stopped dead in the street,
so suddenly that a large woman carrying two well-laden baskets
nearly walked straight into his back. 'Sorry,' he muttered absently,
as she pushed angrily past him.

'What's wrong?' Deepbriar asked.

'The date. Pattridge touched Charlie for a loan, probably to
buy that Christmas present for his Dad, and to take his girlfriend
to the pictures. He told Miss Blake he'd be coming into some
money very soon, and he was going to buy her a ring. Pattridge
was a driver, right? And we know his reputation, even that he
might have got involved with Rudge. Remember the date when he
vanished? Thursday before Christmas last year. Does it ring any
bells?'

'The Somerson robbery!' Deepbriar rubbed at his forehead, missing the familiar weight of his helmet. 'You think Pattridge was in on that?'

Jakes nodded, 'It all fits! And there's something else. The getaway car was found on its side in a ditch the next day.'

'I heard about that. They skidded in the mud.'

'Yes. But you probably won't have heard that there was blood on the front seats. We always thought the driver must have been injured when the car left the road, though there wasn't a lot of damage. We checked all the local doctors and hospitals, but we never turned anything up. The windscreen was shattered, there was glass everywhere, it's just possible the driver was thrown out of the car. Suppose it was Pattridge?'

'It could have been. You think the accident killed him?' Deepbriar was sceptical.

'Maybe. But it might not have been quite that serious. If his face was cut he could have decided to make himself scarce,' Jakes suggested, 'and if he was permanently disfigured he might have thought his girl wouldn't want him any more. Anyway, his injuries would have pointed to his involvement in the robbery, so he could hardly go back to his lodgings as if nothing had happened. Or maybe he died, in which case his accomplices might have shovelled him into a hole somewhere, or just tipped him into the river.'

'Yes, but ...' The constable hesitated. 'Not the river, bodies have a way of coming back to the surface down at the weir. As for burying him ... Sorry, sergeant, it's not my place to criticise, but that's a heck of a large assumption.'

'It was a heck of a large haul, worth indulging in a bit of amateur grave-digging for,' Jakes said. 'Eighty thousand pounds in used notes, being delivered to the factory for wages.'

Deepbriar let out a low whistle. 'I didn't realise it was that much.'

'The villains chose the right week, it was more than double the normal amount, because staff had been putting money into a Christmas saving scheme, as well as getting paid their annual bonuses.'

They carried on towards Belston police station through the darkening end of the afternoon.

'Was there any hint that Rudge was involved?' Deepbriar queried.

'Plenty of them, but if he was behind it he'd covered his tracks pretty well, there was no evidence at all.'

'What line of business is he in? Legitimately, I mean.'

'Good question,' Jakes said. 'We know he's owns half a dozen houses on the Burrow Road, and it's said he's involved in the motor trade. And transport of course, he's supposed to be behind one of the big firms that do the run to London and the channel ports.'

'I heard some of his men were stirring things up on the picket line during the strike. I suppose if that company was one of his rivals he wouldn't mind seeing them in trouble. You think Rudge could be the man Pattridge was working for when he was doing these odd driving jobs?' Deepbriar pondered.

'I wouldn't have thought so. Since he mentioned them to his girlfriend they were most likely legal, and she said that was in Falbrough, not Belston.'

Deepbriar nodded and changed tack. 'Didn't I hear that the van delivering the payroll was sent at an unusual time, and by a different route that week?'

'Yes, the bank manager cooked up the idea with Somerson,' Jakes replied gloomily. 'There were only supposed to be four people who knew about it, and one of them was the driver.'

'He wasn't suspected?' Deepbriar asked.

'He'd been with Somersons all his life and was about to retire with a generous pension, but he was so badly hurt in the attack that he didn't live long to enjoy it.' Jakes sighed. 'The fools didn't even send along a guard, they thought nobody would suspect the van was carrying that amount of money if the old man was alone.'

'You say there was a fourth person in on the secret,' Deepbriar said. 'Who was that?'

'The bank manager's secretary. Everybody was pretty sure she must have been the one who gave the game away, but she was questioned by half a dozen different coppers and not one of them could shake her, she swore she hadn't told a soul.'

'But the gang were lying in wait, so they had to know the route,' Deepbriar mused. 'Maybe there was something that was missed at the time, somebody else who could have found out. Was there anything on paper? A map, or written instructions?'

'No. And nobody could have overheard what they were talking about either, they met in Somerson's office, and we checked it out, that building's two hundred years old and the walls are solid stone, about a foot thick. Three floors up, and it wasn't the day for the window cleaner.'

Jakes turned in under the blue lamp that shone bright in the increasing gloom. 'I don't know that there's ever been a case that left us with so little to go on.' He stopped for a quick word with the desk sergeant then led the way to an empty room. 'Right, let's see what Mr Pattridge's friends left behind. A bank wrapper or a Somerson's envelope is probably asking a bit too much.'

'Why not wish for an incriminating letter in Rudge's own handwriting, while you're at it,' Deepbriar said, emptying the bag out on to the table, tipping it upside down and giving it a shake. It didn't look a very exciting haul: a pair of worn shoes; three socks, all darned at toe and heel; a shirt with the collar missing; a pullover, thin and rather faded from much washing; a single cuff link in the shape of an anchor, with half the silver plating rubbed off, and an envelope addressed to Mr A Pattridge at 5 Alma Villas, Belston.

'There, what did I say?' Deepbriar offered the envelope to Jakes, but the sergeant motioned to him to open it.

'From Hemming and Cole, Estate Agents and Valuers. "Dear Mr Pattridge,"' he read aloud, '"Our representative, Mr Michaels, will be happy to meet you at 3 pm this Wednesday to discuss the purchase of Low Rooking Garage and attached cottage."' He checked the date. 'A few days before the robbery,' he said.

Jakes whistled. 'So Pattridge was thinking of buying himself a bit of property.' He waved a hand over the items on the table. 'It doesn't look to me as if Mr Pattridge could afford a gallon of petrol, let alone a garage.'

Deepbriar felt around in the bottom of the bag in case he'd missed anything, and pulled out a photograph, worn around the edges and with a crack across it, as if it had been folded and kept in a pocket or wallet. It was a picture he'd seen before, of two boys proudly holding their new watches, standing on either side of their father. On the back, written in pencil but hardly faded at all, as if the inscription was more recent than the picture, were the words 'Happy days'.

The Belston police station canteen was much larger than the one at Falbrough, but thanks to the flu epidemic it was almost empty when Deepbriar and Jakes walked in. A long-faced uniformed sergeant sat alone in one corner, while by the window two constables who looked as if the sum of their years would barely add up to Deepbriar's age, were sharing a plate of sandwiches. Jakes went to the counter and ordered tea. Without consulting Deepbriar he bought two rather unappetising slices of fruit cake.

'Hello, Ted,' Jakes said, taking his tray to the table where the solitary sergeant was sitting. 'This is Constable Deepbriar, from Minecliff. Constable, this is Ted Cosgough. He was desk sergeant at Northern End when I was as green as those two infants over by the window.' He put the cake down in front of the man and drew out a chair, giving Deepbriar a nod of invitation to do the same. 'Thought you might be getting peckish, Sarge.'

'Thanks.' The man stirred slightly and reached out for the first slice, dipping it into his almost empty mug of tea. 'I could do with a refill.'

Deepbriar took the hint and returned to the counter. The lugubrious sergeant had to be Jakes's source of local information.

They watched in silence as the man devoured both pieces of cake, dipping each mouthful in the fresh mug of tea. He then washed everything down with yet more tea, finally pushing the plate and mug away, and looking at Jakes. 'I hear you're searching for a missing man.'

'Two,' Jakes replied, with a rueful look at Deepbriar; evidently it was not the time to mention Tony Pattridge.

'Nobody in Belston's going to miss Joseph Spraggs much,' Cosgough said, fishing in his pocket for a packet of cigarettes and a match.

'Especially not Sylvester Rudge,' Jakes agreed.

'You heard that? When our chief inspector heard about Mrs Spraggs coming in and accusing Rudge of being involved he put out a few feelers, discreetly of course. It didn't take long to find out Spraggs had made an enemy of Belston's favourite businessman; they'd had a few words, but as far as anyone could tell that was as far as it had gone.'

He paused, taking a long draw on the cigarette. 'Anyway, if you really think it's a murderer you're after, it's not Rudge's style. Anyone who gets on the wrong side of him might be in danger of getting roughed up a bit, and one or two minor villains have left town in a bit of a hurry after he's fallen out with them, but I never heard of any of his enemies doing a total vanishing act.'

'There's another reason why he doesn't seem a likely suspect,' Deepbriar said, and he explained about the prior disappearance of young Joe, who shared the name of the missing man, but had nothing else in common with him.

Cosgough shook his head. 'That can't have been Rudge's chums,' he said, 'he doesn't suffer fools gladly. They'd be nursing a few broken bones if they made a mistake like that.'

'But who sets out to kidnap a man without knowing exactly what he looks like and where to find him?' Jakes mused.

'A contract killer,' Deepbriar said, 'if he was just given a name, and maybe the place where he could pick up the man's scent. How about this? Joe Spraggs was making a delivery to Falbrough a few hours before he was abducted, and we know the older man, Joseph, was often in the Queen's Head. Suppose young Joe went there for his lunch that day? Anybody asking for a man by the name of Joseph Spraggs might have had the wrong one pointed out to him.'

'You've been reading too many of those American penny dreadfuls, constable,' Cosgough said. 'Contract killers? Come off it!'

'So you think two men of the same name going missing within a few days of each other is a coincidence? That's about as likely as an outbreak of flying pigs,' Deepbriar replied, unabashed.

'He's got a point,' Jakes said. 'But let's get back to Rudge. Mrs Spraggs says he threatened her husband, so he's got to be our best suspect. Maybe the other Joseph Spraggs had also come up against Rudge in some way, and whoever was given the job of dishing out his comeuppance got the wrong man. Then when they picked up the right one, and he was supposed to just get a bit of a beating, perhaps he had a heart attack or something.'

'Or they went a bit too far, killed him by mistake. Then they disposed of the body, and came up with this idea of packing a few of his clothes so everyone would think he'd left home.' Deepbriar concluded.

'Guesswork,' Cosgough was disparaging. 'You know better than that, lads, you haven't got a single fact to hang a case on.' He was silent for a moment, lighting another cigarette from the butt of the first. 'Tell you one thing, though. If Rudge was involved, you can bet he was out of town at the time. And that he'll have a cast-iron alibi.'

Chapter Seventeen

There was a long drawn out silence at the table, as Jakes and Deepbriar considered what Cosgough had told them. 'So maybe we should go and ask Mr Rudge where he was the first week of November,' Jakes suggested at last.

'Not a good idea,' Cosgough said. 'Rudge eats police officers below the rank of chief inspector for breakfast. But you're in luck, as it happens I can tell you. It was the first thing we checked when Mrs Spraggs made her complaint. He was in London, seeing an old friend and getting his teeth fixed in Harley Street or some such place.'

'Was he gone by Saturday the first?' Deepbriar asked.

'Took the evening train on the Friday,' Cosgough said. 'Which is one thing that suggests Rudge wasn't in on it. Spraggs didn't go missing until the following Thursday, and that's the day Rudge came home, on the late train, the one that gets in at half-past nine. On past experience I wouldn't expect him to run things that close.'

'But young Joe did his vanishing act on the Saturday afternoon! You must admit, sergeant, it does seem to fit. I don't suppose you know where Rudge was last Christmas?' Deepbriar went on nonchalantly.

Cosgough laughed. 'You're thinking of the Somerson case. He went in the opposite direction for that one. North of Scotland. Staying with posh friends at a castle. Lord and Lady whatnot, sheriff of the shire and Justice of the Peace or some such.'

'What about the men who work for him?' Jakes asked. 'I've heard he always keeps a couple of strong-arm types close to hand.'

'He didn't take them to Scotland with him, but we couldn't find anything that put them near Somerson's van.' Cosgough was suddenly thoughtful. 'It seems they did go to London with him though. So if there was a mistake made, it's just possible he was using an outsider, who didn't know exactly who this Spraggs was.'

'Or what he looked like,' Deepbriar said. 'Joe's half Joseph's age for a start.'

'We were hoping you might be able to give us some idea about who he would have used, Ted,' Jakes said. 'Is there a list of his known associates?'

'There's nothing official,' Cosgough replied, 'Not with Rudge and the chief constable rubbing shoulders at functions every night of the week. Nobody would dare commit anything to paper. I can give you a few names. Spraggs was a minor player, and as far as we know he never worked directly for Rudge, but let's see. Wilky Bright. He's always hanging around. And Gordon Frith, though he's inside now, doing time for assault.'

'Wilky,' Jakes said. 'We heard about Wilky in connection with somebody else. Any more?'

Cosgough dragged smoke deep into his lungs. 'There's one who fancies himself as a ladies' man, always smartly dressed. He's small fry, trying to muscle in on the big time; where Rudge is he's usually not far away. I can't think of his name. Berty is it? No, Barty, Barney. Barney Rimmer, or Simmonds … something like that. It'll come to me, and when it does I'll let you know.' He pushed himself to his feet. 'Nice talking to you lads, but I've got to get back to work. If you're trying to finger Rudge for this business I wish you luck, he's been running rings round the law for thirty years, I can't see us stopping him now.'

'He's right,' Jakes said, slumped back in his chair once Cosgough had gone. 'It's all nothing but guesswork. We need evidence.' He looked at his watch and straightened suddenly. 'And finding it will have to wait. I'm sorry, Thorny, but I'm off duty until Monday. My sister's getting married tomorrow, and if I'm not at my Mum and Dad's house by seven o'clock there'll be hell to pay.'

'What do you suggest I do?' Deepbriar asked, following Jakes from the canteen. 'Anything you want me to follow up?'

'I still think Bronc is our best bet, if we could only find the old man's body, that would give us a place to start. Did you get anywhere with getting permission to search the aerodrome?'

'The only person who could tell me who holds the key was away until next Wednesday. According to the Ministry, the local police should know who it is,' he added gloomily.

'And that's you.' Jakes turned and grinned at him. 'Ain't life grand? I'll see you at Falbrough on Monday morning, but until then you're on your own. Only one piece of advice, Thorny, stay away from Rudge, we don't want the chief constable on our backs.'

It was barely daylight. Apart from the new layer of fallen leaves lying sodden in the mud, Wriggle's yard looked very much as it had the day Deepbriar had gone there looking for young Joe; the gate stood open and the ancient lorry was parked facing the exit. At first glance the place was deserted, but as he leant his bike against the fence a metallic noise caught the constable's attention and he walked around the Atkinson, to find Joe Spraggs picking up a piece of pipe to load into the back.

'Good morning, Mr Deepbriar,' the young man said. 'You're out and about early.'

'Morning, Joe. Didn't want to miss catching you,' Deepbriar replied. 'You know we're looking into what happened to your Dad's cousin, the other Joseph Spraggs.'

'Yes. Do you really think he was supposed to be the one they carted off when they came here?'

'It seems that way.'

'Mum said his wife was frantic because nobody would listen to her. Emily's still upset, she keeps going on about it. I suppose she's imagining how she'd feel if I hadn't turned up again.' Joe frowned. 'I'm glad the police are taking it seriously. I mean, Joseph's one of the family, even if he is a bit of a black sheep.'

'Actually the police at Belston had done a bit of asking around about Joseph Spraggs before his wife came to see me,' Deepbriar said, 'so they'd made a start. They should have told her. Not that they got very far, and we're not doing much better, but at least we're looking. That's why I'm here, I need to ask you a question.'

'Right you are.' Joe heaved the last length of pipe into the lorry and slapped some flecks of rust off his sleeves, then he turned to face Deepbriar. 'What do you want to know?'

'That other Saturday, the first of November. In the morning you made a delivery to Falbrough.'

'That's right. They're building a new estate where the nursery used to be. Mr Wriggle got the contract to supply all the pipe work.' He gestured at his load. 'This is the last of it.'

'As I recall, you'd taken a packed lunch with you. But did you by any chance go into the Queen's Head? Maybe for a beer at lunch-time?'

Joe shook his head. 'No. I don't think I've ever been inside the Queen's Head, not that I remember.'

'Did you call in anywhere else that day? The post office, or a shop?'

'No. I didn't even stop at the transport café on the way to Gristlethorpe, like I usually would, because I didn't want to be late for the show. Is that all you wanted to know?'

'Yes, that was it.' Deepbriar did his best to hide his disappointment; his theory about how the mix up over the two Joseph's had occurred, had just been thoroughly demolished. 'Thanks, Joe.'

Deepbriar cycled homeward sunk in gloom. It didn't look as if he had much talent when it came to detection. He had nothing to work on, he could only follow Jakes's vague suggestion that he should continue looking for Bronc, but he'd be going over old ground and looking for a trail that was getting colder by the day.

Back at the police house, Mary was busy in the office.

'You weren't gone long,' she said, putting a file back on to a shelf.

'No,' he agreed absently.

'I think I'm wasting my time here. Can't you think who they might have given a key to? How about the Colonel, he's a military man?'

'I had already thought of that,' Deepbriar replied. 'I asked him yesterday.'

'Bert Bunyard's farm is nearest to the gate, but if he'd had a key he wouldn't have had to break in through a hole in the fence,' Mary remarked. 'You know, I don't believe they ever sent that letter telling you about it. Maybe the person at the ministry forgot.'

'Could be. Perhaps there isn't a key,' he said, sniffing, 'not in Minecliff anyway.'

She was already flicking through the papers in another file. 'There's only that one folder left to check, perhaps you'd do that. I have to go in a minute, or I'll miss the bus, and there'll be no beef for your dinner tomorrow.'

'All right, love, thanks. I think you're right, there was no letter. I'm sure if I'd been told who the key holder was, I'd remember.' Deepbriar lifted down the remaining file. 'It won't be in here, there's no way I'd file it under traffic.'

'Unless it got caught up with something else. You might as well look, since it's the last one.' She left him to his fruitless search, coming back a few minutes later with her coat on, carefully inserting a lethal-looking pin through her red felt hat. 'Bye, love.' She pecked him on the cheek. 'What I don't understand is, if you want to have another look at the airbase, why don't you go in the same way as before?'

'Because last time I could say I was following a suspect, which makes it all right to use the hole in the fence, although even for a police officer that's officially classed as trespassing.' He sighed. 'The ministry are a bit over zealous if you ask me. I'll just have to make my search unofficial, and anything I find will need to be discovered all over again once we get hold of the key.'

She laughed. 'Poor old thing. You've got a face as long as a wet weekend. Why don't you have your elevenses a bit early? There's a fresh fruit cake in the tin.'

Thorny Deepbriar took his wife's advice, and along with a generous helping of Mary's cake he sneaked an exciting ten minutes with Mitch O'Hara, so he was in a more cheerful frame of mind when he wheeled his bicycle out again and headed up the hill. Instead of taking the route by which they had recovered Ferdy Quinn's pig, he went to the main gates. These were made of two layers of thick mesh and stood nearly eight foot high; topped with barbed wire, they made a formidable barrier. Bert Bunyard had hinted that somebody went in that way, but if so they must have had a key, because the chain and padlock showed no signs of tampering.

The passing years had left the road into the airfield very over-grown, but only in a few places had the concrete vanished entirely beneath a layer of dirt and weeds. Deepbriar bent down, taking a closer look at the ground. He could barely believe what he was seeing. There were tracks. A vehicle had gone in here, some time ago; a week or more maybe, he couldn't tell exactly, but there could be no mistake. Despite the rain that had fallen since, there were still faint indentations where the wheels had passed. The marks weren't clear enough for him to be sure it was the same vehicle that had left the tracks in Wriggle's yard, but they looked as if they were the right distance apart. Was this what Bert Bunyard had seen?

Full of a fresh determination, the constable hurried to the place where the badger trail passed under the fence. There were miles of old concrete roads on the airfield, simply getting back to the gate on this side of the fence would have taken him half an hour on foot. He crouched to force his way through the gap, holding the bike by the saddle and pushing it in front of him. A pedal snagged on a low branch at the very moment that the front wheel hit a root. The bike slewed sideways, the handlebars twisted and the whole machine bucked as if it were suddenly alive. With no room to get out of the way, Deepbriar was sent crashing to the ground with the bike landing painfully on top of his legs.

It was amazing how many projecting parts a bicycle had, and at that moment all of them seemed to be sticking into him. At the expense of more bruises, a scratched face and a nasty tear down the sleeve of his greatcoat, he pulled free. Muttering words he wouldn't dare use in front of Mary, he wrestled the bike through the gap somehow, emerging smeared with mud from the wheels and grease from the chain. Hot, cross and dirty, Deepbriar eventually pushed the machine on to the concrete surface and climbed into the saddle.

Back at the entrance, this time on the inside, he scanned the ground. The tracks were no easier to see, and they faded out in a couple of yards, leaving nothing to suggest which way the vehicle had gone. He sat astride his bike, one foot on the ground, deep in thought as he stared down at the slight indentations in the grass. Had dead men really been brought this way? Bronc, Spraggs, maybe even Tony Pattridge? Could the cellar where Joe was held have been an air-raid shelter?

'Hello, Mr Deepbriar.'

The constable jumped as if he'd been shot, almost tumbling over for the second time that morning.

'Sorry,' Harry Bartle said apologetically as he came free-wheeling along the concrete track and braked alongside Deepbriar. 'I didn't mean to startle you.'

'You shouldn't be here, Harry, this is Air Ministry property.' Deepbriar was ruffled by his display of nerves. 'Did you come through the fence?'

'Yes. Sorry,' Harry said again, 'I didn't think you'd mind. I followed you.' He grinned. 'The whole village knows this is where Bert hid the pig. You know, I think plenty of other people know the way in. Billy Tapper and his mates have been ferreting up here more than once, and George Hopgood knows somebody who's been rooting about looking for scrap metal.'

'If that's true he could find more than he's bargained for,' Deepbriar said, 'that's why the fence is there, because there's unexploded bombs all over the place.'

Harry shrugged. 'He never had much in the way of brains. Serve him right if he blows himself up. But you've not come looking for unexploded bombs. Did Bert hide something else up here?'

'That's no business of yours, even if he did,' Deepbriar said sharply. 'As it happens I'm concerned with more serious business than Bert Bunyard's feud with Ferdy Quinn.'

'You're still looking for Bronc.' Harry's eyes shone with detective fervour. 'You think this is where the murderer hid the body, is that it? The aerodrome is an awfully big place for one man to search on his own, Mr Deepbriar, can I help?'

'Certainly not. This is a police matter, Harry. You're trespassing, and I can't allow you to stay. This isn't like looking for a man who's worst crime is leaving a couple of gates open. You'd best get off home.'

'Right you are.' Crestfallen, Harry turned his bicycle round and rode slowly back the way he'd come. Deepbriar watched him go, feeling mean. If there was an official search then there was every chance they'd be calling for volunteers before the next week was out, it wouldn't have hurt him to tell Harry that, instead of sending him off with a flea in his ear.

Then he recalled the notice he'd seen in the file Jakes had borrowed to fool Bert Bunyard. If the county authority decided to lower the regulation height for police officers then Harry would qualify; his dream of joining the police force could finally come true.

Deepbriar opened his mouth to call the young man back, then he had second thoughts and closed it again. Time enough to share the good news when it was certain; it would be heartless to give the lad false hopes.

Somehow the episode with Harry had plunged Deepbriar back into gloom. He no longer felt any enthusiasm for the search, it all seemed pointless. Which is what it proved to be, because although he explored several miles of overgrown roads he found no further trace of the vehicle. As he faced the problem of getting his bike back through the gap in the fence his misery deepened. He decided he'd been chasing a red herring, and that the tracks would turn out to belong to some official Ministry car.

*

'I thought Mary would be back by now,' Mrs Emerson said tartly, standing in Deepbriar's doorway, solid and immovable. Obviously she had no intention of leaving.

With an internal sigh Deepbriar attempted a smile and asked the woman if she would like to come in and wait, praying that she would refuse. Yet again that day he was to be disappointed. With a decisive nod she shouldered her way past him.

'I know dear Mary will want to see me, I've been going through my libretti, and I've brought three for her to look at.' She bustled through into the living-room with Deepbriar following disconsolately at her heels. 'We have far too much talent to waste our time on Gilbert and Sullivan. Are you familiar with the works of Verdi? There's one aria from *Aida* I simply adore. Let me sing you a few bars, I know you'll recognise it.'

'Oh no,' Deepbriar said hurriedly; his day was going from bad to worse. 'Not without warming your voice properly, don't risk straining anything.' He searched frantically for some subject to distract her. 'Tell me, Mrs Emerson, was your husband keen on opera?'

She shook her head. 'Poor Edgar, I'm afraid he wasn't musical, although the dear man always encouraged me with my art.' Her face took on what she obviously thought was a wistful expression and she leant towards the constable as if sharing a confidence. 'I miss him, you know, Thorny. Life can be hard for a widow. One gets so lonely.'

'But you have many good friends, I'm sure.' This was barely better than listening to her singing. 'You and Mr Emerson lived somewhere north of Belston, didn't you?' he asked.

'At Overside,' she said. 'The manor house.'

Deepbriar nodded. He'd recognised the picture he'd seen on the wall when he and Inspector Stubbs had visited to ask about Bronc. 'That's a very beautiful old place. It must have been hard to leave.'

'But it had to be done.' She gave a theatrical sigh. 'Overside Manor was our home for nearly twenty years. For me it holds too many memories. It's never a good thing to cling to the past.'

Deepbriar nodded. 'I'm sure you go back sometimes. It must be a comfort to go to the churchyard and know your Edgar is there, close to the home you shared.' This, he thought, was safer ground; all the widows he knew attached great importance to the ritual of tending their departed husband's grave.

Mrs Emerson's face suddenly went a bright shade of pink, and her breathing seemed to be troubling her. Deepbriar looked at the woman in confusion.

'Is something wrong?' he asked, wondering if she was about to have a seizure.

'No, of course not, I'm quite well, thank you. Whatever makes you think ...' The words tumbled out, as her plump face cycled rapidly through a range of emotions. After a moment she regained control and offered Deepbriar a wintry smile. 'You'll have to excuse me, it's my artistic temperament. Talking about such things is so distressing. Ever since I was a child I've preferred not to dwell on unhappy events.'

She turned away from him and began rooting in the bag she'd brought. 'Do let me sing a little of this aria for you,' she gushed, 'it won't take me a moment to do some exercises and warm up my vocal chords ...'

The sound of the back door opening had never been so welcome. 'That will be Mary,' Deepbriar said thankfully, 'I'll go and tell her you're here.' He made his escape, and a few minutes later was safely hidden in his office. It was only when he read the first paragraph of a new chapter of 'Mitch O'Hara and the Thousand Dollar Dame' for the third time, that he realised he couldn't get the woman's strange behaviour out of his mind. Mrs Emerson's greatest pleasure in life was to talk about herself, and she happily dramatised the least little event in an attempt to appear more interesting, yet only now did it occur to Deepbriar, that in all the time he'd known her, she had never said one word about her husband's death.

Later, joining his wife for lunch once their visitor had gone, he asked Mary about it.

'Now you come to mention it, that is odd,' Mary said. 'Bella has told me every detail of her father's last illness, she had to nurse him for nearly two years, you know, it was very hard on her, but she's never told me much about Edgar. I expect it's still too fresh in her mind.'

'But it must be more than a year ago,' Deepbriar said. 'And most people love talking to you about their trials and tribulations, you're such a good listener.'

'Flatterer,' she said, doling an extra spoonful of soup into his bowl. 'I'm sure there's some perfectly simple reason why she prefers not to talk about him.'

Back in his office an hour later, Deepbriar picked up the telephone, and dialled the number of the vicarage at Overside. It just happened that Father Gregory, the vicar there, had once done a spell as curate in Minecliff; he and Deepbriar shared an enthusiasm for church organ music, and it seemed like a good moment to get back in touch. After ten minutes of enjoyable reminiscences, Deepbriar came to the point, and was greeted by total silence at the other end of the line.

'Father?' he prompted, wondering if the connection had gone dead.

'Yes, I'm here, Thorny. But do you know, I don't think I can help you. Edgar Emerson isn't buried in my churchyard, because he didn't die in my parish.'

'Didn't he? But he was one of your parishioners?'

'Oh yes, he was a regular churchgoer, more so than his wife. But he died in Peru.'

'Peru?' For a moment Deepbriar thought he must have misheard. 'You did say Peru? South America?'

'That's right.' Father Gregory sounded a little uneasy.

'Did he travel a lot then?'

'No. It was all a bit odd. The Emersons hadn't been in church for a couple of weeks, and I hadn't seen them in the village either, so I decided to call. Mrs Emerson answered the door herself, which was unusual, because they always kept a maid, even through the War, though then the girl was an evacuee. Anyway, I asked after Mr Emerson, and she stared at me in the most peculiar way, and then told me he was dead. Naturally I offered my condolences, and asked how and when it had happened. And that's when she said he'd died in Peru. As far as I know neither of them had ever travelled abroad before, even during the War Mr Emerson had never been further away than Norfolk.'

'So what did he die of?' Deepbriar asked.

'I never found out. To be honest I was so taken aback by the news that I rather failed in my duties as pastoral advisor. I was going away on a sabbatical a few days later, and by the time I returned the house was up for sale, and Bella Emerson was moving out. We spoke once or twice more, but I never did learn any more about the circumstances of her husband's death. But you surely can't think there was anything suspicious about it?'

Father Gregory gave an uneasy little laugh. 'I hope you're not suggesting that Bella is getting her widow's pension under false pretences?'

'No, of course not,' Deepbriar said insincerely.

'Of course, she always had a tendency for self-dramatization, and her singing voice is truly awful, but she's an honest soul at heart.'

'I'm sure you're right,' Deepbriar replied. 'Forget I asked, it isn't important. Tell me, have you been to St Peter and St Paul's at Possington since the restoration was finished? The organ sounds wonderful. That swell to great coupler ...'

If there was something suspicious about the fate of Edgar Emerson, some mystery in Mrs Emerson's strange reticence on the subject, the constable could think of no way to find out for the moment. There must be officials who dealt with deaths that occurred overseas, and doubtless on Monday he could track one of them down and discover the details of Edgar Emerson's sudden demise, but for now, short of subjecting the man's grieving widow to the third degree, he was stuck.

Deepbriar did his best to concentrate on the matter in hand. He tried to think how Mitch O'Hara might have tackled the problem of finding Bronc's body, but much as he enjoyed reading about the detective's exploits, when he considered the American's methods he concluded that they depended very much on luck; any time O'Hara despaired of making any more progress, some previously unheard of character would turn up with exactly the piece of information he needed.

There was nothing wrong with a sizeable slice of good luck. With that in mind Deepbriar decided to patrol the village on foot, making himself available in case anyone had something useful to tell him.

It was a raw December Saturday, and very few of the villagers were out and about. With too much time for his thoughts to wander, Deepbriar's ruminations returned to the subject of Edgar Emerson. Outside the shop he met Mr Harvey, a stalwart of the Amateur Operatic Society and one of Bella Emerson's staunchest supporters. It had been he who discovered the absence of the fake plaster case when he helped check the props cupboard in the village hall.

'Mrs Emerson called in to see us before lunch,' he said, when

Deepbriar brought her name into the conversation, 'and I must say Mrs Harvey and I were a bit worried about her, she wasn't her usual self at all. It's not like our dear patroness to be so subdued, and she jumped like a cat when the postman knocked at the door. She said she'd been to see you and Mrs Deepbriar, I trust nothing happened to upset her?'

'Not that I'm aware of,' Deepbriar replied thoughtfully. Bella Emerson's behaviour smacked strangely of a guilty conscience.

'I don't think she's been the same since that business with the tramp,' Mr Harvey went on. 'It's very unsettling, a thing like that. I mean, imagine, a murder happening in your back garden! It's enough to make anyone nervous.'

'Murder's a serious business right enough,' Deepbriar said stolidly, but his mind was jumping wildly to conclusions. Perhaps his earlier supposition was right, and they had a contract killer on their patch! Perhaps the Emerson's marriage hadn't been happy. Perhaps the idea of playing the part of the merry widow had persuaded Bella to take matters into her own hands.

Chapter Eighteen

'Constable Deepbriar, I am so sorry, I tried to telephone you but the exchange couldn't get through. I believe there was a fault on the line.' Miss Lightfall wrung her hands together in an apologetic frenzy. 'Coming all this way on such a cold morning, it's so good of you, and finding it's wasted....'

'I'm not needed then,' Deepbriar said. He could hear the rich tones of the organ spilling through the open door of St Peter and St Paul's, and it wasn't Nicky Wilkins playing, because he was larking about with two other choirboys as they bundled through the vestry door. Possington had its organist back.

'Mr Crimmon didn't tell me until yesterday evening that he was fit to play,' Miss Lightfall said, 'it was rather naughty of him.'

'Not to worry,' Deepbriar said stolidly, 'I'll come in for the service, now I'm here. No point rushing to get back to Minecliff.'

'So sorry,' Miss Lightfall repeated, as Deepbriar followed her under the handsome Norman arch and in through the doorway. He sat in a pew at the very back of the church, positioning himself behind a pillar, where nobody would notice if he didn't manage to stay awake during the sermon.

He'd not slept well, and when he'd finally dozed off he'd been plagued by vivid dreams, all of them unpleasant. In one nightmare it wasn't Bronc who had had his throat cut, but Harry Bartle. The young man's body lay in a pool of blood outside the NCO's mess up at the abandoned airbase, while enemy aircraft circled high overhead. Deepbriar flinched as one aeroplane dived, but instead of dropping bombs it dropped a pig, which came hurtling towards him, squealing on a high monotonous note as it fell. He woke with a start, a split second before the animal hit him, to hear the kettle whistling in the kitchen. Mary was making tea.

Despite his fears Deepbriar didn't sleep during the service.

Father Michael's sermon was short and to the point; he preached the virtues of love and truth, inviting prayers for the missing Bronc, and urging anyone with information about the mysterious goings on in Minecliff to talk to the police, or, if they felt that was impossible, to consult him. 'God's justice is certain,' he said in conclusion, 'but so too is his mercy.'

Father Michael stepped down from the pulpit and delivered a prayer, then with a shuffling of feet and clearing of throats the congregation rose for the final hymn. No sound came from the organ. Seconds dragged by. An uncomfortable silence descended but still the music didn't start. As the pregnant pause dragged on, people began to fidget, until finally Father Michael coughed loudly, and said, 'we will now sing hymn 256, "Come unto Me, ye weary, and I will give you rest." Let us lift our voices together in praise of our Lord's charity.'

A frantic rustle of paper could be heard from behind the curtain which screened Mr Crimmon from view; the resultant giggle from the boys in the choir was drowned as the organ's rich harmonies filled the church.

Evidently wishing to make amends for his slip, Mr Crimmon played with more than usual gusto, and the congregation responded in kind, their singing echoing from the roof. From behind his pillar Deepbriar added his own full-throated bass, wondering if the Vicar's appeal would bring any results.

As everyone filed out after the final blessing, the sound of the organ swelled to a new pitch, until it must surely have been audible in Minecliff. Deepbriar stayed where he was, sitting hidden in his pew, enjoying the great crashing ebb and flow of music echoing in the high roof. At last, long after the nave was empty, Mr Crimmon launched into the Adagio from Beethoven's Pathetique, playing so poignantly that Deepbriar's found himself almost moved to tears by the haunting theme, so different from the organist's previous triumphal outpourings.

The last strains died away, leaving behind nothing but the drift of dust in the low shafts of winter sun that had crept in through the windows. Getting up and walking as silently as his size ten boots would allow, Deepbriar went to meet the organist as he stepped down from his high seat.

'Mr Crimmon,' he began.

The little man had a faraway look on his face, and coming suddenly upon the constable he stopped dead, his face blanching deathly white. 'Ohh.' The breath escaped from Crimmon's lungs as if he'd been punched, and he seemed to shrink.

'I'm sorry,' Deepbriar said, finding it hard not to laugh at the man's total confusion, 'it's lucky you're not the criminal type or I'd think you were suffering from a guilty conscience, Mr Crimmon. It's not surprising you were still lost in the music. I had to come and tell you how much I enjoyed your playing. I've never made any instrument sound the way you did this morning.'

'Wha-a-a.' Crimmon swallowed hard and managed to pull his wits together, although he still seemed distracted, his gaze wandering to the rank of pipes above their heads. 'Some things,' he said at last, 'are more important than others, don't you agree?'

'Well, yes,' Deepbriar said, though he had no idea what Crimmon was talking about.

'This organ,' Crimmon went on, nodding to himself with an air of satisfaction, 'will go on playing beautiful music long after I'm gone.'

Father Michael came from the vestry then, and Crimmon gave him a vague smile and hurried away, hugging his music to his chest as if it were a buffer against the cares of the world.

'Is he all right?' the vicar asked. 'I've never known Mr Crimmon to sleep during my sermon before.'

'Maybe he wasn't asleep,' Deepbriar replied thoughtfully.

Monday morning found Deepbriar sitting in the magistrate's court, waiting for Bert Bunyard's case to be called. Jakes had spoken to him briefly when he reported to the police station. The sergeant told him he was going to visit the estate agent who had written to Tony Pattridge about the sale of Low Rooking Garage, to find out if the missing man had turned up for his appointment, and if he was considered to be a serious buyer.

Compared to spending hours hanging about in the stuffy courthouse, Deepbriar thought that Jakes's morning sounded pretty exciting, and he was fighting to stay awake by the time the name of Albert Horatio Bunyard was finally read out, followed by the long list of charges. After some deliberation the magistrate ordered Bert to be tried at the Quarter Sessions, and declared himself ready to set bail for his release in the meantime, providing the police had no objection.

'If the defendant agrees not to enter any property belonging to Ferdinand Quinn, nor to approach Ferdinand Quinn, as a condition of bail,' Deepbriar said, 'we would have no objection, Your Honour.'

'You hear what the constable says, Bunyard?' The magistrate stared over his spectacles at the man in the dock. 'Will you promise not to molest Mr Quinn, or to trespass upon his property?'

There was an indistinct mumble from Bunyard, then a grudging agreement, though he had to be prompted by the clerk of the court to address the magistrate with proper respect.

'Very well. Released on bail, on a recognisance of five pounds.'

Deepbriar made his escape, thankful that he had no more cases coming up. As he descended the steps outside the court he met Jakes coming the other way. 'That's good,' the sergeant said breathlessly, 'I thought I might have to come in and fetch you.'

'Why, what's happened?' Deepbriar asked, his earlier lethargy forgotten.

'There's been a tramp seen in Derling, and the woman who telephoned us thought it might be Bronc. I didn't want to go without you, it's not easy to identify a person you've never even seen. That's the trouble with tramps, nobody takes their photograph. Come on, I've got a car. It's a bit of luck this flu, they don't often let me drive.'

Not bothering to point out that the simplest way to identify a living human being was to ask them their name, Deepbriar followed the younger man, and folded himself into the front passenger seat of the police car. Jakes drove far too fast for the constable's comfort; after one glance at the speedometer to see that it read fifty five miles an hour, he kept his gaze firmly fixed on the road, while his mind veered between prayer and trying to figure out how likely it was that Bronc would leave two coats and his hat in Minecliff, not to mention a couple of pints of blood, before travelling to a village some twenty miles away.

Opening his eyes again just in time to see Jakes take a blind bend on the wrong side of the road, Deepbriar decided he needed something more concrete to divert his mind from the possibility of his imminent demise. 'What did the estate agent say?' he asked.

'Pattridge turned up for the appointment. And he was keen to buy. He was due to call at the agent's office the following Monday with the deposit. Needless to say he didn't turn up. The agent wrote to him, but the letter was returned with "gone away" on it. Low Rooking Garage was sold to somebody else about three months later. It's a dead end, but it's yet another piece of evidence that suggests something untoward happened to young Mr Pattridge.'

'Three men can't just vanish,' Deepbriar said.

'It looks increasingly likely that they did. While I was in town I called on another of Joseph Spraggs's old chums. He was a bit more wary of naming names than Mrs Spraggs, but I got the impression he wouldn't be surprised to hear that Sylvester Rudge had something to do with Joseph's disappearing act. Though like Ted Cosgough, he was inclined to the view that Rudge wasn't likely to resort to murder.'

'Rudge himself wasn't around the day Spraggs went missing. That might make a difference. It would be murder at one remove, so to speak.' They went speeding through a village and zipped across the arterial road. 'Didn't you see the lights?' Deepbriar asked, wondering if his new-found career with the CID would survive if he gave his superior officer a caution for dangerous driving.

'On amber,' Jakes replied cheerfully. 'Proceed with caution, constable.'

There was nothing of caution in Jakes's driving, but they were only half a mile from Derling by this time, so Deepbriar gritted his teeth and kept silent.

'We're looking for Mrs Marshall at Derling Grange Farm,' Jakes said, as the village green flashed by. 'Any idea where it is?'

'You just passed it,' Deepbriar said. 'On the left.'

Taking advantage of a side turning, the sergeant wrenched the car round with a squeal of brakes, and headed back the way he'd come. 'Neat, eh?' he asked, grinning. 'I don't often get behind the wheel of one of these. Stubbs prefers to use a driver from the pool; he says it's easier for us to work on the case if we don't have to concentrate on the road.'

Stubbs, Deepbriar decided, was a diplomat, and a sensible man.

Mrs Marshall, a plump woman dressed in a stockman's coat tied around the waist with string, and with her head swathed in a woollen head square, told them she had seen the tramp that morning as she brought her cows in for milking. 'I'm not absolutely sure it was Bronc.' she said, with a sidelong look at Deepbriar's uniform, worn that morning because of his appearance in court. 'But I'd heard the police were looking for him, so I telephoned the police station as soon as I got back inside.'

'Exactly where did you see him?' Jakes asked.

She answered with a question of her own. 'You're not going to arrest him, are you?'

'No, but we hope he might be able to help us with our enquiries,' Jakes said.

'It's nothing he's done,' Deepbriar explained, seeing the woman was still hesitant. 'He's needed as a witness.'

'Oh, that's all right then. I remember old Bronc coming through here when I was a little girl, I wouldn't want to get him into trouble.' She pointed to a small patch of trees on a nearby hill. 'He was on the track up there. It goes over the top and down on to the Polthrup Road. There's a café, where the lorry drivers go, and there's usually somebody who's prepared to buy a cup of tea for a tramp. At this time of year with the weather being so cold, I'd guess that's where he'd be heading.'

Jakes turned the car around in the farm yard. 'Which way?'

'To the right.' Deepbriar instructed. Suddenly inspired, he added, 'I don't know the roads that well, you'll need to go slow or we'll miss the turn.'

The ABC Café lay on the junction of the Polthrup Road and the new arterial road; an ideal spot to attract the passing trade. Through the haze of steam and cigarette smoke inside, the two officers inspected the clientele. Two lorry drivers sat hunched over plates of sausage and mash, while a man in a grubby trilby and a brown mac sat by the window nursing a large mug; a parcel wrapped in brown paper and tied with string lay on the seat at his side.

'That's not him,' Deepbriar said, disappointed; somehow he'd hoped, against all the odds, that this might be Bronc, alive and well. 'That's Digger Biggins.'

The tramp looked up as the two policemen approached, and gave Deepbriar a toothless smile. 'Howdo, constable. What brings you so far from home?'

'What now?' Deepbriar asked, surreptitiously easing his belt out a hole. They were heading back to Falbrough, having made the best of a bad job by inviting an overjoyed Digger to join them for a plateful of the ABC's choicest offering of sausage, eggs, bacon and fried bread, washed down with plentiful amounts of strong tea.

'Blowed if I know.' Jakes was despondent. 'Let's face it, we've got nowhere. We're looking for Bronc because he just might know something about the abduction of Joe Spraggs, which just might be linked to what happened to Joseph. That case in turn bears some similarity to the disappearance of Tony Pattridge, who vanished nearly a year ago. All we've done is add more mysteries to the ones we already had. We think Sylvester Rudge could be involved, but apart from a few rumours, we've only Mrs Spraggs's word for that.' He shook his head. 'Inspector Stubbs isn't going to be impressed.'

'He's not back until Wednesday,' Deepbriar said consolingly.

'But that's only two days. And we still haven't got hold of the key to the airbase. I managed to speak to somebody at the Ministry this morning. They're waiting for the man who knows who the key holder is, but he won't be back in town until tomorrow night.' They had almost reached Falbrough. With sudden decision Jakes turned off towards Minecliff. 'There's no point waiting, we'll go in through the fence and take another look around. I came prepared this time, I've got some wellingtons in the back.'

Mud clogged their boots and splashed up their legs as they trudged along the headland, past the rusting warning signs and on to Air Ministry land. The airstrip looked bleak and neglected, a grey December sky hanging low above their heads, and a cold wind blowing from the north. They looked into a concrete guard post and descended steep steps to an air raid shelter, then moved on to examine a circular gun emplacement, finding nothing but a roll of tangled barbed wire and a couple of empty beer bottles.

'What about that?' Jakes asked, staring at the mausoleum, prominent on its slight rise. Your friend Joe told you he was shut up in a place with stone walls, didn't he?'

Deepbriar gazed up at the building and shook his head. There were narrow slits right near the top, glazed with panels of stained glass. 'He said there were no windows.'

'It was probably the middle of the night,' Jakes said. 'He wouldn't be able to tell in the dark.'

'The sky was clear,' Deepbriar told him, recalling the starlight as he stood outside the Speckled Goose on the first of November. And by the time the audience left the village hall the moon had risen.

'It wouldn't hurt to take a look, though.' Jakes led the way. The approach to the mausoleum was overgrown with weeds and brambles, but a paved area in front of the door remained clear.

The door, which was decorated with carvings of a bizarre mix of skulls and cherubs, was of solid wood, probably an inch thick. There was a huge lock, only slightly rusty, with a flap that could be swung aside to reveal the keyhole. Jakes took a magnifying glass from his pocket to take a closer look.

'I don't think the lock's been tampered with, though it's clean, no dirt or cobwebs in there, so it could have been opened recently,' Jakes said. He turned slowly, looking at the surrounding weeds and scrubby bushes. 'That bit looks as if it could have been trampled.'

Deepbriar fought his way through the brambles to circle the building. 'No sign of anybody forcing a way in,' he said when he got back to Jakes. 'The windows are too small, even if you could reach them, and it would take a tank to get through these walls.' He bent down and scanned the patch of ground Jakes had indicated. 'Might be animals,' he commented. 'There are deer up here, and plenty of rabbits and foxes.'

'We know somebody had those gates open though, and they brought a vehicle in,' Jakes said. 'Let's suppose they were heading here. Where's the nearest bit of roadway?'

'Over there.' Deepbriar pointed, and they thrust their way through the undergrowth to find the strip of concrete. Several minutes later they had reached no conclusions. If somebody had driven here they had left no obvious tracks, though the two men found plenty of places where the grass had been flattened.

'What's that?' Jakes said suddenly, diving into a patch of brambles. He backed out with a scrap of paper held in his hand.

'Well?' Deepbriar asked eagerly.

Having had a good look at his trophy Jakes handed it to the constable. 'If that's a clue then it's not much of one,' he said, pulling a thorn from his thumb and sucking at the resulting bead of blood.

Deepbriar looked at the piece of paper. It was almost square, about two inches across, totally blank except for the corner where two rough edges showed it had been torn from a bigger sheet. Close to the torn edge was a thick line, joined by a slightly thinner one at right angles. On the very edge of the tear was a circular mark, almost like a black ink blot.

'That's a funny shape, it doesn't look like any letter that I can recognise,' Jakes commented. 'And it's not written on the line. Could be part of a signature I suppose.'

'It's not lined paper,' Deepbriar said. 'Yet it doesn't exactly look hand-written. It reminds me of something, but I can't think what.'

Jakes sighed. 'There's just a chance it means something. Let's see if we can find any more of it.'

They searched until the light began to fail, then gave up and headed back to the car. 'I'll drop you in the village,' Jakes said, 'no need for you to come back to the station.'

'And what do we do tomorrow?' Deepbriar asked.

'I'm having the photograph we got from Mrs Spraggs copied and sent out, and I've got an address for another of Spraggs's friends, I thought I'd go and have a word,' Jakes replied, 'but that doesn't need both of us. What about the mausoleum? We're back to keys again. Any idea who'd be able to open that door?'

'I'll see if I can find out. Of course it could be the same person who's got the key to the gate. Anything else you want me to do?'

'Yes,' Jakes gave a humourless laugh. 'Find Bronc's body, and Spraggs. And while you're about it, catch the villains who robbed Somersons, and ask them if Tony Pattridge was driving that car when it went into the ditch.'

Tracking down the key to the mausoleum proved no easier than finding the one that opened the gates to the airbase. The vicar did his best to be helpful, finding the address of the two elderly ladies who were all that remained of the Abney-Hughes line, but there the trail went cold. They had no idea who held the key, although they were able to give Deepbriar the name of the family's solicitor, which was Kerridge. When the constable traced the firm and telephoned them, it turned out that Mr Kerridge had passed away some three years before, and the two remaining partners were both out. Their secretary promised to call Deepbriar back as soon as one of them returned.

Deepbriar was at a loose end. He turned things over and over in his mind, and found it kept coming back to yet another mystery, as if his subconscious was seeing a link with the cases he and Sergeant Jakes were investigating. Feeling a little guilty, since Bella Emerson was Mary's friend, he set about discovering how her husband had died.

It took several phone calls to locate the right department at the Foreign Office, only to be totally stonewalled by an official who insisted that all such enquiries must be made on form 12/B/54DO. Uncertain of his ground, Deepbriar requested that such a form be sent to him, and obtained a grudging assurance that this would be done.

Feeling sour and bad tempered after his encounter with the civil service, the constable spent a couple of hours on paperwork, then went thankfully through to the kitchen to join Mary for a meal, careful to avoid any mention of the Emersons. After lunch he prowled restlessly around his office, his mind travelling in pointless circles. He sat at his desk and stared at the wall for a while, but that didn't help either. At last the phone rang.

'Minecliff police station,' Deepbriar said, expecting to hear the refined tones of the solicitor's secretary. Instead it was Phyllis Bartle, from the Speckled Goose. 'Thorny, I'm sorry to bother you,' she said, 'I don't suppose you've seen Harry, have you?'

'Harry? No, he hasn't been here.'

'Right. Well, it wasn't likely I suppose.' She sounded uneasy.

'What's up?' Deepbriar asked.

'He went down to the school on his bike, first thing, taking round the crate of soft drinks for the children's Christmas party,' Phyllis said, 'and a bottle of sherry for the staff. He said he had something else to do before lunch, but that he'd definitely be back before twelve to take care of the pub, because me and Don were supposed to be going out.'

Deepbriar looked at the clock. It was a quarter to three.

'I know it's silly to worry,' the woman went on, 'but it's not like Harry to be late, not without letting us know. You know what us mothers are like, we start imagining accidents.'

'I'd have heard by now if he'd been knocked off his bike,' Deepbriar told her. 'I'm sure he'll turn up soon. You don't know what it was, this other thing he wanted to do? He didn't give you any hints?'

'No. I thought he was a bit funny last night though, at closing time, but Don says I'm imagining things.'

'Funny in what way?'

'Sort of excited,' she said. 'Like he was that time he came out to help you look for the man who'd been up to mischief at Ferdy Quinn's. That's why I thought I'd try phoning you.'

At the school Mrs Harris greeted the constable cheerfully. 'No truants today,' the headmistress said. 'You obviously did the trick with Kenny Pratt.' Her cheeks dimpled in a smile. 'I hope you didn't give him nightmares.'

'I'm the one with the nightmares,' Deepbriar replied, only half joking. 'All I did was give him some tea cards with sports stars on, in return for a promise.'

The headmistress shook her head. 'I thought I'd tried everything with that boy. The workings of the infant mind never cease to amaze me. So, if you're not after my reformed truant, what can I do for you?'

Deepbriar explained about Harry missing his lunch-time duty behind the bar of the Speckled Goose.

'He left here as the children were coming out of assembly,' Mrs Harris said, 'that would be about nine thirty. I offered him a cup of tea but he was in a hurry.'

'He didn't mention where he was going?'

She shook her head. 'I don't think he was going straight home, but that's all I can tell you. I didn't watch him leave.'

'So we don't even know which direction he turned,' Deepbriar mused, 'not much help.'

'I'm sorry. But surely you don't think anything's happened to him? He might have got a puncture.'

'I expect it's something like that.' Deepbriar agreed. But it only took a few minutes to mend a puncture. And if his bike had more serious problems there were buses; whatever happened Harry should have been home by now. The constable thanked the headmistress and left, standing outside the school and looking up and down the road, as if it could tell him where the errant Harry had gone. His eye caught sight of the solitary house on the hill. Oliver. The boy kept watch from his windows most of the day, and he might at least be able to confirm if Harry had turned towards Falbrough, or taken the Possington road.

As he cycled up the hill, Deepbriar had an unpleasant sensation in his stomach which had nothing to do with his digestive system. Harry might have gone off to do a bit of amateur detecting, and got himself into trouble; calling on Oliver Rose could be a waste of precious time. But what else could he do? The possibility that Harry was to be added to their list of missing persons was too awful to contemplate.

'Mr Deepbriar! You must have known I was thinking about you,' Mrs Rose said, almost dragging the constable through the door. 'Oliver's got something to tell you.'

Chapter Nineteen

'I don't have long,' Deepbriar began, as Mrs Rose ushered him upstairs to Oliver's room. 'I came to ask if Oliver was watching the road at half past nine this morning.'

She paused to look back at him, bemused. 'Half past nine? I don't think so, because the nurse was here until nearly ten. It was after that.'

'What was after that?' it was Deepbriar's turn to be baffled.

She smiled at him as she opened the door to her son's room. 'Let him tell you. I was so relieved, I'd been really worried, not knowing ... Oliver, look who's here.'

'I saw you coming up the lane, Mr Deepbriar.' Oliver was sitting in his usual chair, with the telescope on his lap. 'You didn't look nearly as happy as the other day.'

'No, I've got something on my mind,' Deepbriar said.

The boy nodded, very solemn. 'Like me,' he said, 'when I didn't tell you about the black car. I'm very sorry.'

Deepbriar stared at him. 'Are you saying you saw the black car? The one that knocked old Bronc down?'

Oliver nodded again. 'And I've seen it other times, too. I saw it today.'

'It was about one o'clock,' Mrs Rose broke in, 'I came up to sit with Oliver so we could eat our dinner together, and I happened to look out of the window as this car was coming down the road from Falbrough. At first I wasn't sure Oliver had noticed it, but then I realised he'd gone white as a sheet, just like he did that day you were here. Of course, when I thought about it, the whole thing made sense.'

'What made sense?' Deepbriar asked, totally at sea. 'What was so special about this car then?'

'It was a hearse,' Mrs Rose said.

'But ...' the constable began.

'It all started when Oliver was staying in Falbrough hospital for a few days,' Mrs Rose explained. 'In June. There was a boy in the same ward who was a bit older than Oliver. He used to like pushing the other boys around in their wheelchairs.'

Oliver nodded vigorously. 'One day he took me down the main corridor, where we're not allowed, and I was afraid we'd get in trouble, but Brian said it would be all right, and he'd make sure nobody saw us. I couldn't stop him anyway, so there wasn't much point arguing.'

Mrs Rose tutted loudly, but Deepbriar waved her to silence. 'Go on, Oliver.'

'When we got to the end the door was open and we could see outside, and there was this big black car with a door at the back.' He stared down at the floor. 'Brian said it was really unlucky, seeing that sort of car. He said it meant that somebody was going to die, and that whatever happened I wasn't to tell anyone.'

'You see, that's how he got the silly idea in his head,' Mrs Rose said. 'A lot of superstitious nonsense. He's been worrying about it ever since.'

'Let me get this straight,' Deepbriar said. 'The day I came to ask you about, at the beginning of November. You saw one of these cars then?'

Oliver nodded. He reached for his notebook and leafed through the pages. 'I saw it on the first of November, and again on the second,' he said, showing the constable the page. 'I didn't like to write it down because it was unlucky, so I just put this instead,' and he pointed to a roughly drawn skull and crossbones.

'And you saw the same car on the day your mother and father went out and left you with the nurse? Not just one that was similar, exactly the same one?'

'I think so. And today, at dinner-time.'

'Where was it going?' Deepbriar could hear his pulse beating hard in his head.

'Towards the village. It was funny, because it went behind the trees and we didn't see it come out again.' He pointed, then looked at his mother. 'We thought it must have stopped some-where, though there aren't any houses along there.'

'No, there aren't,' Deepbriar agreed. But there was the lane that led up to the aerodrome. His mind was leaping to half a dozen conclusions at once, but he forced himself to smile down at the boy. 'So, you're not afraid of this car any more?'

'No.' Oliver spoke decisively, though with an uncertain expression in his eyes.

'There's no need to be,' Deepbriar told him, 'your mother's quite right, what Brian told you is just a silly superstition, left over from a time when people believed in the evil eye, and witches, and that sort of nonsense. You're much too sensible to bother with that. I don't suppose you took down the number this time?' He finished hopefully.

The boy shook his head. 'I couldn't see it.'

'Never mind. You've been really helpful. But there's something else I have to ask you. Have you seen Harry Bartle today? He'd have been on his bike, probably coming away from the village.'

'No, I'm sorry.'

Deepbriar turned to the boy's mother. 'How about you, Mrs Rose?'

'No, I don't think I've seen Harry for a couple of weeks. Is it important?'

As he pedalled furiously back to Minecliff, Deepbriar's mind was racing. It couldn't be a coincidence that the hearse had been seen again, and on the very day that it seemed yet another man had vanished. Deepbriar refused to think about the possibility that Harry Bartle might be dead; it was too much like a scenario from a Mitch O'Hara story. Things like that couldn't happen in real life.

Deepbriar turned to practicalities. There was only one funeral car in Falbrough, belonging to Aubrey Crimmon, but there were two undertakers in Belston, one of them a big firm which had at least three cars. Oliver had thought it was the same car he'd seen each time; on the day of Colin Pattridge's funeral, it would have been Aubrey Crimmon taking the old farmer to his final resting place, but one hearse looked very much like another, he couldn't be sure the boy wasn't mistaken.

The use of a hearse explained how Joe had vanished; it was an ideal way to move a man around. Once he was unconscious he could be hidden inside a coffin, and nobody would suspect a thing. Anyone seeing the hearse might wonder who had died, but Joe had been abducted late on Saturday afternoon, and returned in the middle of Sunday morning when most people were in church, or still enjoying a leisurely breakfast. Only Bronc had seen the car at close quarters, and then he too had disappeared.

Reaching the police house, Deepbriar left his bicycle by the kerb and ran indoors, but when he picked up the telephone, intending to call Sergeant Jakes and request assistance, he was greeted by the voice of Miss Strathway at the local exchange.

'I'm very sorry, Constable Deepbriar,' she said, 'but I can only connect you to numbers within the village. Some calls are coming in from other exchanges, but we've been having trouble since Saturday evening. I'm waiting for the engineers, they shouldn't be long.'

Resisting the temptation to swear, Deepbriar asked to be put through to the pub, and spoke to a worried-sounding Phyllis, who confirmed that Harry still hadn't turned up.

'Was he talking to anyone in particular in the bar last night?' Deepbriar asked.

'It was fairly quiet,' she said. 'Just a few regulars.'

'Joe Spraggs wasn't in? Or Peter Brook?'

'No. Let me think. Harry had a word with Old Bob, and Alan. Will Minter called in about eight o'clock and bought them a round, but he didn't stay long. Oh, and Bert Bunyard was here, he was drinking a bit more than his usual, said he was celebrating, though he didn't say what. He stayed till closing time. Come to think of it, Harry bought him a drink, just before Don called last orders.'

'Maybe that's it.' Deepbriar recalled the way Bunyard had clammed up when he'd asked him about Bronc. At the time he'd let it pass, thinking Bert was merely trying to get his own back after they'd tricked him into making a confession. 'I'd better have another word with Bert.'

'Is that where Harry went this morning? To see Bert Bunyard?' Phyllis asked.

'I don't think so. Try not to worry, I'm sure Harry will turn up,' Deepbriar said, with a confidence he didn't feel. 'Just be sure and let me know when he does.'

The constable spoke to the operator again and asked her to call him as soon as the line was repaired. 'It's urgent,' he said, resisting the urge to tell her it was a matter of life and death; since he'd learnt of Harry's disappearance everything had taken on an air of unreality. It was like one of those dreams where every attempt to wake up simply led him deeper into fantasy. 'I have to contact the police station at Falbrough.'

Once he'd put the receiver down Deepbriar went in search of his wife, and told her what he'd learnt, jotting down the main points in his notebook and tearing out the page to give her. 'Miss Strathway will call as soon as she can get through to town, and when she does, you have to speak to somebody at the station, preferably Sergeant Jakes, but the desk sergeant will do if he isn't there. I'm going up to the aerodrome.'

'Not on your own?' Mary protested. 'It will be dark soon, what use will one man be if there's a gang of criminals up there?'

'I can't just sit here doing nothing,' he said, bending to give her a kiss. 'Don't worry, I'll be fine. It may all be a storm in a teacup anyway. If Harry comes home in the meantime Phyllis will come and tell you, and you can send somebody to find me.'

Having fetched a couple of tools from his shed, and checked that he had a spare battery for his torch, Deepbriar took to his bike again. A fine drizzle had started. As the constable wheeled across the village street he saw a hunched figure leaving the village shop, an ancient canvas bag swinging from one hand. Maybe luck was on his side after all; it was Bert Bunyard. The constable swooped, coming to a stop in the farmer's path.

'What you doin'?' Bunyard demanded. 'A'most 'ad me over you did.'

'I'll do more than knock you over, Bert, if you don't come clean. You're going to tell me what you saw up at the old aerodrome when Bronc went missing.'

'An' if I don't?' Bunyard asked belligerently.

'If you don't,' Deepbriar said, dropping his voice, 'I'll tell the magistrate you've been over at Quinn's farm again, and we'll have you safely locked up in Falbrough nick before you can say "knife". And when your case comes to court I'll see you put away for a couple of years, no matter what it takes.'

Bunyard's face darkened. 'Bliddy coppers,' he muttered, 'can't bliddy trust nobody these days.'

'All you have to do is tell me what you know about Bronc, and about that hearse.'

'If you already know then what you askin' me for?' the man growled.

Deepbriar's heart sank. He had almost hoped Bert would explode his theories. 'Because I need to know exactly what you told Harry Bartle last night.'

Bunyard spat into the gutter. 'Young 'arry's always ready to lick your boots, why don't you ask 'im?'

'Because I'm asking you,' Deepbriar hissed, 'and if you don't stop messing me about then you'd better make sure your boy Humphrey can look after himself for a good long spell, because you won't be there to take the beasts to market or do the shopping for him.'

'Didn't tell him much,' Bunyard said sullenly. 'Only that I saw them Crimmon brothers in that black carcass carrier, drivin' across the airstrip the day Bronc went missin'.'

'What, Cyril Crimmon was with Aubrey?'

'Not that long thin drink o' water,' Bunyard said scornfully, 'the younger one. Barney. 'im that was always gettin' in trouble when 'e was a kid.' He gave an unpleasant smirk. 'That mother o' theirs was no better'n she should have been, the only boy what looked like 'is father was the first. By the time Barney turned up 'er old man was goin' barmy, an' 'e never sired a great lump like Aubrey, neither. Funny though, them three was always close, looked out for each other, like.'

It was as if all the cogs of a piece of machinery suddenly fell into place and began to turn smoothly and soundlessly. Barney Crimmon! That was the name Sergeant Cosgough had been trying to think of, the name of the man always hanging around Sylvester Rudge, trying to impress him.

'So you told Harry about seeing the Crimmon brothers. Anything else?'

'Might o' mentioned that other car, that little red un in Gadwell Lane what you asked me about. Reckon that belonged to Barney, though I didn't see 'im clear. Wearin' a fancy coat 'e was, fawn colour, with a soft brown 'at.'

The description fitted that of the stranger seen talking to Bronc in the porch at the Speckled Goose on the Monday, the last day he was seen. Barney Crimmon could have been finding out where Bronc planned to sleep that night.

'You'd better be telling me the truth, Bert, or you'll be sorry.'

'Fine one to talk about the truth, you are,' Bert said, 'makin' threats against an innocent man. I could report you.'

Deepbriar didn't respond, getting back on his bike and turning away.

'Don't you go tellin' no lies about me!' Bunyard shouted after him, the words echoing in the empty village street.

The afternoon was already darkening into night. As Deepbriar turned towards the aerodrome he felt a shiver run up his back; who better to dispose of a body than an undertaker, given their access to graves.... The thought hit him so suddenly he almost fell off his bike. Who was most likely to have the key to a mausoleum if it was no longer in the hands of the family?

Deepbriar went directly to the gates, intent on not wasting time. He didn't have any tools powerful enough to cut through the chain that held the gate shut, but a few minutes hard work with a pair of pliers provided him with a hole in the wire fence. Once he'd wheeled his bike through he paused to study the ground inside the gate. There were new tyre tracks in the mud. He went back to the gap in the fence and pushed the edges of mesh roughly back together, with some vague idea that it would be better if he left no obvious signs of his visit. Swinging his leg back over the saddle, Deepbriar set a direct course for the mausoleum.

It was full night now. He was reliant on the dim beam from his cycle lamp to show the way as he pedalled along the cracked concrete road, and he wondered what had happened to Harry's bright new battery lamp. Presumably his bike had been left somewhere, like Joe's, but where? Had Harry gone to Belston looking for Barney Crimmon, or to the undertakers in Falbrough?

A ghostly white shape flickered into the beam of light, and Deepbriar bit down an exclamation of alarm. It was a barn owl, flying low. It screeched as it swooped away towards the rows of Nissen huts to his left. Deepbriar braked. The bird had come from directly ahead; maybe it had been disturbed in some way. He turned off his lamp and for a few moments he could see nothing, then gradually his eyes adjusted, and he could make out the pale surface of the road. Cautiously, aware of every sound the bicycle made, even the slight hiss of its tyres on the concrete, he pedalled on.

The mausoleum appeared first as a faintly grey patch against the dark sky. When he was a couple of hundred yards from it, Deepbriar dismounted and pushed the bike out of sight behind a mound of brambles, to continue on foot. He approached slowly, carrying his torch in his left hand, finger poised on the switch, while his right was gripped tight around his truncheon.

There was no car, black or otherwise, parked anywhere near the mausoleum. No sound disturbed the silence; some instinct told Deepbriar that he was alone. He turned on the torch and inspected the ground beneath his feet. The area he and Jakes had examined the day before had been trampled since their visit.

The grotesque carvings on the door looked menacing in the flickering torch light, the skulls staring sightlessly from blank sockets, the cherubs leering unpleasantly at him. Deepbriar shone the torch at the lock. It hadn't been tampered with, but there was no way of telling if it had been opened recently. He pushed the cover from the keyhole and bent closer.

A sound, as terrible and yet as sweet as any he'd heard in his life, came faintly from behind the locked door. Harry Bartle's tuneless tenor was murdering a popular song. It took a few moments to recognise it as an attempt at 'Tea for Two'.

Deepbriar put his mouth to the keyhole and shouted. 'Harry!' The caterwauling stopped, and he shouted again, then shone the torch through the keyhole, hoping there was no flap to obscure it on the inside.

'Mr Deepbriar?' Relief and incredulity in his voice, Harry shouted back. He must have moved closer, for the words were plain and clear. 'Is that really you?'

'It's me Harry. Are you all right?'

'I am now. I never thought....' He paused, and when he went on the tremor had left his voice. 'You've got them then? You know what happened?'

'Only what I've guessed. Tell me how you got here,' Deepbriar ordered. A further look at the door confirmed what he and Jakes had agreed on the day before. Without the key or a sledge hammer he had no hope of getting Harry out. He turned off the torch, half an ear cocked for sounds from the direction of the gate. 'And make it quick.'

'It was Bert Bunyard. He had a bit to drink last night, and it loosened his tongue. He told me he'd seen Aubrey Crimmon and his brother up here in a hearse, the night Bronc disappeared.'

'You should have come and told me.' Deepbriar said angrily.

'I know. I thought about it, but I wasn't sure if Bert was telling me the truth. Besides, they might have had a legitimate reason for coming here. Crimmon is an undertaker, for all I knew he could be responsible for taking care of this place. Anyway, there was something else Bert told me, about a car that he'd seen parked in Gadwell Lane. He thought it might belong to Barney Crimmon, so I decided I'd find out if that was true, and if it was then I'd have something definite to tell you.'

Harry made a sound halfway between a laugh and a sob. 'I didn't think about it being risky. When Mr Crimmon taught us he'd never even take a ruler to us, no matter how much we played up in his lessons. We always reckoned he was soft.'

'You went to see *Cyril* Crimmon?' Deepbriar was confused. 'But he wasn't the one Bert saw in the car.'

'I know. That was the point. Anyway, I knew Mr Crimmon's first lessons always started at eleven when I was at school, so I took a chance that he still started work late, and dropped in just before he left home. I'd got an excuse all worked out, because the last time I saw him, he told me I ought to give up singing and try to learn an instrument instead. I was going to ask where I could find somebody to teach me to play the flute.'

Deepbriar suddenly remembered the scrap of paper Jakes had found; he knew now what it was. It had been torn from the corner of some sheet music, and nearly every time he saw Cyril Crimmon, the man had a bundle of scores clutched to his chest. Unlikely as it seemed, the music master had been here as well. Whatever was going on, he was involved.

'So what happened?' Deepbriar asked.

'Well, he was getting ready to go out when I arrived, and we stood talking at the door for a bit. He told me he'd find out about tutors if I was really interested. When a car went by it gave me the chance to ask about his brother, and whether it was him I'd seen driving an Austin Healey. He looked at me a bit strange, then he sort of shook himself and asked if I'd like to come in for a cup of tea. I thought it was odd, but since he hadn't told me about the car I said yes.'

'He'd got you sussed,' Deepbriar hazarded.

'Yes.' Harry sighed. 'I couldn't get him to talk about his brother at all, let alone the car. It's all so easy when Dick Bland and Mitch O'Hara do it. Mr Crimmon just kept talking about music, and whether I might do better with the piano instead of the flute, then he started telling me how much he enjoyed playing the organ at the church. That was when he mentioned you, saying that he knew we were friends.'

It was the constable's turn to sigh. 'And that didn't ring any alarm bells? Come on, Harry, I didn't think you were that slow.'

'Sorry, Mr Deepbriar. I made a real hash of things. I sat in the parlour like a proper nitwit while he was making the tea in the kitchen. He brought two cups in and gave one to me. I don't think

I drank more than half of it, then suddenly I felt sort of sick and sleepy.'

'And the next thing you knew, you were shut up here in the dark.'

'Yes. It's the mausoleum, isn't it? The one belonging to the Abney-Hughes family. I wasn't sure, it's pitch dark, but I fumbled my way around a bit, and I could feel these great stone coffins.' He paused. 'I don't know what it is, but you wouldn't believe the stench in here.'

Deepbriar bit his lip. He'd believe it all right. Harry had probably been lucky not to fall over old Bronc's body while he was exploring.

'Can't you get this door open, Mr Deepbriar?' There was a sudden urgency in Harry's voice. 'They'll be back, won't they? Mr Crimmon and his brothers?'

'I'm afraid they will, and no, I can't see any way of getting you out. I brought a few tools, but nothing that will get through an inch of solid oak. Try not to worry, Harry, there'll be reinforcements coming from Falbrough.' Childishly, he crossed his fingers as he spoke, either for luck or to ward off the evil of telling Harry something he scarcely knew to be true. 'It's odd, there must have been a bit of daylight left when you came to, and there are windows in the top of these walls. Even now, the sky isn't completely dark.'

'It's pitch-black in here,' Harry repeated. 'I suppose ...'

Deepbriar didn't hear what Harry supposed, because at that moment a dim light showed in the distance, and there was the throaty rumble of a motor. Somebody was coming. Jakes must have got his message. Deepbriar breathed a sigh of relief. But then he realised that the car was showing only sidelights. Whoever was driving didn't want to be seen from the village.

'Harry,' he said urgently, 'I think it's them. If we're going to get you out of there I can't do anything until they've got the door open. It might be an idea if you hide yourself. See if you can get out of sight.' Without waiting to hear the young man's reply, Deepbriar crept away from the door and around the side of the mausoleum. He stood with his back to the stones, trying to keep his breathing slow and silent, and listening to the growl of the car's engine as it drew closer.

There was a crunching sound as the car's wheels pulled off the roadway, then the motor stopped. A hinge creaked as the car door opened. Hurried footsteps sounded, muffled by the trampled turf. Deepbriar leant cautiously from his hiding place until he could see the car; it wasn't a hearse, but a sports car, left with the driver's door standing wide open. It seemed that the youngest of the Crimmon brothers had come alone.

Deepbriar relaxed as he heard a key inserted into the mausoleum's lock. He'd soon have Harry safely back home; one man he could deal with. Flexing his grip on his truncheon and checking that his finger was ready on the switch of his torch, Deepbriar pushed away from the wall. Something snagged hard at his leg and he stumbled, his arms windmilling wildly. He pulled free from the clutches of the brambles, but he had wasted several precious seconds, and his quarry was already out of sight.

From inside the mausoleum came a thud and a muffled cry, then the sound of something falling. His heart in his mouth, Deepbriar rushed the doorway. He had expected Crimmon to be carrying a light but he found himself facing an impenetrable darkness. With a flick of his finger he turned on his torch. The beam caught Barney Crimmon full in the face, making him squint, dragging his attention from Harry Bartle, who lay on the floor at his feet.

The torch light reflected dully off something in Crimmon's hand. A knife. An inch of its tip was stained red. Halted for no more than a moment by the interruption, the man lunged towards Harry's unmoving form.

Chapter Twenty

'No!' Deepbriar shouted desperately. 'Police! You're under arrest, Crimmon. Drop that knife.'

A slow grin lifted the corners of Crimmon's mouth. 'I don't think so.' He was standing right over Harry and his arm drew back for the fatal blow. In response Deepbriar launched himself, swinging the truncheon wildly, terrified that he'd been too slow and praying that his attack would force Crimmon to abandon Harry.

There was a split second when it seemed that the knife must stab down into the helpless man between them, but to Deepbriar's relief Crimmon straightened. 'Interfering bloody flatfoot,' he snarled. 'You first then. Come and get it.'

Deepbriar moved to one side, and as Crimmon followed, lured away from Harry Bartle, he turned off the torch. Moving like lightning, Deepbriar kicked back with his foot, slamming the heavy door shut. Total darkness descended and he dodged to the right, light-footed despite his bulk.

Something thudded solidly against Deepbriar's left arm, just below the shoulder. He grunted, flailing with the truncheon at the place he thought Crimmon must be, but encountering only thin air. Deepbriar took a cautious step, silent as a cat, then he paused, listening. There was no sound, he couldn't even hear Crimmon's breathing.

Feeling faintly ridiculous, Deepbriar stretched his arms out in front of him, hoping they would impede Crimmon's aim and save him from a fatal body blow; he had to put some distance between himself and the knife before he turned the torch on again.

His flesh cringing at each step, expecting the knife to strike him at any second, Deepbriar crept forward, setting each foot down with exaggerated care, hoping he wouldn't trip over Harry and give himself away. Completely disorientated, he had no idea which direction he was taking. Three steps and he was still alive and untouched. Four. Maybe he was going to live after all.

Ears straining, he heard faint rustlings and scrapings echoing round the mausoleum's high roof then abruptly a different sound intruded into the silence, a sound muffled by the thick wooden door. Another car was coming.

Deepbriar kept moving until he encountered a wall. He set his back to it, hauled in a breath and turned on the torch. Barney Crimmon stood with his back to him, a few yards away, head cocked as if he was listening to the approaching car. The man snapped round as the light came on.

'That will be half a dozen officers from Falbrough,' Deepbriar said, taking a wary step back towards him. 'Don't make things any worse for yourself, Crimmon. Put the knife down.'

Outside, doors slammed and there was the sound of footsteps. Two men at least, Deepbriar thought; he was glad Jakes hadn't come alone, things could still turn nasty if the other Crimmon brothers arrived. The door opened and a bright light shone in, eclipsing that held by the constable, and almost blinding him.

'I'm glad you came, sergeant,' Deepbriar said, squinting into the light. Silhouetted against the glare was a slight figure, too small to be a police officer. The man paused for only a second then crouched down to examine Harry Bartle, who still lay huddled on the floor.

Behind the newcomer was a much larger man. He stepped inside to set the lantern down before stepping back to block the doorway. Deepbriar's heart sank. He was looking at the solid black-clad figure of Aubrey Crimmon.

'About time,' Barney said. He smirked at Deepbriar. 'Looks like I'm the one with the reinforcements, constable.'

'What I told you is true, more police are on the way,' Deepbriar said. 'If you give yourself up before they get here I'll put in a good word for you at the trial.'

'You're bluffing,' Barney Crimmon said. 'But you've got nerve, I'll grant you. The kid too, trying to jump me from behind the door like that.' He scanned the floor and bent to pick up the torch Harry must have knocked from his hand. He tossed it to the undertaker, who stood silent and motionless at the door. 'Stupid of course, but brave.'

'If you've killed him ...' Deepbriar grated.

'He's still alive,' Cyril Crimmon said, straightening up from beside Harry.

'That can be remedied,' his younger brother said, the blade reflecting shards of rainbow light as he tossed the weapon casually from one hand to the other.

'No!' Cyril protested. 'He's hardly more than a boy. You can't.'

From the doorway, Aubrey spoke for the first time. 'You weren't supposed to come here, Barney. We told you it was over, you should have gone while you had the chance.'

'I'm going nowhere.' His gaze flickered over each of his older brothers in turn. 'You really think that would solve anything? You're both in this as deep as I am. Were you planning to make a run for it too? I suppose you were just going to let this little meddler go, like the other one. If you'd let me deal with Joe Spraggs in the first place there wouldn't have been any of this bother.'

'He'd done nothing,' Cyril said, sounding terrified. 'Please Barney, it's time to go.'

'Run if you want,' Deepbriar said, 'but you won't get far. Either way, there's no point killing Harry, because we're on to you, Crimmon. We know you've already killed three men.'

'Three?' Barney Crimmon shook his head mockingly. 'You've got it all wrong. I didn't kill Tony. The fool got thrown through the windscreen when he put that car in the ditch. He broke his stupid neck.'

'We're wasting time.' Aubrey Crimmon put a hand into his inside pocket. 'I thought we might find you here, so I brought some money, Barney. We'll keep these two out of commission for a few hours while you get clear. Drive to the coast and find a boat that's crossing the channel.'

'I told you, I'm not going.' The younger man, the knife still in his hand, moved towards Harry. 'We'll clear up here and nobody will know any different. Out of the way, Cyril.'

'There are more police on their way,' Deepbriar said urgently. 'Killing us isn't going to help you.'

'If they were coming they'd be here by now,' Aubrey said, 'but he's right, killing them won't solve anything.'

Barney ignored him, his left arm extended to push Cyril out of the way.

'No!' The musician's long fingers clutched at his brother's sleeve. 'You can't!'

'Got no stomach for blood, have you, Cyril,' Barney said,

easily thrusting him aside. 'It's a good job we didn't need your help getting rid of the tramp.'

'Aubrey,' Cyril pleaded, 'stop him.'

The undertaker hesitated, and seeing his chance, Deepbriar launched himself across the five yards that separated him from Barney Crimmon, raising his left arm, surprised to find how heavy the torch had become in the last few minutes. Deepbriar dodged Aubrey's belated grab at him and plunged on, as if intent on bringing the torch down on Barney's head, distracting him from the weapon in his other hand. The man ducked expertly aside, his knife arm sweeping round, aiming to slice up between Deepbriar's ribs to find his heart.

The truncheon came ramming through in a powerful swing, to catch Crimmon full in the face. It smashed his front teeth and his nose, sending a spectacular spray of blood arcing across to hit the horrified Cyril, who shrieked and flinched back to cower against the wall.

Deepbriar's momentum carried him on, and for a heart-stopping split second he was staring death in the face. The torch slid from his fingers. Crimmon's stabbing blow was still coming, but Deepbriar's luck held. Encountering the thick leather of Deepbriar's belt beneath his greatcoat, the blade slid upwards. It sliced through every stitch of his clothing but barely grazed his flesh.

As Aubrey Crimmon leapt to grasp him from behind the constable delivered another blow, this time hitting Barney's elbow with a bone-jarring stroke that knocked the knife from his hand.

'Leave him alone!' the big man had an arm round the constable's neck, jerking his head back. 'You leave my little brother alone!'

Deepbriar choked, the truncheon flying from his grasp. He took hold of Aubrey's arm, but it felt like a bar of iron, solid and immovable beneath his clutching fingers as it crushed his windpipe. Time slowed. Deepbriar's whole existence was suddenly centred on the need to keep breathing, to somehow drag air into his lungs. It was as if he stood outside himself, watching his silent struggle for survival, while Aubrey Crimmon increased the pressure on his neck. Calm, almost detached as the strength ebbed from him, the constable knew that he was losing. A black void lay in wait, only seconds away. And after that, death.

'That's enough.' Jakes's voice echoed round the mausoleum.

Through a haze speckled with bright spots of light, Deepbriar saw the space around him suddenly filled with blue-clad men. Two of them pulled the undertaker away from him, and Deepbriar slumped against the flat top of a huge stone coffin, gulping in air. More officers had grabbed Barney Crimmon, but there was no fight left in him, and he yelped in pain when they touched his injured arm. Jakes bent briefly over Harry Bartle, and gave swift orders to another of his men.

Recovering a little, Deepbriar pushed himself upright, and the heavy slab he'd been leaning on moved, stone grating against stone; it wasn't properly bedded down. Straightening up, he became aware of the terrible stench Harry had mentioned. There was a narrow gap between the coffin and the lid, and the side of the sarcophagus was smeared with a rust-coloured stain.

'Look,' Deepbriar said, beckoning Jakes.

With help from a uniformed constable the two men eased the coffin lid aside a few inches. The smell was overpowering, and Jakes gagged, turning away.

'Bring that light,' Deepbriar ordered, and a constable obeyed, handing the lantern to him. Using his right hand to pull aside the dirty sack that had been exposed when they moved the lid, Deepbriar held the light high in his left, and found himself looking into a pair of staring eyes. He'd never seen the man alive, but he knew they'd found Joseph Spraggs.

It was suddenly very hard to hold on to the lantern. He needed to grasp it more firmly because it had become very slippery, but his fingers were reluctant to grip, and his arm felt weak. With something like amazement Deepbriar watched fresh blood dripping freely on to Spraggs's dead face. He looked at the deep rent in the sleeve of his coat, and the big damp stain that surrounded it. Only then did the stab wound below his shoulder begin to throb with pain.

'You're a lucky man,' Jakes said, as he wound a makeshift bandage round Deepbriar's arm.

'That was skill, sergeant,' Deepbriar said lightly, trying not to wince as Jakes tied a knot. 'Pure skill.'

'I wasn't talking about this, I was talking about your wife. She's one in a million. She sent me the message that got us out here in time to save your neck.' Jakes nodded grimly. 'Literally, as it happened.'

'I told Mary to call you as soon as the telephone line was repaired.'

'Yes, but it wasn't. Mrs Deepbriar had the sense not to wait. She sent a young boy on his bike. Came dashing into the station as if his pants were on fire. Lad by the name of Kenny Pratt, I expect you know him.'

'Indeed I do,' the constable replied, suppressing a grin. Kenny would be expecting a good few tea cards when he learnt he'd saved two people's lives. That thought brought him back to more important matters. 'How's Harry?' he asked.

'Showing signs of coming round. He's lying in the back of the hearse, Constable Giddens is keeping an eye on him while we wait for the ambulance. My guess is, he tried to jump out of the way when Crimmon stabbed him, and his head hit the wall. The knife didn't do much damage. He's got a good strong pulse and his breathing's normal, I doubt if he'll have anything worse than a bad headache in the morning.'

'Thank the Lord for that,' Deepbriar said fervently. 'I'd never have forgiven myself if he'd got himself killed. Maybe this will cure his enthusiasm for amateur detection.'

'He's the one who didn't grow tall enough to join the force?' Jakes hazarded.

'That's him.'

Jakes grinned. 'Then there could be a better cure. They've confirmed the new regulations. He can apply to become a police officer in a couple of months time.'

When the ambulance arrived to take Harry Bartle and Barney Crimmon to hospital, the latter under guard, Deepbriar refused point blank to go with them. 'I want to be here when they lift Spraggs out,' he said. 'Please, sergeant.'

Jakes sighed. He had sent for Inspector Stubbs, and was expecting him to arrive at any time, probably with the police doctor. He didn't think either of them would approve of him allowing Deepbriar to stay, but it was thanks to the constable that they'd just arrested three men, at least one of them a murderer. 'All right. But you go back to Falbrough in the next available car and get that wound stitched.'

They didn't have long to wait. By six o'clock the lid had been removed from the last resting place of Marmaduke Abney-Hughes, to reveal that he had been sharing the great carved sarcophagus with three uninvited guests. Beneath Spraggs's body were the remains of old Bronc and Tony Pattridge.

'You knew we'd find them here,' Jakes said quietly.

'I thought it was likely,' Deepbriar replied.

'I don't blame you for wanting to stay and see the case through to the end,' Inspector Stubbs said, 'but you'd better get off to the hospital now.'

Deepbriar nodded, too weary to explain; it hadn't just been a matter of professional pride. Old Bronc had been a solitary man, but it seemed right that somebody who'd known him should be there at that moment.

'Are you sure you're fit to be on duty, constable?' Inspector Stubbs looked at Deepbriar quizzically. 'Not that we're sorry to see you. Another two men went down with the flu yesterday, and I'm due at Belston again this afternoon.'

Behind the Inspector's back Sergeant Jakes grinned at Deepbriar and lifted a cheerful thumb; Stubbs's absence would leave him in charge again.

'I'm fine, sir,' Deepbriar insisted, gently patting the sling he wore. 'The wound's been stitched. As long as I don't try any physical jerks with my arm for a few days I'm sure I can make myself useful.' He picked up a pen. 'I'm right handed, I could take notes,' he offered.

Stubbs nodded. 'Jakes told me you wanted to be in on the interview with Cyril Crimmon. We've got nothing at all out of Aubrey, and Barney's not been exactly forthcoming either. Of course we've got a pretty good case against them, now we've got the bodies, not to mention catching them about to add you to their list of victims. Still, we're hoping Cyril's going to spill the beans.'

Cyril Crimmon had never been a big man, but he seemed to have shrunk even more in the few hours since Deepbriar had last seen him. He didn't look up as the three officers walked in, his gaze fixed on the table top between the fingers of his long hands.

'What do you know about the death of Anthony Pattridge?' Inspector Stubbs asked, once the preliminaries were out of the way. Crimmon looked surprised, as if this wasn't the question he'd expected.

'Barney didn't kill him. Nobody did, it was an accident. He was driving too fast and the car skidded, and when it hit the side of the road he was thrown through the windscreen.'

'How do you know all this? Were you involved in the robbery at Somersons?'

The music teacher shook his head. 'No. Barney was. He told me what had happened later. He'd had an idea that Aubrey could get rid of the body by putting it in a grave the night before a funeral, burying it so the coffin would go on top, but Aubrey thought that was too risky. He suggested the mausoleum instead. They came to see me, bringing the body with them in the hearse, and asked for the key.'

'You had the key?' Jakes asked, surprised.

'Yes. Rupert Abney-Hughes was a friend of mine. When he was lost at sea his great aunts asked me to wind up his estate. That included taking responsibility for the mausoleum.' His eyes took on a distant look. 'At first I wanted nothing to do with Barney's plan, but then he offered me money. A large sum of money. I found I couldn't refuse.'

Stubbs nodded, as if this revelation confirmed his suspicions regarding human nature.

'Sir?' Deepbriar said tentatively. 'May I ask a question?'

'Go ahead.'

'What did you do with the money, Mr Crimmon?'

The musician gave him a faint smile. 'I think you know,' he said. 'I had the organ repaired. I'd already raised nearly two thousand pounds, but it had been incredibly hard. Getting the rest together would have taken years, I'd have been lucky to live that long. You must admit, it was money well spent.'

Stubbs looked at Deepbriar, who quickly explained.

'That doesn't excuse what you did,' the inspector told Crimmon, 'ill-gotten gains don't become legitimate just because you use them for a good cause.'

Crimmon sighed. 'I know. Although if I'd done nothing more I don't think I'd judge myself too harshly. I know young Pattridge died when he was on the run from the police, but all I did was help to hide the body. I never thought Barney would be capable of murder.'

'How did you get involved with the disappearance of Joe Spraggs?' Stubbs asked.

'You have to understand how it was with Barney,' Crimmon said, biting his lower lip. 'He'd always been demanding, even as a child. And we indulged him, my brother and I. Aubrey was five and I was ten when he was born, inspector. Our father was in a mental institution, after being brain damaged by an injury at work, and our mother was out fifteen hours a day, trying to earn enough to give us a decent schooling. That left me and Aubrey to look after Barney.'

As he wrote all this down, Deepbriar recalled the words Aubrey had shouted at him as he broke Barney Crimmon's grip on the knife: 'You leave my little brother alone!' He must have used that same phrase a hundred times in the school playground.

'So, in the case of Joe Spraggs?' Stubbs prompted.

'Barney asked me and Aubrey to kidnap Joseph Spraggs for him. He told us it was what Sylvester Rudge wanted, and that he was too scared to refuse. Evidently Spraggs had crossed Rudge in some way.' Crimmon's voice trembled. 'I didn't want to get involved, but Barney said Spraggs would get a beating, that's all. We just had to lock him up in the mausoleum and he'd do the rest.'

'But you got the wrong man.' Jakes said.

Crimmon nodded. 'I'd seen that name in the school register for five years. Joseph Spraggs. It never occurred to me that he had a relation of the same name. Barney got hold of the stuff to put in his tea, then he went out of town, to give himself an alibi; evidently that's what Rudge had done, and Barney didn't want to risk anyone connecting him with Spraggs's abduction. Nobody was likely to suspect me or Aubrey. Actually it all went very smoothly, but when Barney came back we found we'd made a mistake.'

'So you decided to let Joe go.'

'Yes. Barney didn't want to, but I persuaded Aubrey it was the best thing to do. I insisted. I was sure Joe hadn't seen us.' His voice dropped to a whisper. 'That was when I made a big mistake. I let Barney keep the key to the mausoleum.'

'You got hurt that morning,' Deepbriar put in suddenly. 'Sorry, sir,' he added, as Stubbs turned to look at him.

'No, that's all right constable.' Stubbs looked back at Crimmon. 'Well?'

Crimmon nodded. 'Young Spraggs kicked my hand. The wound turned septic and I felt quite ill, I couldn't even go to work. I was glad not to be involved when Barney and Aubrey went after the other Joseph Spraggs, I just decided to put it all out of my mind.' There were tears in his eyes, and he dashed a hand across his face to wipe them away.

'I never thought Barney could kill anyone, but when the old

tramp disappeared I began to suspect something. In the end I went to see Aubrey. He admitted he'd helped Barney put two more bodies in the same sarcophagus.'

'Do you know why they took off the tramp's coats?' Jakes asked.

'Evidently Barney panicked,' Crimmon said, 'and he had some idea of burning the clothes and burying the body. By the time he'd calmed down and fetched Aubrey to help him it was nearly dawn. Aubrey took charge, and Barney didn't tell him about the coats until they were up at the mausoleum. They decided they'd be safe enough where they were.'

'So Aubrey had no problem with the fact that his young brother had committed murder,' Stubbs said.

Crimmon shook his head miserably. 'I suppose he deals with death all the time, he didn't seem to think he'd done anything wrong.'

Stubbs nodded. 'And like you, he'd become accustomed to doing what Barney said.'

'Yes,' Crimmon said eagerly. 'That's it exactly. Barney was really quite a good little boy, you know. Mischievous perhaps, but always so cheerful. We couldn't help ourselves, it was easy to spoil him.'

And turn him into a murderer, Deepbriar thought bleakly.

Harry Bartle, a gleaming white bandage round his head, came out from behind the bar of the Speckled Goose and put the brimming pint pot down in front of Thorny Deepbriar. 'On me,' he said, 'and as many more as you want.'

'One will be fine,' Deepbriar said, taking a mouthful and savouring the taste, 'Mrs Deepbriar's keeping my supper warm. Really,' he added, reaching into his pocket, 'I just came to show you this.' He took out an official letter. There were holes in the four corners, where it had been pinned to a notice board. 'I need to take it back with me, but I thought you'd want to see it for yourself.'

He leant back and enjoyed his drink, surreptitiously watching the younger man's face as he took in the printed words. Puzzlement turned to incredulity, then to joy. After that an odd expression Deepbriar couldn't place flickered across Harry's features.

'What's up?' Deepbriar asked. 'I thought you'd be pleased.

Only a couple of months and you can apply to join the force. Don't tell me you've changed your mind!'

'Not exactly. Only I didn't do too well, did I? My first attempt at solving a crime nearly got both of us killed.'

'That's amateurs for you,' Deepbriar said, grinning. 'Once you're a professional like me, you'll never find yourself in that sort of situation. I mean, what kind of fool tries to take on three men, one of them armed with a knife, and another nearly twice his weight?'

Harry's face cleared and he laughed. 'As long as I've got you looking out for me I'll be all right anyway.'

Deepbriar nodded solemnly. 'And one piece of advice,' he said. 'Get yourself a good wife. But for Mrs Deepbriar I don't reckon either of us would be here right now.'

A few minutes later he let himself into the house, to be greeted with a wonderful aroma of beef and onions. Mary came to meet him. 'Thorny,' she whispered, 'before we eat there's somebody waiting to see you. I put her in the office, she didn't seem to want to come into the parlour. It's Bella.'

With a sigh Deepbriar re-buttoned his tunic, in too good a mood to mind much. Mrs Emerson sat in the visitor's chair, her fingers shredding a little wisp of handkerchief. She jolted to her feet as he came in. 'Thorny, oh dear. I thought I'd got it all ready in my head, but now I'm not so sure ...'

He sat her down and made soothing noises, then he took the seat opposite and waited. 'I have to make a confession,' Bella Emerson said. 'Mary has been such a good friend, and you too. I can't go on deceiving you.'

'Would this be something to do with Mr Emerson?' Deepbriar hazarded.

'There!' She pouted. 'I might have guessed you suspected something, you policemen are so very clever. Yes. There's a reason why I never speak about the way Edgar died. He didn't really die in Peru. He never went further afield than Liverpool in his whole life.' She flushed. 'Oh dear, I knew this would be difficult. The fact is, he's still alive.'

'Alive?' Of all things, this wasn't what Deepbriar had expected.

'Yes. He left me. It was very sudden. He just walked out, and sent a letter a few days later saying I was to arrange the sale of the house. I was quite devastated, I loved living at the Manor, and I never guessed he wasn't happy.'

'Men often go a bit crazy when they reach a certain age,' Deepbriar offered, feeling a twinge of pity. 'If he met a younger woman—'

'Oh no, there was no other woman. He's living alone in Broadstairs. Well, not quite alone, I understand he has a dog.' She shuddered. 'Horrid dirty animals, I would never allow one in my house.' She stood up. 'Well, now you know my secret. I'd be grateful if you'd tell Mary for me. Of course I know I should come clean, as they say, and tell the rest of the village, but I'd rather not.'

'Well ...' Deepbriar began, but she gave him no time to finish.

'I'm at your mercy.' she said, smiling tremulously. Like a heroine of the revolution off to face the guillotine, she swept from the room.

Deepbriar swallowed the last mouthful of stew, placed his knife and fork neatly together and sat back. 'You know,' he said, 'I think you're the best cook in the whole county.'

'Either that knock on the head is still having an effect on you, or you want something,' Mary Deepbriar said complacently.

'Neither,' he replied. 'It's a sorry state of affairs if a man can't compliment his wife. You didn't ask what Mrs Emerson wanted.'

'I thought it might be police business, she was being a bit mysterious.' She stacked the two plates.

'She had a guilty secret,' Deepbriar said, 'but I'm supposed to tell you all about it.'

'Maybe I already know,' his wife said, as she went through into the kitchen.

Deepbriar picked up the empty dish and followed. 'Know what?'

'That she isn't a widow. Her husband left her. I don't know how she came to make up that silly story about him dying in Peru, the wretch is living in Broadstairs.'

'How did you know that?'

She turned from the cooker, lifting out the apple crumble. 'We women have our sources,' she said with a smile. 'I've known ever since Bella moved into the village. Oh, by the way, we've decided on our next production. It's not Puccini after all.'

'No?' Deepbriar's heart leapt. 'Please, tell me you're doing Gilbert and Sullivan.' Add that to Bella Emerson's shame over the disclosure about Edgar and surely she'd move out of Minecliff.

Mary shook her head. '*Carmen*,' she said.

Deepbriar barely suppressed a groan. Another murder. Poor Bizet.